DAVID IRELAND was born in 1927 on a kitchen table in Lakemba in south-western Sydney. He lived in many places and worked at many jobs, including greenkeeper, factory hand, and for an extended period in an oil refinery, before he became a full-time writer.

Ireland started out writing poetry and drama but then turned to fiction. His first novel, *The Chantic Bird*, was published in 1968. In the next decade he published five further novels, three of which won the Miles Franklin Award: *The Unknown Industrial Prisoner*, *The Glass Canoe* and *A Woman of the Future*.

David Ireland was made a member of the Order of Australia in 1981. In 1985 he received the Australian Literature Society Gold Medal for his novel *Archimedes and the Seagle*.

David Ireland lives in New South Wales.

NICOLAS ROTHWELL is the author of *Heaven and Earth, Wings of the Kite-Hawk, Journeys to the Interior* and *The Red Highway*. He is the northern correspondent for the *Australian*.

ALSO BY DAVID IRELAND

The Chantic Bird
The Unknown Industrial Prisoner
The Flesheaters
Burn
A Woman of the Future
City of Women
Archimedes and the Seagle
Bloodfather
The Chosen

The Glass Canoe
David Ireland

Text Publishing Melbourne Australia

Copyright Agency
Cultural Fund Proudly supported by Copyright Agency's Cultural Fund.

textclassics.com.au
textpublishing.com.au

The Text Publishing Company
Swann House
22 William Street
Melbourne Victoria 3000
Australia

First published by Macmillan Publishers Australia 1976
This edition published by The Text Publishing Company 2012

Cover design by WH Chong
Page design by WH Chong & Susan Miller
Typeset by Midland Typesetters

Printed and bound in Australia by Griffin Press, an Accredited ISO AS/NZS
14001:2004 Environmental Management System printer

Primary print ISBN: 9781921922411
Ebook ISBN: 9781921921021
Author: Ireland, David, 1927-
Title: The glass canoe / by David Ireland ; introduction by Nicolas Rothwell.
Series: Text classics.
Other Authors/Contributors: Rothwell, Nicolas.
Dewey Number: A823.3

CONTENTS

Hard Core
by Nicolas Rothwell

THE most steadfast tradition of Australia's cultural establishment is its resolve to forget the recent past. If there are achievements, dishonour them; if there are masterworks, neglect them, consign them to some discreet scrapheap of obscurity. The past can make people uncomfortable: many of those who survive from that strange place know more than us; they have seen more; their perspectives, most alarmingly, are different, and cast doubt on the universal validity of our own.

Of course this phenomenon is pretty familiar everywhere. Writers, artists and dramatists routinely go into a reputation slump once dead, or once their urgent heyday is done. They seem somehow tainted by their time, caught up in its delusions, representative of trends and attitudes we incline in later, more enlightened, years to disparage or mock. Often these disappearances are permanent: the mid-grade and the modish fade away, and we never hear their names again; they become no more than pale references for historians, evidence of views and customs that would be unthinkable without the lengthy explaining notes of scholars.

Sometimes, though more rarely, those vanished names return, like comets swinging back into proximity with the sun, their magnitude increasing as their approach draws nearer and the tail of blazing light behind them lengthens across the sky. Is the time at hand for the reappearance of the Ireland comet? Can he be assigned a place in the thin firmament of fixed Australian literary stars?

The story of David Ireland's rise and eclipse is a tale from an earlier century, when literary romances were all dramatic elevations and giddying falls from grace. The writer was born in Sydney and raised in the city's north-west. He took a range of jobs that find echo in his books: as a greenkeeper, as a refinery worker. By 1968 he was a novelist with a work in print; in 1971 he published *The Unknown Industrial Prisoner*, a book that received the Miles Franklin Award, as, in 1976, did the book you now hold in your hands. This was the reputation peak. The books, and prizes and honours, kept on, for several years, and one can almost imagine an alternative time path in which Ireland's late saga, *The Chosen*, released to virtual silence in 1997, had a vast success and its author enjoyed an Indian summer of prestige and acclaim.

Almost. But no. Crack open the pages of *The Glass Canoe*, reader in waiting, and you'll see why. The book has traction. It pulls you in. It's the hard core. It's art, not entertainment; action, not plot. It's the lurking, dark beast of fear and beauty at the heart of Australian life. It is all we know, and all we seek to put behind us, and all that the literary world has struggled to evade and overcome. It has a geography, physical and social: it's what lies beyond the beach; beyond the shore; Australia beyond the line of coastal suburbs and their aspirations. The set-up is simple. Ireland works this way: he disdains surface marks of coherence, he has no time for the long forms of narrative. It's fragments, for him, snatched scenes, glimpses that show all.

This book is an anatomy: it tells the tale of The Southern Cross, a hotel, fairly clearly situated in Northmead, western Sydney, downwind of the Clyde refinery stacks, far from the city centre 'where tall buildings stood, rich castles lit up all over like burning buildings with fire still feeding inside'. The hotel regulars are the book's cast. They drink, they brawl, they dream, they weep. The episodes are short; they stitch together; they make up a mosaic. The view those fragments build up is hard to bear. The world is empty; its routines revolve round alcohol, blood and sex.

Even for a reader of our time, replete as our environs are with images of sensual abandon and cinematic gore, the going is tough. Indeed it is almost unthinkable that a modern publisher would dare to send the *Canoe*, stuffed as it is with words of sexism, with prejudice and with brutal, escalating, unending violence, out into the world of literary festivals and cultural promotion tours. What did Ireland's contemporaries think, when they reviewed him and elevated his reputation, if briefly, to the skies? The quality of the writing spoke, of course, for itself. It was sinew, it was the feel of life. And in its quality of attack it had no competitors, just as it has none now. The context was also striking. The publication time was the twilight of Whitlam's Australia. The gilded paragon of Australian letters was Patrick White, who had won the Nobel Prize for literature in 1973, and who published his sprawling, mythographic, moralising *A Fringe of Leaves* in the same year Ireland's slim *Canoe* appeared—and it is an amusing thing to think of these two new releases in the bookshops, perhaps at Lesley McKay's in New South Head Road, Double Bay, competing for the shelf space, but needing to be kept apart for fear their utterly divergent worldviews might produce a spontaneous annihilation of the cosmos.

Critics were kind, if cautious. The venerable Douglas Stewart in the *National Times* felt Ireland had identified in the pub 'the last shaky refuge from industrialism'. The Penguin blurb suggested there was a degree of sardonic humour in the scenes of carnage and despair Ireland had sketched: 'Perhaps it's all to be taken on a bent elbow with another swallow.' They were different times. Australians knew what Ireland was painting was there: you could still stroll down from your neat townhouse in Carlton or Edgecliff and wind up in a hotel where men with horizon eyes gazed at the race-screen and the aroma of stale beer hung like a sentence in the air. And of course you still can today, but those parts of Australia are now, for the most part, safely cordoned off, far from where books are read, and the books that once portrayed that other Australia are no longer seen as central to our literary life. Ireland's writing journey continued: the establishment moved on to other, gentler books, with attitudes that did more to polish the moral virtues of the reading class.

The inescapable suspicion forms that Ireland was admired, and celebrated, not just as the hard voice of the people but as the chronicler of that world's demise. And *The Glass Canoe* is cast as the tale of the old hotel's passing. Even in the early pages it looks to the narrator figure like an illuminated tomb, 'a sort of past solidified in masonry'. The Southern Cross is on the verge of being rebuilt. Its regulars are the flotsam of history, the losers on the refuse heap. But was that Ireland's tilt? One reads *The Glass Canoe* today with very different eyes. What is permanent in the book stands out. It is the least judgemental of books. Ireland sees horror. He sees beauty. He casts them into poetry and sets them down. Where is this beauty? In looks and gestures. In the need for tribe and place. In League's awe and majesty, 'when Danny's on the burst and swerves just before taking a pass from the half and that swerve takes him past a stiff-arm the ref didn't see and wouldn't have seen, and then he takes three strides...' Where is it? In life's bitter traps: 'In the street, at the lights, men were rotting in their cars, fighting nothing, only fearing; fearing crashes, fearing cops. Their blood whitened in fear and got thin.'

The book makes up a tapestry: many perspectives, many actors, their words, their breathing, the ways they mesh and move. The landscape, the sun and moon in the sky above the city, the gleam of the rainbow in fuel oil spilt on the pavement, the different kinds of grass blades in a greensward: fragments, a world of fragments—but over it all, spread over it like the heavens, an authorial perspective. That perspective is the thing that hits the reader most forcefully. Ireland is presenting, in his hotel, an Australia: an Australia now largely without literary voice. It is vernacular Australia, and it would be tempting, but not quite right, to see as its spokesman the articulate inebriate who steps up to the bar to speak from section to section, Alky Jack: 'Never be ashamed of being an Australian,' he'd say. 'There's plenty just as bad as us in the world.' His audience looks around: the saloon's a shambles, dirt everywhere, smoke too—now gone, its curtain never to be glimpsed again in a back bar's filtered light. Alky Jack resumes: 'Anything can happen. We started off in chains, we do our best when we're not pushed, we pay back a good turn, say no to authority and upstarts, we're casual, we like makeshift things, we're ingenious, practical, self-reliant, good in emergencies, think we're as good as anyone in the world, and always sympathise with the underdog.'

It's not Ireland's simple view, and he subverts it in the book right away—but it's hard not to feel those words were written with a bit of love as well as a degree of irony. Hard not to feel that Australia is in your hands when you hold this book. An old Australia, wild, and picaresque, one worth a few words, the words Ireland pronounces, almost like a blessing, as he ends his phantasmagoria, still, as in every sentence, at perfect pitch: 'I went to the bar to get us a small fleet of glass canoes to take us where we wanted to go. I thought of the tribes across Australia, each with its waterhole, its patch of bar, its standing space, its beloved territory. It was a great life.' How resonant the past tense sounds, a deeper tense now, as we glance back today on this jewel in our literary tradition, long out of print. How much we have lost that still lives with us.

The Glass Canoe

SHOOTING BUTTERFLIES

Down the back of the Southern Cross kids were shooting butterflies. Occasionally pellets tinkled harmlessly off the tinted glass windows of the saloon bar or made little dints in cars in the car park.

They never shot at the big neon sign riding high above the pub. It was a proud sign: THE SOUTHERN CROSS. They had a natural reverence for neon.

Butterflies flew free. They dazzled the eye and the mind with their freedom. Flight was something we could never know.

At night when the butterflies had gone to bed and there were no moving targets to hit, they'd pot fireflies. We don't get fireflies down the back of the Southern Cross; fireflies were street light globes. Somebody put little shields round the globes to keep out rocks from shanghais or the human arm, but BBs or slugs couldn't be kept out. Sometimes the street was in darkness for a mile in both directions. They were sodium lights. Perhaps that was the difference.

I used to do it once, but I'm not a kid anymore. None of us was too happy about it: globes weren't moving targets. It was against the rules to aim at a butterfly when it stopped, you had to go for it on the wing. It made for a lot of stray shots.

In summer, what with daylight saving, the air-rifles would be popping till nine at night and by then the drunks from the pub would be too full to chase us. Anyway, they were our fathers or brothers or someone up the street.

When I could pass for eighteen I was initiated, and became a man. I went inside the pub and bought the beers. Before that we used to sit out in the cars and let Mick go in, or Flash, because they looked eighteen. At fifteen I was fresh-faced, I took longer to graduate.

On hot days we jumped fully clothed into our bottomless beer glasses and pushed off from shore without a backward look. Heading for the deep, where it was calm and cool.

The Mead was our territory, the Southern Cross our waterhole. The next tribe west drank at the Bull, and on the other side the nearest tribe holed up at the Exchange. While your tribe's waterhole flowed, you never went walkabout to another tribe's waterhole.

Unless there was trouble, some little matter to be settled.

After you have a fair bit to drink of an afternoon the future is sort of blank; the present is all there is. Sometimes you wonder. Where will I be when. Not often, though. Next moment you see a splash of rust on the tiles about belt level. Rust? Wet a finger, touch it. Ten to one it's sticky.

It brings your wonderings smartly back to the present.

Out the door you see, around four o'clock, men coming from all directions, walking lightly between flying traffic, flittering and darting towards the Southern Cross, moths towards the light.

By five the place is crowded. The noise.

I had this job in an office for a while and what the pub noise reminded me of was going down to the factory. As soon as you opened the door the blast

3

hit you. It was everywhere. There was so much of it that one of the old hands was taken sick one day and trying to tell someone what was the matter, but this guy couldn't hear and thought he was just raving on, and turned away and the old joker kicked the bucket right there on the concrete floor. I didn't like that noise, it tried to take you over, leaving no room for anything else. You couldn't think. Unreal, it was. I got out of that job quick.

The noise at the pub was just as loud, but quite different. You could sort of swim in it after a while. By the time you got four or five schooners into you there seemed to be a cushion in your head, anyway. But that's not why I loved to let it wash over me and carry me along. It's because it was people-noise, not machine-noise. What silences there were—not many— were shallow. Like a few inches of water over sand-flats.

The first time I drank any decent amount I got back home and wrote down on a bit of paper what I felt, like the feeling on the backs of your hands, your lips, the way your eyes feel. Where that paper is now I haven't got a clue. I was very young.

They call me Meat Man. They reckon when I grow up I'll be as big in the meat department as Fuse. He's an old rodeo rider, very bandy. Instead of being a ton of dynamite with an inch and a half fuse, Fuse is eight stone wringing wet but in the meat department he's

4

never been beaten. When he's challenged in the matter of length he'll only bring out enough to win the challenge. No one has ever seen the whole thing.

Yet for all that he isn't a pants man.

Men came round, usually Friday and Saturday, and sold things cheap from the backs of their vehicles. They'd go to the licensee, ask could they sell in the pub.

'What are you selling?'

'Shoes. Straight off the boat.' Never which boat, it could be a Manly ferry.

'How much you asking?'

'Five bucks.'

The licensee would push out his lips, look doubtful, say nothing.

'What size do you take?' the hustler would say when he saw it was the only way.

'Eight.'

Out would come eights. 'They're yours.'

'No.'

'Go on, take 'em. Do me a favour.'

6

'I don't know . . .'

'It'd please me if you would.'

'OK. Thanks. Sure, go for your life.' And the salesman would put fifty cents on the next ten pairs to cover it. After all, he got them very cheaply. Left in the hand they raised blisters.

They'd bring oysters, prawns, and one man with a big wicker basket always got a good sale for his garlic sausage. A lot of sales went to hungry drinkers who'd been there since ten in the morning if it was Saturday, or hadn't been home for tea if it was Friday.

Shirts, vegetables, fish, kitchen sinks, tyres, stoves, meat from the abbatoirs, timber, copper wire, welding rods, bolts of cloth. You could get anything, and if you wanted something you'd tell someone, who told someone else and it was there next week.

What with the snack bar, you could stay at the pub all week if you had nowhere to go. As long as you had a car to sleep in for the cold weather.

It was home. The world and history passed by on wheels. Life stayed outside. Babies were started, and born. Weddings, shootings, promotions, dismissals, hungers, past and future—all were outside.

Morning, like a brand new baby, would come up on broken glasses, pools of stale sick and the odd car left behind by drinkers who couldn't make it but were cluey enough to call a cab. Not that the boys in blue were waiting outside the pub to put the bag on departing drinkers; if they did that they wouldn't have room enough at the station for all the excess oh-eights from just one pub, let alone if they did it outside all the pubs in the district.

Let's get away from the politics and back to the pub.

The red bar was the only bar I've ever been in that had no mirrors. We were busy enough watching each other, we had no time to look at ourselves.

Christmas Eve the pub was rocking with the din of voices and shouts when over all there was a tremendous crash. The din stopped. There was a mass move to the doors. Up the street a truck lay on its side and three other vehicles, two cars and a low loader, were stopped at peculiar angles to the road. In the truck was a party of do-gooders surrounded by wrapped Christmas presents for the kids' Home, except most of the volunteers and presents were no longer in the truck.

Out of the dark figures came, and more from newly stopped cars. They crept over to the presents and began to help themselves. All the volunteer cheer-bringers were injured or dazed, but the harpies that came out of the night didn't mind, they pulled Christmas presents from the hands of the people only just conscious enough to grip the edges.

In a body the boys from the Southern Cross ran up the street taking cover from the streetlights on factory lawns and flattening themselves against fences. They descended on the harpies and did them over, all but two good runners who left their cars in the street and headed up the steep hill to the lake.

The boys headed back to the pub, full of virtue, talk, bruised knuckles and thirst.

Much later, the two runners sneaked back, walking soft as spiders.

At night the Southern Cross often looked, even to me, an illuminated tomb. A sort of past solidified in masonry. The traffic tried to run by all the faster to stay in the present or the past might grab them. But to us, our tomb was where life was: outside was a world fit only to die in.

The dark, a live monster, leaned on the roof and tried the glass doors. Its eyes were black, fathomless as death.

My mother died not long after the traffic there got real bad. We used to live in a house right on the main road, one of a row of the old Caroline Chisholm cottages—they're demolished now and a car sale yard there instead—and when they widened the road and it got busier and busier, she got sick.

At night the house shuddered with the big refrigerated freighters, semi-trailers, low-loaders, cement trucks and all the rest. You couldn't use the front door. Day and night it was, the sound going through you like knives in a cutter, and her dying. I held her hand once and felt her pulse dragging. Like knots in a bit of cotton, only not spaced evenly.

When I was old enough and with her dead, I got out of there and went to live up near the lake. The lake was a fresh water catchment on high ground, fed by ground still higher, so you can see the Southern Cross was well down in a hollow. The kids get in the lake area after dark and carry on. Every now and then, when they get too bad, the ranger gets police help and they go through and hunt the kids out.

I live in an old house. There's half a dozen of us there. We all chip in to pay the rent. Most of the time I have a room to myself, and I like that.

I christened the house FORTRESS AUSTRALIA, a phrase Alky Jack used. It was big and rattly, nothing fitted flush any more. No locks on the doors.

I painted the name on the front wall, in different coloured letters. The people round about don't like the letters being so big, but they're shy about telling us. They leave us alone.

Up at the lake the birds' song is so clear you'd think it was words they sing.

Saturdays, depending who was cellarman, you'd have to watch out for the cocktail. The man that was supposed to come round to check had his hand out, so they forgot to put that purple dye in the slops tray. At the end of the day they'd take the pressure off the half empty keg and slip in the slops. An old guy that used to work there told me the first keg of the day was usually pretty right, but on a Saturday, say, about the third keg, they'd pull from the cocktail.

It used to get a bit cloudy.

You wouldn't think they'd need the slops to earn more of our money. Fuse showed me the cellar one day and how the kegs are lined up one after the other. I followed the plastic pipelines with my eye and noticed a point where the beer lines met with a tap on the wall.

'That's the water,' he explained. 'Flush out the system.'

'What if they just left the water tap on?' I asked. 'Just a dribble, even.'

He didn't answer me. He still worked there, then.

Saturday the noise would rise and begin to take over before twelve and go on all day till ten with only a small lull or two in the afternoon, when the race broadcasts were on and the pub dead still.

One Saturday, two guys appeared at the door with clipboards and pens at the ready and began to ask questions of the first people inside the door. They were doing a survey, but when they asked questions and got no answers but blank faces, they looked at each other. What was this? Then the race call finished and the noise rolled back like the waters after the children of Israel.

No use asking this mob questions. They went.

The cars outside, one by one, three a second, passed like a stream of time. I tried to imagine what it was like for a deaf person watching that traffic. Maybe a sort of formal game. But creepy.

No one minded too much what others did for sex. There was a sit-down cubicle in each bar toilet and two out in an old toilet shed. One day when it was raining like a bastard and I was busting for a pee as soon as I got out of the car, I ran into the old shed and began letting it out when out of the corner of my eye I saw movement. I turned to look in case it was a hand with a bottle, but it was only two harmless old men in the far cubicle. One had his trousers down and was touching his toes. Actually his hands gripped his knees. They were just at that stage of drunk not to mind me having a butcher's.

I don't mean they were homosexuals. It's not easy to be old, and still get a woman. Look at the jails. Guys inside for a few years get to like it, but when they get out they mostly go straight back to women.

* * *

Another old man came along the street every day with a sack slung over his shoulder. He picked up riches others discarded: bits of timber, bottles, wire, cans and things people threw from cars.

Once he put an airline bag in his sack and later found a human hand in it. A child's hand, it was.

Every time I saw him the beer tasted thick and nourishing, like roast beef. One day I saw him coming and bought him one, but when I held it out to him he glared at me and spat.

Didn't want my roast beef.

They told me he was illiterate, couldn't write his name. He wasn't that old, either, fifty-five or sixty. Sun, wind, rain had aged him. He looked eighty.

These things in the past few pages are general things I put down first when I got the idea of making a book about the Southern Cross and our life here.

I think now I'll tell you about some of the people of our tribe.

It's raining hard and my darling's away on a business trip.

This would be as good a time to start as any.

First they were boys, primitive hunters of fruit and adventure, skirmishing in backyards and paddocks, living in trees, spying out far hills, swimming creeks and rivers and the compulsory surf, shooting butter-flies; out all day, returning to shelter to sleep. The horizon was boundless.

17

Teenaged, they became apprenticed to learn the pastoral world of snorting, grunting, purring machines, bikes, cars, tractors, trucks and buses, and grew among flocks, herds, whole wheat-fields of workers whose labour and lives were farmed by the powerful; learning to imitate sheep, or even sheepherders, jackeroos, slaughtermen. The horizon had shrunk.

A few years more and a job displaced them, now part of the adult herd, to the refinement of the factory-city. They were wage and small-enterprise sheep and cattle amongst the unattainable riches of civilisation; among tall, unfamiliar buildings, unimaginable processes, incomprehensible aims, scratching a living on the edge of the educated world. The horizon was work, pub, races.

As sheep they were exploitable and gave their bodies for a full belly, but the adolescent apprentice one layer down was bewildered, and the hunter boy deep inside who had never changed was a pitiable refugee, two removes from his original culture, stranded in an alien world. Stranded? Locked. In their own bodies they had travelled man's road from primitive hunter, through herder of flocks, to our present settled-city civilisation. Where *they* were the sheep, the hunted.

And yet these sheep were something more when they were drinking. The golden drops stirred something inside that wasn't human.

When that something woke up it looked like the

guy was in the grip of a storm, thrashing around. Or a sort of growth inside that switched all the savage circuits to ON.

It was more than a growth—it was a live thing. Like a monster inside. Looking out through the pupils, working the controls, smashing.

Maybe it was all too human. Maybe it was the hunter and destroyer of life inside them that had never made the transition to a settled life husbanding plants and animals.

Once upon a time they were decent men, unaggressive, hardworking, tired at the day's end. They drank to erase the ache and the tiredness.

Now there's only a few of us do a hard day's work, even though we're as poor, relatively, as our grandfathers.

We drink to erase everything.

On the back wall where the clock is, above the pool tables, there's a crack in the bricks. It goes up from floor level, slantwise, wide enough to hold our cue chalk. Guys rest cigarettes in it—it's jagged and goes up by steps and stairs—combs, papers, and push dead matches into it out of sight. It points up at the clock like a finger.

DANNY

He had an inscribed football in a place of honour on his mantelpiece at home. He wasn't often there, but his parents allowed the ball to stay, with its inked names all over it. It was the ball the Mead had won the under-twenty grand final with, and the team's signatures were on it. The same team had come up through the juniors from the under-elevens and won every grand final. Rugby Union, but not rah-rah boys.

Danny knew every football statistic of Rugby League from the year dot, and a lot of the statistics of the code he played. You know the sort of thing: who was in the second-row for France in the second Test in 1953, how many tries Gasnier scored, whether Fulton grounded the ball for that second try on the ice at Warrington, how old was Gus Risman when he played his last Test for England. His memory was fantastic.

He worked for the council for the basic wage and took sickies on Mondays and Fridays; Friday to start the weekend early and Monday to get over it. He held the Stop and Go signs when they had the road up.

It was part of his personal code not to make use of his memory for money. Besides, he wouldn't work indoors. As long as he had enough in his pocket for a beer. Even this didn't bother him. He was into blokes all over the pub for two, five, ten, any amount. One thing about Danny, he never forgot: always paid. You might have to wait a bit. He bit me once and I only had enough cash for two more drinks, it was early on and there were plenty of guys with brass and I said no. He didn't believe me and thought I was holding out and from that day I've always had enough in my pocket, but he never put the bite on me again.

How he came to get the ball for his mantelpiece, he was a great player. After the under-seventeens the grog got him, and although he played great games up into the under-twenties, he was on the way down. In the local all-age team he played a few good games, but he'd be on the field and after two bursts upfield there he was crouching, bringing up his heart. And often blood. It was the grog.

He played five-eighth, he was very quick, his sidestep was fantastic, but his life was practically over.

At school he was no good at metalwork, always breaking off things and getting the lathe stuck. He

21

stood up to the English teacher once and swapped a few punches in class, but he was good at history.

Now he's history himself.

The folks at home didn't think too much of him. His old man used to belt him, and to make it worse his brother was a good boy, never got drunk, saved his money, always home in time for tea, while if it was Friday Danny might start the day at seven in the morning at Dorrie's in Parramatta until it was time to go to the Southern Cross at ten and stay there all day.

The boys said, 'If he went on the waggon or in a convent somewhere to dry out, he'd be the best five-eighth in Australia.'

They said this sort of thing but words didn't do him any good. Every birthday he'd down his pint in one go, no matter how drunk he was. And he had birthdays right through the year.

You never saw him with a girl, but sometimes a few of the boys would go up to this Sandra's place and go through her. They'd give her something, or take a few cans up. She didn't mind. Once he went up alone, gave her some drinks and was going to town, rasping away, when the others crept up outside the window, and one—Mick, I think—put his hand in the window and touched her between the buttocks. She liked that and went for her life, nearly throwing Danny. Just as he reached the vinegar stroke, Mick dated him.

Danny flew off forwards, did a somersault over the pillow and landed on his back with his feet in the air against a wardrobe.

'You rotten bastards!' he yelled. 'I could've broke my neck.'

He was very touchy on the subject for days after.

He drank more and more and finally the beer wasn't enough to give him a glow, what with his insides breaking down and pains all the time. Fishhooks in the stomach. He got on the Bacardi and that really used to flatten him. It flattened me the only times I got on it. I fell over, out like a light. Trouble is, you get used to zotting down schooners and you try to drink spirits the same way.

Around that time he copped a load at some harlot's place at Burwood. He was going to the doctor's and had penicillin needles, seven in a row. He told the others it was his guts. They might not like to be drinking from glasses he'd had.

Once in the Leagues Club—he doesn't go there now, he's barred—he told me he'd knocked off more houses than you could poke a stick at. You know, rich places round Pennant Hills, money, jewels. Saturday night capers, on foot.

I didn't believe him. How would he stand, let alone climb into windows, on a Saturday night? Full as a boot.

But he did get nine months once for something. Did it at Long Bay.

'I'm never goin' there again. Sooner put a bullet in me head. You have to say Sir to the screws every time you talk, have to get a pass to go three feet, and you're locked up from four in the afternoon till seven or eight in the morning. Nothing to see, and here I am locked up with an idiot. How would you like that?'

I'd never been in jail, only police stations, and I didn't even like that.

Maybe, when they stop telling him he was so good and everyone gets tired of putting up with him going off his brain every week and sympathy runs out, he'll pull himself up. That's what I used to tell myself.

A few of them went to Parramatta nicely pissed one Saturday night looking for trouble. They found it. During a little scrap up a dusty lane someone hit one of Danny's mates with an iron bar. Dropped him cold as a maggot. Danny walked up the lane, hands on hips.

'Which one a you cunts hit my mate?'

In the dark someone kneed him in the crutch and Danny went down like a bag of shit.

When he got up later, they went further up the lane and ran into another mob of guys that shouldn't have been out on the street. Only kids and dressed like pox doctors' clerks. Danny and his mate couldn't help laughing until one came from nowhere, ripped a paling off the fence and cracked them both. They ran.

Straight into the arms of two large coppers standing there with their paddy waggon drawn up and doors wide open.

One said, 'You got any money, you lot?'

'I have,' Danny said.

'Drop five dollars on the ground and turn round.'

He dropped the five and turned round. The copper gave him a good kick up the arse and said, 'Piss off.'

They accepted this advice.

Another time they were picked up at the lake. Someone complained about the noise. They'd drunk most of the cans by that time, luckily.

There were eight in the cell. A kid called Vernon they let off straight away.

'Your old man isn't going to like this,' one of the Jacks said.

Another kid gave his name as Gazzard.

'Any relation to the sergeant?'

'He's my uncle.'

Out he went.

'I'm with him,' Danny said.

But the Jacks replied, 'Shut your mouth.'

It was better up the Cross. King's, not Southern. If they caught you drunk in the street they'd put you in the waggon, take you to the old high-ceilinged cells at Darlinghurst, give you a board two inches off the ground to sleep on and leave you alone till nine o'clock.

On the way out you pay a dollar and that's it. Not a bruise. Not a hard word. Gentlemen.

Danny went off regularly, and was getting worse. He'd start singing, he might jump up on a table to perform and beat time, might even jump the bar and serve himself. But he started to get aggressive. He'd karate chop a full table of glasses of beer. Or suddenly demand a lift home and start swinging if he thought you were putting him off.

Once I came out to find him on his belly on the roof of my car, pretending to swim. Pushed the roof in. I called him a dickhead, but he doesn't know what he's doing when he's real full.

He had flashes of the old good humour. He lobbed at the Oriental for a Chinese feed one weeknight and ate like a king. When it was time to ante up with the brass for the meal he found he had seventy cents. His pocket had jingled so he hadn't bothered to check. He sat there pretending to work on the remains of the sweet and sour.

I know, he thought. I'll run. I can see him sitting there, and the sudden grin.

He ran, and was in full flight when he caught the shine on the plate glass door. It was after hours and they locked the door against incomers, and a little old Chinese lady let you out. When you paid.

Desperately he turned and sat down next to some-one. They'd sprung him by this time, though, and a woman walked up and asked the man, 'Is he with you?'

'No,' said the man.

Danny washed a lot of dishes. They must have saved them up for six months, he said.

He wasn't full that night. He was very pleasant when he wasn't full. His blue eyes had lights and his teeth flashed white. He had the whitest teeth around and didn't pay a penny for them.

Someone made an appointment for him with Rent-a-drunk, who duly called to pick him up and take him to some posh party to liven things up. They couldn't find him at home. When they pulled up at the Southern Cross and caught sight of a shoeless apparition with wild hair singing, shirt out and shorts a dog wouldn't sleep on, they left, shaking their heads.

Once, on a Monday, when he started drinking early, he was so full by late afternoon that he didn't make it across the road. He woke at peak hour on the median strip, cars all round him like blunt cattle nosing forward in a field. When he got to his feet all he could see was cars, all roughly the same height, all with horns.

He must have thought they were cattle because he brayed out 'Moooooo!'

I hadn't worked for six months. When the brass ran out, I got a job at a golf course not far away and cut grass, put new trees in, raked bunkers, laid plastic water pipes. Best job I ever had.

There were two streets along either side of the course, which made it a long rectangle. One of the streets had heavy traffic, but also a lot of trees that made it a good stopping place for truckies with big rigs at night when they were ahead of themselves. You know, can't travel more than five hours without a rest, produce your log book, and so on. Not all of them had two log books.

We started early and if you were over near the third green when a truckie noticed another truckie still asleep and late, he'd give him a blast on the horn. This could sometimes lead to mowers digging into the green or nervy golfers diving for cover at the top of a swing. Golfers were out with the dawn, hail, rain or shine. And the athletes and footballers running round the inside edge on the cut grass.

I liked the trees and the curve of the fairways and the dull silver dew. Sometimes, in mid-beer, my heart was outdoors and the world fragrant with cut grass. And when there'd been a dry spell and the dams running dry, one of the club members who worked up at the water catchment would let a bit go at night, accidentally on purpose, and in the morning it would be across the eleventh, twelfth, thirteenth and fourteenth fairways and sliding nicely into the old dam. There were two dams and tanks between to make pumping easier and cleaner between the two and to lower the level in the old dam and build the level in the new dam if there was rain. The water-race between the two couldn't handle a lot. We were at the bottom of a long slow slope and got all the gutters and culverts from the south-west end of the course and some from the north-east.

I hadn't graduated then to cutting fairways with five gangs of mowers behind me on the tractor: I was cutting the rough, which was a two inch cut. I used to wonder what the word meant. The rough was usually better to play from than the fairway since it didn't get watered and the surface was firm. You could lift a ball cleanly.

Kids used to get on the course and swim in the third dam, near the fence at the north end. It was a mistake to chip them. One club secretary chipped them about language, swimming near the eighth, and just being there. In the morning the transfer tanks at the south end had tomahawk cuts all over. Water coming out all directions.

This had its funny side, but when I planted two dozen young willows along the banks of the north dam and next morning most of them were uprooted and on their sides in the water, it wasn't funny at all. I don't like young trees dying.

It was just as funny when you'd find the local kids had ridden their bikes over the greens and skidded them, to turn up the turf. Or when they'd dug little holes in the greens and thrown the spoil into the bunkers.

I can understand them, that's another funny thing. There was no way in the world they'd ever have enough money to spare to join a good golf club.

One wet day there was an almighty crash on the noisier road. Grade A accident, lights flashing, ambulances, tow trucks, sirens, foam, police on Hondas, in Minis, Toranas.

I was spreading top dressing near the third tee and the accident was fifty metres away. A family car pulled up and the man got out and watched, then came back to the car thinking he'd have to keep his kids inside the car against their will.

30

He was wrong. They watched calmly for a few minutes. One said, 'How long does it go on?'

His father said, 'What do you mean?'

'Can we stay for the rest of the programme?'

The other kid was bored.

'I seen that show last week. Can't we change channels?'

The father was stumped.

'Channels? Look, son, this is happening. Now. You can't change channels. There's no channel to change.'

'Switch off the set, then. I want something to eat instead. Where's the next Kentucky?'

In the Southern Cross that afternoon, suddenly all the glasses round the bar lifted in unison. Someone pointed. A foolish grin flickered round the red bar, from glass to glass. Then all heads bowed as we resumed our worship at the red bar.

The more I saw of grass the more I liked it. I guess you get pretty fond of things you see around you every day. Like a farmer runs a handful of dirt through his fingers.

Some lunchtimes I'd have a lie down on it with my face against the blades, and pull up the paspalum stalks and chew the white part.

And the smell of it. Some sweet, some dry and hard, and some, like the clumps of Parramatta grass, didn't care if humans lived or died. Ignored you completely. Hard as nails. You had to admire them for that.

If anyone saw me enjoying the grass they'd think I was mad. I guess if anyone saw me on my knees with my face buried in my darling's soft belly, they'd think I was praying to her.

The days are never long enough. I drink faster.

MICK SAID:

I'd been at this girl for nearly a week and all she'd say was no. This was unusual for me. Normally if I smell a No in the air I give the bird the big A. No risk.

This No has started to get to me.

It's Show time. I took her with Flash and his bit to the Showground. It's night. After we see a few things we sort of get out of the bright lights and find ourselves up near the pig pens with packets of sandwiches. Which we hoe into.

The smell. It's atrocious, but I get hungry and after a while I don't notice it.

As soon as we stop eating, Flash and his bird are into it. Hands everywhere. We take refuge behind a big truck. He's OK, but I get nothing. No use saying I can't get it in, I can't even get a hand on it.

33

I get jack of this, so I say, 'You better have a good night here, enjoy the Show. I won't see you much any more. I'm mixed up in football, there'll be training nights after work and the boys are setting up a mob of us to train in the gym on the other nights.'

There's tears then. And 'I don't want to lose you.'

I put my hand on her tit and whack! She knocks it off.

So I do it again, and this time it stays. This is all right. So next I try to get a finger in and whack! she clobbers my hand.

I do it again and this time it stays there. Now I reckon I have to keep that finger in or she'll go cold, so I undo my belt, one of those fancy things with big shiny buckles, with one hand and lying on my elbow. Boy, I have every muscle straining right out of their sockets. But I keep that finger in.

'I don't want to be pregnant,' she says.

So at last he's free and I put him in under my finger, just pretending it's only the finger. I don't know if she believes it. When he's in I jam up tight, don't let her move. She's so tight I blow in about ten seconds, my hand still there.

Then I hear this low sort of yell. 'Look out! Stop, Mick!'

It is my mate. He's pulling his pants up in a sweat. I look round where he's looking.

The truck has rolled away. Five hundred people,

34

kids and all, are watching, eating paddle pops, sitting at tables with hamburgers and cans of drink.

The other doll's laughing, but my bird is ashamed and worried and red and half in tears, all at the same time.

There are no cops, that's something.

Funny thing, even with all the embarrassment, as I get up to go I notice, in a pool of water, some oil must have dripped from under the truck and there are these rainbow colours on the water, moving and shifting as if they were nervous. Mostly a sort of bright red and a bluey purple. You want to keep looking at them to see what shapes they'll change to next.

We're standing watching the prize bulls and saying it was a bit sad that as soon as they win their blue ribbons they'll be knocked on the head and cut up—girls like you to be a bit sad about killing things—and set out neatly in butcher's shops for people to look at their insides and all their private parts that even they—the bulls—hadn't seen, and all for a quid, when I hear this joker ask someone the time.

I'm just about to tell him, when another bloke in a broad-brim hat bends down under this Santa Gertrudis, grabs its balls, swings them to one side and looks and says 'Eight-fifteen'. The first joker looks at him sideways, says thanks and goes. He hasn't gone ten metres when someone asks *him* the time.

'Eight-fifteen.'

'Yeah?' He hadn't looked at his watch.

'Yeah, I got it off that bloke back there. He just took hold of a bull's balls, looked and told me.'

That country joker did this three times. I had to know how he did it.

'Well, mate, it's easy. You just squat down, grab the bull's balls, pull 'em to one side and you can see the showground clock.'

Country jokers like to take the piss out of Sydney guys.

SOMETHING TO WONDER AT

At my darling's place the radiogram is playing. It fascinates me to see a stupid machine recognise the size of the record and only put the arm over enough to come down right on the outside edge of it.

Maybe it's not so stupid.

I look at it a long time, and think about it, but it's a mystery. In a way, I like not understanding how it works.

Serge was a Russian. He was only middle height, but everything about him was big. Beer and heredity filled him out to such an extent that he gave up the beer to keep his weight down to seventeen or eighteen stone. His expansive nature he could not give up. Anyone within reach was liable to be included in the brawl.

He was a pub fighter. Not like some that went round wherever there was a man with a reputation and waited to take him on. Serge was a pub fighter at the Southern Cross, and only there. He wasn't even king of the pub.

Simply that he fought often, and usually with strangers. Some gig from another part of Sydney, where the local rules on the pool table were different, would protest at Serge putting a colour on the black, Serge would say, 'Outside,' the primeval savage would peep out of Serge's eyes, and that would be it.

Sometimes in the middle of a conversation, the monster would take over and Serge would swing. No change of expression, no verbal form of intention heralded the action. His arms, legs, chest, stomach were so thick you'd wonder where you had to place a punch for him to notice it.

Not that there was time for wondering. If you were slow off the mark and his first swing got you, he'd have a hand in your hair or round the back of your head and pull the head down to meet his vast knee on the way up. This tactic resulted in many a smashed face. If he hadn't had enough exercise at that stage, he'd follow the transgressor down to mother concrete and carefully smash the head down on it until such time as he—Serge—had enough.

His hands wore a covering of skin millimetres thick. He held dry ice in his hands, or a pot of boiling water, without discomfort. People watched his face when he came in the pub to see if the weather could be read there.

It was handy to know early if it would be necessary to duck a chair or a king-hit. When the action started, all laws went into neutral, the only custom that continued was aim and punch.

He had an authoritarian sense of old-style honour. He never spoke of women, or rooting, never of his own or anyone else's women—I don't think women had much place in his scheme of things—and he was a great stickler for clean talk.

'Behave,' he'd growl at some eager swearer, who was f'ing this and that in a loud voice. If the words were natural parts of a conversation he didn't object. He never swore himself.

One night around ten when the pub emptied and a small fight attracted attention up the street some of the boys discovered two old pensioners hard at it behind the bushes on the front lawns of the dairy company, where Serge worked. Full as ticks.

He took charge, pounded over, lifted the old man off the old woman and zotted him on the chin, whereupon he flew through the air four or five yards and lay still.

'Get off her, you dirty old cunt.'

And to the old lady he gave the advice, 'Not outside the Dairy Company,' in a pained voice. And patiently, 'Get up, love, and pull your dress up.'

The onlookers grunted. He looked round warningly.

'I mean pull your pants up. Go on, love.'

Kindness to women. He was someone to keep an eye on, but you couldn't help liking him.

When he came in looking dark, the mob would say, 'He's depressed. Watch him. Something's on. He might go off today.' Always hoping.

But this was what he always said about his mate Ronny. Ronny would be away somewhere for a month or two, and when he came in and started zotting down whiskies Serge would be hopeful of entertainment in the form of an explosion. Ronny would think nothing of drinking himself into a loving mood and wanting close contact with his fellow man. Or fellow boy. Both usually picked smaller opponents. Perhaps that's not fair: there weren't many as big as they were.

It had been a joke, under earlier publicans, that Serge had been barred from the pub for years, but no one was game to tell him.

Men like Mick didn't come into Serge's circle, they kept their own circles some distance away. Like similar peaks in a chain of mountains round the red bar. If you were in Serge's circle, Serge was the peak: if you were in Mick's, Mick was. A member of the circle acknowledged this by joining, or agreeing to join when invited. As in the aboriginal tribes we'd pushed out, there was no chief in our tribe. Just a fairly loose system of elders, who laid down laws and dispensed wisdom from the shoulder. The shadow-men who stood on the sunless side of the peaks, looked enviously at the creators of action. They'd stand over the world if they could.

One day I was two feet away from Serge, and walking past, when the monster got out and let fly a king-hit at a young guy talking to him. I didn't hear what they said, but I guess the young bloke disagreed with him. Soon they were chasing round the bar, Serge ponderously, the young bloke nimbly getting behind him and hanging on, turning with Serge so he couldn't get those fat arms on his head and pull him down to meet the knees. At the same time Ronny's monster took him round the bar to clean it up. Anyone he took a fancy to, he'd grab and belt. Drinkers, pool players, onlookers, the lot.

While they were blueing, I thought of all that energy exploding during the few minutes the fight lasted. Lots of impresarios in the outside world could have used that energy, harnessing it to make a profit. It was purer the way the boys used it. It isn't as if they went off their heads for a good reason—they did it nobly, with no cause.

Chasing someone out the door Ronny got fouled up with an old stranger woman visiting the pub trying to get away from the slaughter. She clumsily tripped, slipped and fell on her belly. Ronny, who wasn't co-ordinating all that well, was lusting for fresh faces to punch, and didn't see her. He tripped over her, swayed and fell back on her. She lay where she was while Ronny went in search of the faces that would ease the itch in his knuckles.

The following day Ronny saw her, really saw her, for the first time. From the dock in Parramatta court. Four hundred bucks fine and a bond. He was a nice-looking guy and I guess the judge liked his direct blue eyes and fresh face. He spoke well too. One thing about Ronny. No matter what work he did, the palms of his hands were always pink and soft, and he smelled of soap. Always.

That day I got away from the golf club early to be in the pub in case they didn't clap him in boob. The way he saw it, going off was just something a bloke did from time to time, and if people got in the way, they got in the way.

We played second row together. I liked the right side, he took the left.

THE KING

Once he was king of Parramatta. Not recognised in social columns, only pubs. He was medium height, built like King Kong.

The only time he ever backed away from a fight was one night near the Bar Roma. Two guys were attacked by about twelve. Just for the sake of the exercise the King goes over and wades in. He's joined by the three with him. In no time the twelve heroes are routed and depart together.

The King is not stupid and never believes an enemy is safely disposed of unless he can see him there on the ground. He walks on, watchful, and sure enough there come the twelve back, this time with sawn offs.

'Who's the hero?' says one of them.

The King and his boys are already round the corner, leaving the first two, who were late getting away. They were big, but this didn't help them. After the kicking stopped they lay on the footpath until a roving police car saw them and got an ambulance.

Two months later they were still in hospital.

The King said he didn't recognise any of them and couldn't remember their faces, but he was, after all, a fist man. He didn't like guns. Not for personal discussions, anyway.

After he lost interest in being King, what with getting older, he nevertheless always had a retinue of admirers and helpers who would back him up whatever he did. He threw a big shadow, and they stood in it.

Mostly there was no expression in his eyes. One Saturday morning I was talking to him and noticed his eyelids come down, sort of sleepy. He was measuring me for a king-hit. Then the eyes came awake, lids rose back to normal. The monster had got old and tired. I was sorry every time I saw that happen. I would have patted his shoulder, except.

In his spare time and holidays he loved to go hunting. His idea of hunting was to go north to somewhere like Inverell, where he'd be content with forty to fifty rabbits a night and half as many hares.

'No, you don't shoot 'em,' he told me. 'Spotlight. They sit there, hypnotised in the light. You go round and knock 'em on the head. Then you toss 'em in the freezer. Must freeze 'em immediately, so their muscles are OK for cooking.'

The King could bend over, not from the waist but from the hipbones. In the Zoo once I saw chimps do the same thing, picking up nuts. King Kong did it too. Our King could bend and put his elbows on the ground.

And yet, when he spoke of the snap-frozen muscles of clubbed vermin, I'll swear there was a tiny gleam of humanity in his eye, sad as a tear. He went on talking about one of his mates that made a living flying over the countryside dropping chicken heads laced with ten-eighty.

'For the dingoes.'

Poor dingoes. Getting the same treatment the blacks got when they interfered with the white man's crops and herds and flocks. I didn't want to hear any more.

Next time I heard of him he'd settled down even more and had a job as an undertaker's assistant.

'Last week,' he said, watching me with relish, 'I had to go out and pick up this body. When the cops finished, they stood back and I had to get it out of the car. Been there six weeks, killed himself in the scrub with a hose from the exhaust. I knew right away I'd have to put gloves on, you can't touch things like that with your bare hands. By myself, I was. Put the gloves on, reached in, came back outside and tied a handkerchief round my mouth—I breathe with my mouth, nose was broken so many times I don't use it for breathing —and reached in again. Bits of body fell off, broke apart. I had to put the lot in plastic.

'Nothing would ever get the smell out of that car. Nothing. I know the bloke from the saleyard that tried to do it up. In the end he had to auction it. Some silly bastard bought it. But I've seen that before. Never get the smell of a human body out. Gets right in the upholstery, even in the metal.'

Next time I saw him I was driving through Parramatta from the course on the way to the Southern Cross. The traffic held me up a bit and I waved.

'How's business?' I called out.

He wasn't embarrassed.

'Dead!' he roared out from the undertaker's doorway. 'Dead!'

The traffic moved. I moved off, waved again.

He called out after me, 'I'll get you one day! I'll plant you!' In the rear vision mirror I could see the grin on his face from the end of the street.

Once, late at night, he confided to me that he wrote poetry. I didn't mention it again and neither did he.

MY THEORY

I worked out a theory about marriage after watching guys and knowing something about their women and home life.

The bum at work is usually the boss at home. The boss at work is most often a bum at home, picked on, vulnerable. Middle management and supervisory staff float round in a limbo: half bum everywhere, half boss somewhere.

The theory is: Status in marriage is inversely proportional to the surrender value of the marriage. That's for the men.

For women, it's the reverse. Their status is directly proportional to what they'd get from a surrender of the marriage policy.

SHARON

This theory didn't work with Sharon. She was the boss and would have been no matter who she married. She was the barmaid at the Southern Cross.

There were plenty of barmaids: she was THE barmaid. She'd been there since Adam was a boy. Her husband was a little feller, smoked a pipe of sweet tobacco.

I don't smoke. Never been able to get the habit, though I've tried dozens of times. Just the same, I used to stand near him sometimes, to get the sweet smell of his pipe.

The sort of woman Sharon was, if you wanted to swear and carry on, that was all right but you had to swear with a smile if it was near her or she'd reach out over the bar and paste you one. She reckoned she had a duty to her old man and always made him feel he was number one. He got a chilled glass.

She christened the Koala Bear, who eats roots and leaves, the Rambling Rose, who roots against walls, and even made passing reference to Rosebud. If you remember, Rosebud was the last word on the dying lips of Orson Welles in *Citizen Kane*. But in my pub rosebud means something different from a child's picture on the back of a cot. It's a kiss you give your bird fresh out of the shower. You just pull the cheeks apart.

Sharon looked after her sick mother twenty-five years crippled in a sitting position with arthritis, and that old lady spent her time watching birds, bright as a button. Sharon's old man was a bus driver, subject to the colloidal cyste that afflicts cops on bikes and taxi drivers from the bumping up and down, but he didn't die of that. When he dropped, they opened him up and found his lungs were set solid with dust and all these tiny fibres of asbestos through his air passages, from brake linings of cars and trucks and buses. The very things he earned a crust from. I reckon that's what it means, giving your life for your job.

I like Sharon. I think I'll give her a copy of my book.

YOUNG SIBLEY

He was the only one to call me Lance. I guess he was the only one remembered. They called me Meat Man ever since kindergarten. Or just Meat. The teacher called me Lance, but the kids forgot.

Sibley was success-oriented, as they say. His sister was a prominent child in the entertainment racket, and Dad an eminent butcher.

I always used to come out ahead of young Sibley in class and I felt bad about it. It wasn't as if I tried. But he knew and we knew, right from when we were very young, that all he had to do was get in the university quota after the Higher Certificate and he was on the way to a profession. His family expected it. I'd risen in the world too. But only up the hill.

After high school he'd drop in on us at the pub every few months, to see if we were still alive, have one beer and beat it. He had strong healthy views on drinking too much piss and getting a beer gut and dying at fifty. We didn't mind. Sibley was Sibley. We took roughly the view that you can't blame a man for his family.

He dropped in a while back, got a beer without saying hullo to anyone and sat at a table, pulling out papers and things from his pocket and writing. It wasn't a form guide, so it was enough to get attention. Still, Sibley was Sibley. The guys round the Mead had a reverence for education, while not wishing to examine it too closely.

I thought it was a bit ostentatious, waiting till he'd finished writing before he took a sip of his beer. Drinkers all round the bar noticed and got that look.

'Hey Sibley,' I said. 'Still doing homework for the teacher?' I knew he thought of his activities at the seat of higher learning more grandly than that.

Then I remembered and hurried over before he called out Lance. He had pens that wrote red, blue, green and purple.

He didn't answer right away.

'Working on the philosophy of the red bar?' I asked. Then he was ready to talk.

'My thesis,' he said in the offhand way you say My new Mercedes.

'What's it on, Sibley?'

'It's an investigation.'

52

'Sure. Of what?'

'The red bar. Just like you said.'

'No kidding.'

'Lance, the mind of man can have no idea of the fascination this place holds, once you get into it.'

'How are you into it, Sibley?'

'I'm not yet. I'm doing my doctorate in Psych. As soon as I got the idea of investigating the psychology of the drinker I felt like the cow that jumped over the moon. Ten feet tall.'

He was not much over half that.

'You mean your thesis is on the red bar.'

'Exactly. I couldn't have put it better myself.'

'So you'll jump off the red bar and become Doctor Sibley.'

'Right.' His teeth showed, all of them, as he enjoyed the thought. 'Let's say I'll jump *over* the red bar.' I felt like the little dog that laughed to see such fun. What would Sibley make of drinkers? A man that let his beer go flat.

Sibley started to give me a talk.

'Mind you, when I talk of the psychology of drinkers, I'll be up against a sea of prejudice. Till now, they've been taken to be on one of the lowest rungs of the ladder of intellectual development.'

'What?' I said. Then I remembered I was a drinker. My judgment had to be suspect. And how did I know what 'they' thought.

'Past observations tell us that after twenty their mental vigour declines. At forty it's extinct and only instinct is left.'

'What?' I said again.

'These are past opinions,' he said. 'My investigations will update opinion on the subject.'

'What investigations?'

'Tests,' he said casually. 'These old ideas can't be allowed to persist without proper foundations. Imagine—'

'Wait a minute, Sibley. Who are you going to test and how?'

'All the guys that drink here. I'm taking this pub as my sample.'

'How are you going to get them to do tests?'

'I'll be persuasive. Tell 'em it's research, which it is. Tell 'em their psychology will be in books at the university. I bet they never knew they had a psychology.'

'Why don't you go to some other pub?'

'They wouldn't know me anywhere else. They might do me over. Here, everyone knows me. They've seen me around, a lot of us went to the same school, live in the same suburb, breathe the same air. They'll be in it, they think I'm harmless. They know I'm harmless. I might have gone on to university, but they don't grudge me that. They'll tolerate me.'

'Then you go away, then what?'

'I'll get my PhD. If the thesis is good enough, it'll be published.'

I got another drink. Sibley wasn't halfway through his flat beer. He continued the seminar, ticking his points off on his fingers.

'They've always been considered treacherous in their dealings with employers and non-drinkers. After they leave school, they return to the natural surroundings of their fathers. A sort of homing instinct, as in birds. Drinkers can survive in conditions where the non-drinker would perish. All respectable opinions last century.'

'You'd better not tell them any of this.'

'Of course not. And you always were a listener, never a talker. Anyway, to go on. With no history, they have no past; with no religion, no hope; with no forethought and providence, no future. Each drinker is a doomed case; all the civilised races can do is take care that their last hours are not hurried by neglect or cruelty.'

'Hang on there, Sibley. What do you mean civilised races and last hours?'

'They can't survive in our world and in the future, Lance,' he said kindly. 'The non-drinker is a member of the civilised races: the drinker, no matter the language he speaks, belongs to one identifiable inferior race spread throughout the planet. But to go on, some past authorities say that to speak of intelligence in respect of drinkers is a misnomer; they present hardly any of the phenomena of intellect. They are unreflective and

55

averse to abstract reasoning and sustained mental effort.'

'You're describing a drunk.'

'Lance, baby, that's when a drinker's a drinker for Christ's sake.'

Sibley got up to go pee against the stained stainless steel through the damaged door. On the table in front of him were papers. On the top paper I saw a list. Porteus Maze, it began. Knox Cube, Thurstone Hand, Picture vocabulary, Form assembly, Ferguson Form Board, Passalong, Repetition of Digits, Footprint, Draw-a-Man, Pattern Matching, Block Design.

I was worried about Sibley. He was right about not going to a strange pub. But.

He got back and began writing on his bits of paper with the blue pen. I went away to play pool. When I looked up next he was around among the dying race. He wasn't testing them, as far as I could see. Maybe he was explaining, preparing the ground, getting the natives used to the sound of his voice and the way he went on.

Then I saw he was buying them beers. Just like the early colonisers all over the world, giving beads and pretty nothings, which was what beer was to Sibley. I hoped he could grade the wheat from the horse-shit, in what they told him.

His coloured pens were stuck neatly in his pocket, his face lit with missionary zeal; he looked so alive and alert and cheerful it was hard to believe he was real.

Once I saw him tentatively explore the crack in the wall with his finger. He put a finger right in. The wall didn't close on him.

I used to try to get to talk to him early on in the day, when he came in for his heart-starter, but that was no guarantee he'd be sober.

When I say talk to him, I mean listen. I know a lot of his words were nonsense, but no more stupid than other philosophers.

Behind his eyes were stores of scenes and images. A lot of the images were words. His bottom eyelids had come loose and swung out, red and full of liquid. His hair was old ashes, hands crawling with frogskin, face dried out like plums bathed in caustic, left in the sun and wrinkling into prunes. When he turned his head the back of his neck wrinkled like a tortoise.

A graveyard of ghostly ideas flapped silently round his grey brain. His old tongue was his only weapon, the air from his grey lungs his only vehicle. He battled invisible enemies in the wilderness where he stood, leaning against the red bar.

'Think of the life cycle of humans. Compare it to a working day.'

Jack swept the pub yard, picked up glasses. General rouseabout. He was bent, as if the sun pressed heavy on his shoulders.

'You're free in the early morning, this is the baby stage. At school and at work there's regimentation; this is youth and maturity. All of a sudden the children are let out at the end of the day, the workers go home; the senile are put out to die at leisure, retired. Each man each day lives out his life cycle in miniature.'

He stopped for a sip. He was on beer at that stage. Sunlight, soft as talc, spilled in at the door.

'It's like me. What I drink every day is a story in miniature of my drinking history. Milk first thing to stop the pains, water to thin out my spit, a cup of tea, then a beer. Later I'll get on to the spirits, then back to the beer, then last thing some water to work against the dehydration.'

'As for the end of it all,' he said, and hesitated.

'You're not worried about it?' I said.

'I'm not worried.'

'Sure?'

'It's not the dark worries me, it's the getting dark.' Looking to the bottom of his glass.

59

I didn't want to watch him face dying.

Next thing I hear this crazy old voice singing:

'I feel no pain dear Mother
'But Christ I am so dry
'Please take me to a brewery,
'And leave me there to die.'

I look up and he's laughing at me.

The pub considered him harmless, but a deep thinker. Dimly we knew he regarded publicans less than sinners. No one wanted to talk about the things Jack talked about, no one wanted to be a deep thinker, unless it was about the odds on the races.

'Look, son.' He never called me Meat Man. He had no sex life himself. I wonder what old men with no women do? If it's that it's natural enough, but sad. Or maybe when you're old it's better than the real thing.

'Say things from another planet got here and you were alone and tried to answer their questions. Like what's this and how does that work? How would you go?'

'Well, Jack. I could answer some things. I know how electricity gets generated for a start.'

'Yeah, well let's start with something simple. Say they point to the permanent magnet and the copper wiring and the insulation, then to a knife and fork and you tell 'em what they're used for and then they say how do you make them?'

'Well,' I said after a bit.

'Yeah, well. See what I mean. You couldn't tell 'em. If they were all destroyed, how do you start again? Where do you get the ore?'

He didn't have to hammer the point.

'Never be ashamed of being an Australian,' he'd say. 'There's plenty just as bad as us in the world. The Australian just wants to be left alone, he doesn't want to hear nasty things or be bothered by politics, he's not ambitious, he doesn't want too much fun. Look at the bar.'

The saloon bar was a shambles. Pools of beer lay on the red bar and on the floor. The barnlike structure was yellowed by smoke, browned by fly dirt. Doors didn't shut, glass was cracked. Someone had punched a hole in the door to the toilet.

'The Australian knows life's short. Heat waves and the driest drought for fifty years can be followed immediately by floods that wash away houses, people, stock, crops. Anything can happen. We started off in chains, we do our best when we're not pushed, we pay back a good turn, say no to authority and upstarts, we're casual, we like makeshift things, we're ingenious, practical, self-reliant, good in emergencies, think we're as good as anyone in the world, and always sympathise with the underdog.'

I could think of a lot of people in the world that fitted this description and I could think of a lot of exceptions among Australians, but I kept my mouth shut. Alky Jack was the only one that I'd listen to without a beer in my hand for more than three seconds even if he'd dug his words up from a past I didn't know.

'The trouble is, this doesn't make him a good citizen in a democracy. Democracy is not for people who just want to be left alone so long as they do what they're told and don't answer back. The key people in the democratic process are critics, dissenters, reformers. If they're sealed off from the political process, the system grows tired and sick and turns into something else.'

'God save the Queen,' I said.

'She's not a bad little thing, the Queen. I wish the sluts round here could hold their grog as well.'

'And their tongues,' I said.

'True. And their tongues.'

Jack went into a fit of coughing. He rolled his own smokes—uneven looking things. They didn't smell all that good either. The more he smoked to recover from coughing, the more the smoking made him cough. But he either didn't see the connection, or didn't want to. He had more important things to think of. I could imagine him going to bed at night, last thing, holding up two fingers to death. But not beckoning.

'Another thing. There's no greater encouragement to revolutionary dissatisfaction than the realisation that, more and more, only rich men or men with access to riches, can hope to achieve significant public office. Either your own money, or the party's money, or—if you please rich men—their money, but political seats are impossible without a lot of money. Politics are beyond the ordinary man. While he's his own man, I mean. If you allow majority vote to determine what you say in public I think you're not worth pissing on.'

He never once stood on his age as if it was a throne. Never once proved a point by saying, 'That's how it's always been.'

Alky Jack was a man of principle.

'I could lie like a trooper if I wanted, son,' he'd say. 'But I WILL not. Not for me, not for you, not for anyone. Not for gain or good opinion. I won't pretend, I won't take things that aren't mine and I won't do anything I don't want to do. The truth is one thing. Being yourself is another.'

I never knew what to say when he came out with principles.

'Society is opposed to the single unit, man. The bigger it gets, the more production, the more individual misery there is.'

He came out with the thought he always ended on.

'Why does the whole thing have to be built on cutthroat competition?'

He lapsed into silence after that.

Later he said, 'Maybe equal pay's the answer.'

'They've just about got it, Jack.'

He looked at me, disgusted.

'Equal for all,' he said. 'If people were fair dinkum they'd work for the satisfaction of their own competence, their cleverness, the position they attained. Not bloody cash. Not greed.'

I couldn't think of anything to say. He was silent again for a long time.

At the end of the day he'd stumble off to bed, his mind slow, language lagging. You had to be a dill not to know Alky Jack had a mind, but. With something extra he'd have been a great man. But I don't know what that something is.

I used to wonder what he was before he decided to become an alcoholic.

THE PUB WIDOW

Friday nights were busy, drunks everywhere. So much noise you couldn't hear the BB guns popping at the butterflies. In the trees along the creek cicadas sparkled, croaked, throbbed, blared and deafened. You could hear them in the pub.

One Friday, the day of Freddy Mott's funeral, when there were still a few mourners who hadn't bothered to go home and change, dotted here and there in suits too tight and black ties, a woman came to the door of the pub.

There was nothing strange in that, but this woman wasn't a drunkard or a fighter or even an old bag, she was nicely dressed and sort of neat. She carried a small something in her hand but the remarkable thing about her was the look on her face.

If she was a man you'd say he'd come looking for the bastard that just ran him off the road in his nice new car.

But she wasn't a man. She was the angriest woman you've ever seen.

'Listen to me, you useless lot!' she screamed above the hullaballoo and the cicadas. 'I'm Missus Mott. We had Fred's funeral today. When he was alive he spent all his time with you always down here in the pub, so you can have him now!'

She took the lid off the something in her hand and with one furious sweep of her arm let the contents fly all round. Most of it fell on the nearest pool table. Drinkers and poolplayers gaped.

It didn't go far, just settled slowly on the green tables and the floor round about.

Freddy's ashes.

MAC

He tried to keep it dark, but no good. He tried to live it down: it just wasn't on. He'd been a copper and word always got round. No risk. He gave up worrying about it.

They all knew he was a gentleman, which he was, a real human man, but no one ever forgot he'd been a copper, and he never forgot they never forgot.

He never liked getting stuck talking to one particular crew. Not that he was a floater, he'd stay at one place leaning on the bar, but he wouldn't go round stopping at people and striking up a conversation. He stayed there, and they passed him or stopped and spoke to him, then passed on.

When he had a few he'd tell me of his early days in the force. 'This inspector was always drunk and his favourite order was: Out batons and charge, boys!'

His face was a map of long-ago slashes, kicks and fractures. So ugly it was handsome.

And he'd describe fights where he had to go in and restore order.

'Always took a backstop with me. Guard my back. Some of the brawlers, there was only one way to handle 'em. Whack, and down they go. Never bend down, use your boots, that's what they're for.'

And stories of his times up the Cross. King's Cross, not our Cross.

'This Morrie invites me to his place on a Friday night for a feed. Well, I knock him back several times, then after a week or two he seems so serious about it, so dead set to have me, that I say OK, I'll be there.

'I've met him in the street in drag, and he wasn't objectionable, he was well-spoken, clean, and I've said to him, if I did the right thing I'd run you in. Anyhow I lob there this Friday night and the place is a picture. The most pretty, the most comfortable little flat I've ever seen in my life. And I've seen a few. And the spread! You wouldn't want to know, it's some of the best cooking you'd ever see, in a good restaurant or anywhere. He introduces me to his girl-friend, a boy of course, and I forget I'm a policeman for an hour or two and polish off this dirty big meal. It stopped me, I tell you.'

And the girls working the Cross.

'You'd see a bit of trouble down the road and when you get there it'd be two of the girls fighting. Pulling

68

hair, and their funny punches. You know, instead of the arm straightening at the elbow, they tense up the whole arm at a bit more than ninety degrees and swing this from the shoulder. Like the rocker arms on an old printing press.

'Righto you two molls, I'd say. Stop it or I'll hang one on you. And to the one out of her beat, Get up your own territory. I wasn't on the paddy waggon, you see,' he said to me in explanation.

This was some demarcation; the man on the beat didn't take the money out of the mouths of the boys on the waggon.

'What they'd do, they'd round up a few, take 'em round a corner somewhere and charge 'em ten bucks to get out of the waggon. Put it over there in the corner of the seat, you'd say. And when they'd gone there'd be no one to see you pick it up.

'They had to be kept to their territory, or they'd fight all day. You can have a yard full of stallions and there'll be a bit of biting and kicking, then a leader emerges and they all settle down. But you have a yard full of mares and no leader ever emerges. Not ever. Fight all the time.'

If he thought you were pretty much a straight, he'd maybe talk of some of the dirtier side of police work. Like the domestic arguments he was called to settle in houses where the walls practically ran with cack and the smell something you'd never forget. On the floor, everywhere. People that lived like animals and behaved like them.

'Animals aren't dirty, Mac,' I reminded him. 'Unless they're caged.'

'I apologise to animals', he said.

'Yes,' he took an inch off the top of a fresh middy. 'The things humans do you never find in the animal world.'

'They haven't got our imagination.'

'Maybe it's that. Anyway you'd never believe the range of things humans'll get up to in the way of behaviour. Out Parramatta way we had a bloke used to come at night to the nurses' home, get amongst the washing on the lines and cut the gussets out of all the girls' panties. We set traps for him, but even when he was sighted no one could catch him. He was so fit he must have been a long distance runner. He'd been doing it for ten years, so maybe he was over the hill, I don't know, but we combed the force for a young athletic copper. He lay in wait night after night, finally sprung him and chased him. It took him five miles to gain on him and when he caught him he tackled him and lay on him until a police car brought help. He hadn't left that night's gussets behind, there they were stuffed in his shirt.'

'What did he want 'em for?' I said. I wasn't too sure what a gusset was.

'In his boarding house we found five chaffbags of scrap rag, and bottles and bottles of almost clear liquid. I say almost. What's this? we said. I boil 'em, he said. Then what? I drink the water. It was a new twist, even to me.'

Apart from what he told us, we never knew much about him, and not knowing, we suspected a lot.

Mac would never really belong to our tribe.

At the corner of the red bar, Alky Jack was muttering. He might have been talking in our sleep for all we heard him.

My eyes followed his shaking hand up the arm to the wrinkled elbow and saw it in the grave, fleshless, relaxing to white dust. And saw the moment when the last shred of flesh parted, rotten, and the profound skull, free at last from all connections, rolled sideways to rest where an ear had once been.

Was different from the usual run. To begin with, she looked like a little girl. Fourteen, sometimes. Sometimes seventeen.

When she appeared round a corner or you spotted her in a crowd of people you couldn't miss her. There was this light shining out from her legs and arms and face. It shone out to about an inch all round and when you got close to her and put your finger inside the inch, it felt warm.

In the dark, you could see her face clearly. It wouldn't have mattered what else she had or didn't have, the bloom on her smiled like flowers. When she laughed, you knew elves and sprites and fairies still sparkled in the world.

I don't mean she *was* a little girl. She was in business for herself, she earned Christ knows how much brass, but for some reason she was stuck on me. I've never found out why.

She was the sort of girl that would call you Darling about a hundred times running, then ask if she was boring you.

One kiss was never enough for her. You were lucky if you got away with less than about a thousand. No use saying anything: you might just as well have thrown water into the sea.

And if you made love, she didn't pause for breath, she was into it, kissing until you felt you were going under in the sea. And if you made love again, and again, there she was, smiling. If you wanted more, she was there. Ready, and not only ready but waiting, and not only waiting but willing and eager. If you wanted to stop that was all right too.

No matter how tired you were, you got the full treatment; love all the time coming in a golden stream from her eyes. A golden blue stream, would you believe? If you were dirty and covered in sweat, no matter what the dirt was—concrete, oil, anything—she put her arms round you. Never mind her dress, or how you smelt, it made no difference. She loved you and that was it.

If you were late and she was waiting for you on a corner somewhere, she'd get a bit anxious thinking you might be run over, and you'd peep round the corner opposite and see her little face a bit taut, looking this way and that, up and down the street. Then when she saw you this great smile would break out all over her face. It seemed as if her whole body came alive and joyful, her arms and legs sort of smiled too. And people looked at her because of the light shining out of her.

But when you were waiting for her and she suddenly came into sight and saw you right away, she'd run. No one who'd ever had her running towards them could ever forget it. The light, the face, and everything shining, and her pelting towards you, and when she was close enough calling out Darling! And she didn't pull up either. Smack straight into you. And if you couldn't take the impact, there you were both on the ground and she didn't care what bruises she had, you'd be laughing and kissing as if there was no one else in the world.

After Mac had gone I left half a beer on the table and ran out to the car. But driving up from the car park I left the engine running and came in and finished the glass.

Way overhead the helpless moon swung round the earth on Newton's string.

When I got to Sydney and she came down out of her building, she was so desirable her body looked fierce. Sharp rays of something shot out from her skin and hit me. She looked pleased to see me, but when she saw how I wanted and desired her and had a dry mouth, she looked more pleased than any other time. She had a pen in her hand. She'd forgotten she had it.

She saw me looking down, and looked too.

'Here,' she said. And gave it to me with such a love-look that I took it.

I didn't want a pen. I had one.

Later we drove out to the sandstone cliffs looking east to the sea. Where we stopped, to listen to night come.

AUSSIE BOB

He was once an Englishman, but he'd been out here sixteen years and considered himself Australian. In his spare time he taught boxing to the kids at the Police Boys' Club and most of the time I knew him he had one hand injured. I noticed that every time the hand hurt more, he got drunk. He got drunk if he had a bit of sickness. He got drunk if things went badly at work, or if young guys got promoted over him.

'Who wants to get old,' he'd say. 'You're RS these days if you're old. You've gotta be young.' RS means ratshit. I think it tells the story.

Bob drank whisky with a beer chaser or beer with a whisky chaser. One time he drank one way, next time the other. He always poured the last bit of beer in the whisky, to get it all. Sometimes he'd pour it back and forth three or four times, just in case.

'Whisky's good for you,' he said. 'You'll never get worms while you drink whisky. You take a glass of whisky and a glass of water and drop a worm in each glass and see what happens. Whisky shrivels it, water makes it healthy.'

He'd been all over the world for this company he worked for. His favourite story was of when the British were in India.

'I was at a dance and met this real snooty woman about thirty-five. As I was dancing with her I thought This is good, she's rearing to go, and sure enough that night I took her home—to her place, too—and got me end in. They get better over thirty.'

'Like a rattlesnake?' I suggested.

'Yeah, but a day or two later I pass her in the street and raise my hat and say good morning. Young man, she said, remember this. Where I come from sexual intercourse is not considered sufficient social introduction. You could have knocked me arse over tit with a feather.'

A few months after this his two girls went out together with two local kids on a Friday night and got themselves killed. Car smash head on at a ton and a half on Highway One. Just went out for the fun of it.

I sent him a card. He didn't come into the Southern Cross for a while so I thought I might call round at his place with a few cans and maybe cheer him up.

77

In the yard next door a mob of fowls were battering an old hen. Really picking on her. It was probably *her* eggs they came from. Fowls aren't human.

I didn't make much noise. Perhaps I should have. The door was open, no one answered my knock, I could hear voices inside.

I went in, I didn't think he'd mind. As I got further, the voices were kids' voices. Kids of four or five or six. I can't tell what age they are when you get down that far.

I didn't want to interrupt, I just listened. The voices got older. Nine or ten. The kids were saying things like what they did in the holidays, and singing a song or two they learned at school, or reciting poems.

As the voices got bigger, they got louder. I came closer and up to a door that was open a little. I didn't go right to it, there's nothing easier to pick up than a movement close to a slightly open door. I stood about three metres back.

Bob had a tape recorder going, a little old one, and the tapes he was playing had to be his kids' voices. Tears were coming down his face, he wasn't even trying to wipe them away, and falling on to the front of his trousers where the fly is.

I turned away, found a table and put the beer down very quiet, and carefully made for the door. As I got there I heard the voices on tape change to boys' voices—his two other kids—and he shut it off and went to another tape or else ran the same one back. His boys were OK, they were alive and kicking. He didn't need to cry over them.

When he came back to the pub, everyone gave him a few words and said how sorry they were, and this seemed to buck him up. He got drunk his first night back and wanted to fight everybody, bad hand or no bad hand. They all understood except one stranger, who invited him outside. He was going, too, but the boys pulled him back and Mick and a dozen others explained Aussie Bob's case to the stranger who saw the justice of Bob being allowed to shoot his mouth off because of grief for his two girls. Mind you, if a stranger had done the same thing when it wasn't a question of something as solemn and respectable as grief, they'd have joyfully thumped shit out of him.

Out in the pub yard, in a heavy shower a day later, Aussie Bob was fighting raindrops. Punching as they passed him on the way down. At one stage he copped an airgun pellet in the chest and said someone ought to do something about those kids.

The pub lost interest in his private battle. No one thought the kids ought to be stopped. You don't hang the cat because it kills a mouse.

Fate wasn't finished with Aussie Bob. Some months later, in October, his two boys went out in his new high-powered car, bought new for Spring when young men's fancies lightly turn to thoughts of speed, and got killed inside an hour from leaving the house.

That finished Bob. He got on the piss every day, never sober enough to play his tapes of the kids' voices, and finally took to going to work drunk.

His mates did their best to hide him, and on night shift they'd persuade him to get out of sight. When the supervisor came in, Bob was always outside on the plant.

He was on the plant, all right. Lying down on it, sleeping it off under a cylindrical tank, which was supported on four short legs.

It had to fall. Bob had to be there when it fell. The grating supporting it was at fault, and the tank took Bob and the grating down eighteen inches to the vacuum tank underneath. A leg of the top tank fractured the vacuum tank and bits of Bob and grating were sucked into the vacuum tank.

There was no way of telling he'd been asleep. His firm made a presentation to his family, but there was no one to give it to. His wife died when the fourth was eight, he had no relatives in Australia. They put the money into what they call a suspense account, in case he acquired relatives.

None of these things should have happened to Bob: he wasn't made for tragedy; fate or God or something got hold of him and savaged him. Regularly we ironed ourselves out and we did it on purpose: he had it done to him and it was permanent.

ERNIE

He was often in the pub, but not regularly. He'd have to stay away some days in order to practise new sports. He was eager for promotion where he worked and since there was a rapid turnover of bosses he was forced to learn a new sport with every boss. I say forced, but he forced himself. Life was no good if you couldn't talk his favourite sport with the boss, and maybe, with luck, you might get to play with him on the weekend. Who knows what might happen then? You might just hit it off. And next time, when a promotion came up . . .

The only time I ever saw him drunk he kept saying over and over, 'I'm getting smarter. Every day I'm further up the ladder. Every day I'm smarter. Every . . .'

His present boss was a fisherman, and Ernie had heard this from someone other than the boss.

Nevertheless, he took the chance and started to learn about fishing.

He loaded himself up with many dollars worth of equipment and on his first day off took a boat out from Brooklyn and fished in the shallows near a rail bridge. He'd had a few bites and had his bait sucked off and caught nothing and was just about to up anchor when he caught what felt like a dead weight on his line. Thinking in terms of old boots, he pulled. The business end didn't come towards him, but moved from side to side in five or six metre arcs. He'd caught something.

It was a great moment. When it was nearly up the side of the boat he found it was a stingray. Never mind that, it lived in the water and he'd caught it. It was a fish.

The creature stared at him and began heaving for breath.

'Don't do that,' Ernie advised it. 'I don't like that sound.'

He hit it several blows with his sheath knife. After each blow it groaned.

'Don't do that!' He couldn't stand the pitiful groaning. It was still staring at him. He could only afford to take out a rowing boat so he had oars. He bludgeoned the groaning ray to death and pulled its carcase over the side. He soon forgot the groans.

On the way back in the train—he wasn't going to buy any old secondhand car, he wanted to display a brand new late model when he got a car—the thing began to sweat. A flow of fine clear oil came from its pores. He wrapped his pullover round it to protect himself from the wrath of his fellow passengers, and watched while it gradually became soaked in oil.

'Probably keeps it warm in cold water,' he explained to a pugnacious woman opposite with four kids.

'You ruin my children's clothes with that stuff and I'll have every penny you've got,' she said fiercely, and this was exactly the type of threat to make Ernie go to water. He kept his mouth shut in despair.

He wasn't game to take it to his boarding house, so he tried to hack it up at the back of the pub. The skin was thick. We gathered for a while to watch him.

Mick said, 'Waste of time bringing that rubbish home. Shoulda left it in the river.'

Not even Sharon would have a bar of it.

I was the only one to show him any sympathy. I could see he faintly despised me for it, but I was better than no one.

Why is it the weak man will look down on those who tolerate him, and up to those who keep him down? I've never worked it out. When something like this strikes me and I wonder about it, I feel I've found a key and I'm holding it in my hand, but I don't know what it opens.

* * *

When Ernie had cooked a few of the hacked-up bits, he couldn't eat it.

When he threw the bits away in disgust, some plopped in the creek. Ferocious movement slashed the surface of the water and the bits disappeared. The creek was alive with eels.

Ernie kept a salt-shaker in his pocket. When he was sure no one was looking, he'd shake salt into his palm and lick it up. Gave him a thirst. He had no real taste for beer.

He was quite sure no one was looking, but we sprung him every time.

The weather was humid, mushrooms sprouted over the golf course. I got off the tractor every fifty metres and collected hatfuls and tipped them into buckets I wedged behind my legs. If I was stuck on cutting greens and Wal was out, he'd share his buckets with me. At night, a little butter in the pan, they'd melt up and sizzle and come out delicious over your bit of steak or couple of chops.

The dew stayed on the grass often till around nine or ten. Grass-spider cobwebs were weighted down in the middle with diamonds. You got the best sight of them on foot; you could stop and look at one particular drop and move your head one way and the other and see the colours change from gold to blue and turquoise and through to red. And if you did it very slowly you could see the different stages from silver to yellow to gold. And if you got one on your finger and licked it off, the colours and richness disappeared on your tongue.

The weather in the Southern Cross was humid too.

From steel barrels, forced by the magic of gas pressure along slim plastic lines, our liquid golden god spouted out of taps and dew formed on the glass that contained him. Nevertheless we swallowed him.

To give him power over us, that was why. No voice of his own, he was compelled to speak through us.

At other times we jumped into the froth of beer as if it was the spume of surf, like delighted children.

MAKING AN IMPRESSION

Young Sibley was around a lot. He'd got to the stage where he got the guys to make marks on paper, or point to one of a set of choices, or manipulate blocks and sticks of different length. Most of the time all they had to do was point to something, the tests were aimed at a minimum of familiarity with written and spoken language.

Once, Sibley looked up as Alky Jack passed and I looked too. I wondered if we saw the same man.

One day a paper dropped off his pile when he was sitting out the back of the pub at a table. I thought I'd better retrieve it for him before the others got to it. He *could* be writing things that would upset them. He might have forgotten they were taught to read and write at primary school, and most of them still could.

The paper had some guy's name on it, and a summary of the impressions they made on Sibley.

Danny: Neglected at home. Fair intelligence. Health poor.

Ernie: Splendid memory. Most co-operative. Hard to see how he fits in with this group.

Mick: Easily led. Quiet disposition. Anxious to please. Born loser.

Flash: Rather dull. Sexually backward.

King: Good open disposition. Hesitant. Anal passive?

Darkfellow: Companions regard him as violent, unpredictable.

Lance: Plausible disposition. Completed secondary education. Could be assimilated.

Great Lover: Quick witted, mod. intelligent. Conscientious, painstaking.

Alky Jack: Sullen disposition, unco-operative, rambling speech. Fixed ideas. Premature senility?

Serge: Good open disposition, honest, well-spoken, gentle manner. Effeminate?

I stowed it away quick. If the King or Serge saw it, old Sibley was dead. Anal passive? Effeminate? What next? As for born loser—God Christ almighty.

THE SHOW

There were a lot of people round for the Show at Castle Hill, and most of the drinking was done not there but down at the Bull.

Ten of us lined up at the bar and to save time we ordered a hundred middies.

'A hundred? You kidding?' said the barmaid.

'Fair dinkum,' we said solemnly.

She called the licensee, who sat on the problem for ten seconds before answering.

'You got money?' he demanded. The pistol showed in his pocket.

'We got money,' we said, and flashed twenty of it.

'Give,' he said, his hand out.

'Give,' we said, pointing to the bar.

We drank the ten each in an hour. It was a hot day, the beer hardly touched the sides. Who cared if the last five were flat, it was a good laugh.

* * *

At the Show, there were stands everywhere with goods for sale. Where did the word goods come from? I wouldn't have called most of them good.

There was a drinks tent. That was a good. The others went off looking at the ring events, but Mick and I wandered over near a blonde and got talking to her. She pulled us out of sight round a corner.

'She's got a jealous husband,' Mick said, and she laughed.

'How about a bite to eat and a drink?' Mick suggested, and she said OK, but first she had to go off to the Ladies.

'Get her full and you'll be right,' Mick said to me while she was gone.

There we were in the drinks tent. We sat her in the middle so the bottle of wine passed back and forth and she was drinking two to our one. In a short time she was full. Full? She was blind.

She was friends with some people showing machinery at the Show, and borrowed their caravan for an hour. She dragged us inside and both of us went through her several times. She wasn't much, but she really went off her head, and made up for it in enthusiasm.

When we'd had enough and the hour was up, we went to the door of the caravan to see if the coast was clear to go. There was a bloke outside that kept saying to people, 'Have you seen my wife? Have you seen Annette?'

No one had seen her and he didn't look like going, so I opened the door and stepped down.

'Have you seen my wife?' he says.

'I saw her over that way ten minutes ago,' I said, pointing round the corner of the drinks tent. Off he goes.

'Mick,' I call back inside the caravan, 'Get her out. He's gone over there.'

'I can't,' he says.

'What's the matter?'

'She's passed out. She's too floppy to lift. Bugger it. Leave her here. Come on, let's go.'

We went.

Next day we were back there but we kept away from the caravan. But you wouldn't want to know, we run into Annette, with her friend Pam. They didn't know us.

We stopped in front of them.

Mick said to me, with them a metre away, 'Do you know where I can get a fuck?'

Pam said indignantly, 'Did you say fuck?'

'No, I didn't say fuck.'

'I thought you said fuck,' says Pam, winking at Annette.

Annette didn't want to know. The side of her face was puffed, make-up covered it. There was extra make-up at the corner of one eye. Her husband found her after all.

As we walked on, Mick was grinning.

'Some of these blokes got no sense of humour at all. What's the harm? She's on the pill, she's not going to have no kid, I haven't had a load for three years and you're clean aren't you?'

I said I was.

'Well then. Who do these jokers think they are? Jesus Christ?'

He even had the hide to start getting indignant about it. I took him away towards the boxing tent.

The last day of the show we ran into Sammy. Danny was with us.

'Hey, you bastards,' Sammy called. 'Come round the back and take a gander at my new vehicle.'

We went round and there's this Bentley, black, shining and elegant.

'This yours?' says Mick, putting five prints and a palmprint on the duco for all to see.

Sammy runs in with a white handkerchief and wipes off the prints.

'It's not new, exactly. Someone in the government got rid of it and bought a newie.'

Sammy has a lot of brass, he's in the used car business.

'She takes a great shine, eh? You'll never guess what I found in the glove box.' He dives into the front seat and comes out with a little flag on a metal pole about a quarter metre high.

'You watch what happens when I put this on the front.'

He goes to the bonnet and finds a little mounting and sure enough the flag fits into the socket.

'Now watch.' He pulls out a black suit from the back seat, gets us round in a circle to shelter him and puts it on. There's a cap too, and when he has it on he's the perfect chauffeur.

'Now who's got good mocha on?' he says, looking round at us. Sure enough, Danny's gone mad for the occasion and has his grey suit on that he wears to weddings, funerals and smokos.

'Danny, you'll do.'

Danny's pretty right by this time. Not off his head, don't get me wrong.

In they get, Danny in the rear and Sammy driving. They head out to the street by the exit and round for the entrance. We all clear out round to the entrance to watch.

Sammy gives a toot at the gates and gets in without paying. The man on the gate sort of salutes. Others look round at the toot and gape, then crowd over to line the road in. Sammy keeps the speed down to about ten. More people up ahead line the road.

Danny's pissing himself laughing by this time, but Sammy shushes him.

'Keep a straight face for Christ sake. A straight face.'

Danny does his best.

'Now wave.'

Danny waves like it was a bunch of council workers at the side of the road and he was yelling to them to get off their arses.

'Not like that. Like this.' And Sammy shows him to keep the fingers together, and wave side to side, nice and slow. As if it was an effort.

Danny does this, Sammy gives another toot, and a ragged cheer breaks out on both sides.

'These dills think it's royalty,' Sammy says out of the side of his mouth. 'Look, those old ducks are frothing at the mouth. Smile a bit.'

That wasn't hard for Danny. Tears are running down his cheeks.

They come up to the official table.

'Here you go,' says Sammy. The drill is, I stop and you get out. Go up to the official party shake their hands and I'll wait here.'

'What will they be drinking?' asks Danny, between convulsions.

'Champagne, maybe. Wine.'

'No way, mate. I'm no wino.' Danny has his pride.

'Come on, we're stopped. Out you go.'

'No fear, mate. Not me. I'm not up to it. I'm nearly pissing myself laughing.'

'Well, we can't stop here.' People were coming forward, peering in. Sammy looks at Danny. He's shaking. He's died in the arse, Sammy tells himself, and moves off.

'Wave, go on, wave.'

We follow them. They go right round and out the exit. Sammy lets him out a few yards down the road. Danny hops the fence on the bush side and comes back to us.

I look up. There are three coppers leaning against a picket fence, like the three wise monkeys.

First time I ever see three coppers in a row and all laughing.

Sammy could always get things. He got a gross of champagne last week and tried to get the boys round the pub to take a dozen each to flog.

'Great for Christmas presents,' he said. But the tribe weren't traders, they didn't come in. Sammy had to go up the hill to the bowling club, up to the lower middle class: they took them. For a profit of fifty cents a bottle their eyes gleamed with more healthy interest than they showed for the books and bundles of coloured photographs they passed from briefcase to coat pockets while the women bowlers weren't looking.

I was drinking not far from Sharon's taps one day wondering how the radiogram knows the record is a twelve inch or a nine inch or one of those little forty-five-speed things, and also how it knows there's still one more record to come sitting up on the spindle, when there was a great roar from the back of the pub.

Blue raced in waving his arms in a westerly direction.

'That way! Up the hill!'

Everyone rushed for the door and took a screw up the hill. Even Flash, who was down the back of the car park having a screw with a woman from the cheese factory showed himself, alert, ears pricked for trouble.

For a while there was only one glass on the red bar, which was awash with the tide of slops. It was full, a beached ship of treasure.

Blue pointed, they saw a figure darting round a corner.

'That ute there. I saw him pinching tools from that ute. Whose is it?'

No one knew. It probably belonged to one of the old builders sitting in the pub, too tired to be bothered with fights.

It didn't matter. A dozen set out after the thief.

I'd seen a lot of things like this before and not all of them had a thief at the end of the chase. Sometimes you'd catch a decoy up the street with his own property clutched under his arm and a grin on his face and later you'd find someone ratted the cars left open in the car park.

I watched. When they were out of sight, I went back inside for another beer. On the uneven ground, sparrows cocked their heads, alert for sparrowhawks. The beer tasted thick, like fresh milk.

They straggled back in twos and threes with stories of defeat. In fifteen minutes they were all back, the sprinter was away.

No one was happy about it. You could see by the way they began to snap at each other, not exactly looking each other in the eye. They should have caught someone or something. There was going to be trouble.

You could feel it in the air that floated round and over and across between the two long sides of the red bar.

The barmaids felt it. They kept their eyes on their taps and raised them no higher than the glasses on the bar. It would either be trouble between the boys themselves, or they'd find a scapegoat.

It was only Thursday, there was a long weekend coming up. It wouldn't be the best thing if they fought among themselves. There might be several times in the next few days when they'd fight together against strangers, the common enemy.

Strangers. Providence provided one. A big young fellow came in the door, looked round—recklessly—and called for a beer while Sharon was still pouring an order of eight. The pub sort of froze. A few sly glances eased round to where the main trouble would come from: Mick and the visiting King.

The King and Mick had their own language.

'Honestly.'

'Truly.'

'No worries.'

'Well—'

'Fair enough.'

They were agreed on the plan of campaign. The other words which would have made sense of their intentions to the sophisticated world outside were conveyed by eye movements or no movements at all, a shrug of one shoulder or the absence of a shrug, the lifting of a hand to bar level, the inclining of the head forward about ten degrees, a quarter step backwards, an attempt to reach for a glass then the withdrawing of the hand accompanied perhaps by a massive shrug of both shoulders in a forward direction, a pushing forward of the lips—puffing them up as if they were over a mouthguard—so they presented a soft, pliable surface the better for taking punches, a short sharp breath inflating the lungs and mimicking the coming effort, a short sharp expulsion of breath from the nose with mouth closed mimicking the out-breath that accompanies a punch and stiffens the stomach muscles against a counter.

'You drinking?' the King called to the young guy.

He looked over, saw the two of them together, and nodded slowly.

'Drink over here,' said Mick.

'No way,' said the young fellow loudly. Didn't like the look of things. But he'd used the wrong words, the wrong tone. Too sharp, too definite. Refusing hospitality.

'Don't argue,' said the King.

'It's sweet,' said Mick reassuringly. Only an idiot would be reassured by Mick's voice.

'Come here,' said the King. The stranger looked round. Everyone in the place had his mouth shut, watching him. Speculating where the flood would flow. Was he a bleeder over the eyes? Was he bumble-footed, which could mean a fractured skull on the concrete floor which was masked unconvincingly by hard tiles two millimetres thick.

'Why not?' said the stranger, swallowing. His heart peered out of his mouth.

They made room for him so it was a triangle. Mick licked his lips.

'When you're right, Sharon, a beer for our friend,' he said politely.

A few seconds later the King said in a loud voice so all could hear there was an identifiable cause for action and an identifiable person in the wrong, 'Say that again!'

Perhaps the stranger *had* said something, because he took half a step back.

'I'll have you,' said Mick.

'Come outside,' said the King. The stranger couldn't take his eyes off them—because of the danger of a king hit—but he could feel the pub watching. You couldn't back out of a fight. Word of it would follow you to your dying day. 'I remember when he chickened out . . .' and so forth. Your friends would get to hear of it, your wife, kids. His own pub might only be a mile away, but the Southern Cross was another world.

He went with them, looking like a martyr. We followed in a body. They didn't king-hit him on the way, but stopped in the car park.

The action was too fast to describe, the dialogue will have to do.

'You're mine.'

'He's mine.'

'Hold his arms.'

'Let him go.'

'Not like that.'

'No worries.'

'I'll give you the drum.'

'Dead set.'

'Keep his head up or his eyes'll fall out.'

'I've got news for you.'

'He's died in the arse.'

'Sincerely.'

'Is he alive?'

'He's foxing.'

'He's breathing.'

'He's dead.'

'He's history.'

'RS.'

'Let's go.'

'See you.'

'Sincerely.'

'Believe it.'

An hour later the stranger was well enough to get up and come in to the bar. His beer was still there, flat as a tack. The tribe would never handle him for money, so he had his roll, and after a loss no one else would have a go. They'd just let him depart in his own time. Back where he came from, where he belonged, where he should have stayed.

For the next two hours he leaned on the bar getting steadily drunk, a vacant look in his eyes. No one would talk to a stranger in his position even when Mick and the King had gone. But they would answer when he spoke to them. They had their code. The customs of the Cross were stronger than laws of parents, priests and peers.

He'd have a staring fit for a few minutes, rouse himself out of it, then get gabby, calling everyone Sid. It took us a while to realise it was his own name.

Now and then his face got a look as if a thought chimed like a bell in his head. But it was gone before he could make out what it was.

I wondered pleasantly what would happen if more strangers came than there were of us. That would be a test for the old reflexes, as well as the chairs.

On sad days the spatters looked pathetic. But never unfriendly. At least it was human blood.

DO YOU SUFFER FROM
SHAKINESS?

Sibley's next caper was to go round asking questions. He'd write down some of the answers, for others he'd tick off a slot in his columned sheets of paper. What a place to work for a doctorate. Around a pub all day I'd become a Doctor of Beer in very short order.

'If you were a baby again and could grow up, what would you want to be?' was one of his questions. 'Where would you live? What sort of house would you like? What job? Where would you go for a holiday?'

The drinkers would make short work of these, Sibley would note the answers conscientiously, and go on.

'Do you have chest pains, belching, constipation, tender skin, headaches, convulsions, urinary hesitancy? Are you accident prone? Are you touchy, angered by orders, irritable? Do you suffer from shakiness?' It was weird. Most of the answers had to do with the golden sea on which they were afloat seven days a week, but he seemed to think he was recording their psyches.

'Dizziness? Stiff muscles and joints? Do you wear yourself out worrying about your health?' Some of the guys laughed and Sibley looked pained, trying to get them to see it was a scientific search. 'Do strange people or places make you afraid? Are you shy and sensitive? Do you shake and tremble, come out in cold sweats, do you wish you were dead and away from it all?'

No matter how serious he tried to get them to be, they still pissed themselves laughing. He'd have to buy another round to get them to stop.

Watching him, I wondered if he shared the tribe's harmony with nature, with furniture factory, rubber works, woollen mills, tractor yard, cheese factory, jail, mental asylum, hospital; with natural features of the landscape such as corner shop, power lines, bitumen, red roofs, traffic.

Or was he in harmony with a nature we didn't know and could never apprehend?

Sunday afternoon we had a hailstorm. Out of the blue. Drifts of little white balls of ice covered front lawns and piled up against fences. A mile away there was no ice anywhere, but up at the Lake it was like Christmas in another country. Little kids had happy fights with them and trod round in heaps of hailstones in bare feet. Old folks from Europe stood on verandahs gazing at the whiteness, saying nothing.

Ernie used to bring his work problems to the pub. He had no home to take them to.

His new boss, in conversation away from work, was a freak for rational spelling. Not a word about fishing. No matter the historical associations of placenames or the Latin derivation and lateral connections with other languages of ordinary words, he wanted spelling made phonetic. That is, phonetic according to present pronunciations. He wouldn't have understood if Ernie had said a new spelling will eventually change the pronunciation and sometime in the future the spelling will need further alteration to bring it into line again with future pronunciation, but neither would Ernie.

One trouble with Ernie was his literal mind. No sooner had the boss confided this apparently cherished belief to Ernie than Ernie thought how nice it would be for him if he put into practice what the boss believed.

'Knock off all e's, that's what I'll do for a start,' he said.

This gave him heer and ther, com and go and invit and separat, hir and fir, strik and arbitrat.

He incorporated this aberration in his work.

The boss carpeted him.

'Ernie, you're not ready yet for our industrial conditions. You don't seem to understand that what a man says in private, what's on a man's heart, isn't meant to be put into practice in business or industry. Industry has its own rules and you bend to suit them or you're useless. If that's the case, there's no room for you. You might be happier elsewhere.'

Ernie didn't give up so easily.

'I did what had to be done,' he said when we tumbled that he'd crawled his way back. His job was his life.

'You know what that boss of yours does to his bumboys, Ernie,' Mac said. 'I've seen him at it. He's walking along with them, cracks a joke and when they're bent over doubled-up laughing at it or pretending to, he dates them.'

Mac made a blurting noise with his mouth and gestured vigorously upward with his thumb.

'He won't ever date me,' said Ernie stoutly. 'I'll knock his block off.'

In the background, Sibley's voice: 'Do you speak English. Have you ever been to the city.'

Ernie had no home, but he had home troubles, Mum was confined for her own good in a hospital where she wasn't allowed out except for exercise.

Every time some new broom went through the hospital and saw the poor old things there for no other reason than that they were hard of hearing and so appeared idiots when they were asked questions, or nearly blind so they fell over things easily, and started to do something about it such as getting them discharged to convalescent homes as a stage on the way to the 'community'. Mrs Jones would get up on the table wherever they sent her and leave an unmistakeable message for all the staff to see and clean up. Back she'd come again. Hospital was home.

'I've got 'em licked,' she'd say to Ernie.

'SSShh, Mum,' he'd say, hoping no one heard. He didn't want to be lumped in with people who had relatives in mental hospitals.

But he knew how to act to the other old people. If one got out and there were no nurses around, he'd grasp her gently on the shoulders, turn her round and say, 'You want to go that way.' And point her back in the direction of the ward. And off she'd trot. She *did* want to go that way.

Two blocks away the commercial district started. On signs, in windows, in the home, voices would say, 'You want one of our mowers, or TVs or refrigerators and then you'll be happy.' And the populace would trot off in the direction of the sales room, deposit in hand. They had the cash; why not?

Ernie was a dead set prick—we all thought so—but he looked after his Mum's nineteen cats religiously. The number changed constantly, but he didn't mind. They always ate.

Ernie got caught up in a move to have the employees of Reclina-Matic join one of the big unions. It was only a small factory, but they had the standard hierarchy with the same names for the positions as if it employed ten thousand and had a turnover of two hundred million.

Ernie saw the boss's face one day after someone else had made his alley good by dobbing them, so Ernie covered himself by supplying the name of the ringleader and the rest of those willing to go along.

He was scared of being laid off. He might not get another job right away and from what he heard the young clerks down at the unemployment office treated you like dogs. Not dogs: drunken blacks. And spoke to you as if you were sick in the head. This society was the only one they had or knew: if a person was without a job and poor he was inadequate; if he was inadequate he was mentally ill. After all, if he was inadequate and treated as if he was normal, where would the pressure be on the rest to appear normal?

A man he knew, Ek, laid off some time before, was making a good living in the cleaning business. Ernie was suspicious of anything that seemed to have no roots in production. As if cleaning floors and windows wasn't a real job. He didn't think of floors and windows and companies' desires for good appearances as things to be manipulated in his own favour, he thought there must be an object produced at the end of the line and carried away in a vehicle. Anything less was dangerously insubstantial. Even though his own part in production was making marks on bits of paper.

He knew about efficiency, and told us, not that we wanted to know. But when we asked him what the end of efficiency was, he got in a tangle.

'Ernie, if efficiency means getting rid of as many workers as possible, does it mean getting rid of as many machines as possible?'

'Yes,' he said, warily. 'Fewer machines, less maintenance.'

'And if you do that right through the country, you can use the scrap metal all right, but what about the scrap men and women?'

'Yes, Ernie, who's going to buy Reclina-Mats then?'

'It's always the same with you blokes. You never face the fact you can't stop progress.'

'Surveys show Reclina-Mats lead to heart disease, Ern. All this lying about, no exercise. They're going to put a warning on them. Medical authorities warn—.'

It was his shout. His pockets were long and his arms got shorter and shorter. They had to prod him.

'Ernie,' said Alky Jack. 'Is there anyone in the firm, or in the companies all over the country, who's indispensable?'

Ernie thought a bit. One of those business mottoes came to his rescue, the printed cards hung in supervisors' offices.

'No one is indispensable.'

'So in theory it's possible machines one day will do the work of the sweeper, the truckdriver, the clerk, the machinist, the assembler, the supervisor, the wages man, the accountant, the manager, the PR man, the company lawyer,'—and they all nodded after each one to show they'd weighed the possibility of machines doing each function—'the manager, the directors, the chairman of the board. Since,' he explained in case they hadn't got the message, 'if those jobs can be described and if they follow rules and laws and so forth, they can be put on computers.'

The word computer was magic. They nodded.

'And if information can be put on them, who needs teachers? Computers mark the papers now. They can diagnose illness as long as they're programmed fully enough, and that's only a matter of detail. One day they'll drive public transport, they'll even be in

111

charge of your car so you can't drive through a red light or crash into someone or change lanes if there's a car alongside you.' Alky Jack paused. I looked at him. He'd live to be eighty, the spunky old bastard.

'Think of any job and I'll show you a way electronic machines can do it. Now, Ernie, is that progress?'

Alky Jack waited for an answer. I couldn't think of anything; I'm not into progress. I think there's different things, different times. New things balanced by the loss of the old things they replace, or the old ways. But I didn't want to be caught talking a lot of nonsense beginning with the two silliest words in any language: I believe.

No one spoke. We looked at Ernie.

'Don't look at me. He was talking to you mob just as much as me. Anyway, we were talking about efficiency, not progress.'

'Oh,' said Alky Jack. 'The way people talk I thought they were the same thing.'

'I think you're all commos,' Ernie said.

Me, I think there's three estates: communists, capitalists and the poor, with the third estate the most numerous. Put them all together for a day or two and there's no difference. Except you might hear the sound of munching as they sorted themselves into the two primal estates, weak and strong.

No one answered Ernie's charge. They'd be the last people in the world to go commo.

The group broke up. Ernie had to go and practise golf. The newest manager was on six handicap.

Sibley was saying, 'Do you listen to the radio. Do you read papers or magazines. Do you write letters. Do you go to the pictures.' Someone said, 'Do you fuck.' Sibley said yes. The voice said, 'Then fuck off.'

Next time I saw Ernie was in the warehouse of the Reclina-Mat factory. Efficiency hadn't at that time replaced the workers and staff and consumers with one large machine. A man was walking along looking straight ahead—like the man in the ads where the girl looks up admiringly, suckering him on—and Ernie was looking up at him while the man told a story. When it was finished, Ernie stopped, doubled over with obligatory laughter. The man looked down at him, bent to one side and dated him energetically with his thumb. Ernie straightened in surprise, but carefully went on laughing.

As the traffic cleared and I drove on I wondered if Ernie suffered. I hoped not. I was headed towards the city, where my darling was. Where tall buildings stood, rich castles lit up all over like burning buildings with fire still feeding inside; where departing ships mourn out at night into the main stream.

Where older citizens pick into green tin boxes of rubbish for something of value.

FOOTIE

The pub football team staggered up from the Southern Cross around seven o'clock some time in February.

If they were lucky they would get in four or five weeks training before the competition started in April.

Some didn't come straight from the pub, they worked till seven. By half past eight or nine, training was finished and all hurried dirty down to the beer again, which went off at ten.

Training was on a double field on a slope. Kids played there in the daytime and dug holes you could hide a dozen beer cans in.

During the season, on the field, any old-fashioned notions of amateurs playing for the sake of the game and helping an opponent to his feet and fair's fair and who cares who wins as long as we enjoy our football were not merely forgotten: they'd never been learned.

You didn't rip one in because last year or last round or last match that bastard ripped one in to you: you hit him first and on principle, to soften him up. To let him know he had to watch something besides the ball.

There was no philosophic acceptance of defeat. You lost not because you weren't good enough, but because you made mistakes. That centre wasn't brilliant: your cover defence was lousy.

If a manager lost the funds and later drove round in a new car, that was human nature. You would talk to him and drink with him and not a word said.

At the yearly football dinner, after you'd tried your hardest to get double portions of chicken and you'd cornered the jugs of beer up your end of the table, and you'd all gathered on stage to sing together to an audience of waiters and thirty guys had fallen forward in a heap off the stage down the steep steps and you'd grabbed all the leftover prawns and ducked out to put them in the car, and you were rolling, staggering, singing, fighting drunk; after all this you quarrelled with the management to keep the place open another hour.

When you went away to Orange with a team and played up the night before and got beaten on the Saturday and kicked out of the pub that night, you formed up in marching order and climbed the wall to the verandah on the first floor and marched in through the windows and slept in the lounge on the carpet.

And when you had a benefit night for the Dark-fella who got killed doing a delivery run in his truck, there was a detective-sergeant on the roulette wheel.

And when Red was sent off for swearing at the ref, and instead of going off punched the ref and was disqualified for life and the club rubbished the whole team so the team could no longer play, no one said a bad word against the club or against Red, they drank with Red and laughed about the game, and thought the club must be right and spent both training nights and Saturday in the Southern Cross as if nothing had ever happened and there was no such thing as football. They were free to go to the races now, but only went when they were at Rosehill. They didn't like to be too far away from the pub. Something might happen and they wouldn't be in it.

Now and then someone talked about reviving the team, but it was more in the nature of philosophical speculation and the talk would get on to great games of the past. Like the time the whole team turned up drunk when Anzac Day was on a Friday, and a team of large players from Randwick-Botany slaughtered us twenty-four three and offered condolences and best wishes for the future after the game to our team of mainly small players, and in the second round the small players murdered them eighteen nil.

Or the games in the Juniors with Birrong that ended in free-for-alls.

That wasn't good enough for Bob and me. We got everyone to put their names on a football and we deflated it and set it up in the pub. We'd blow it up again if the team revived.

It would be great to get out in the paddock again, running upfield, the ball under your arm, head down, a bit of blood on your lip; waiting for the satisfying bump as your shoulder invaded ribs and stomachs; the crunch as the packs went down and the opposition took a step back; the exhilaration as your centre or winger dived over the line at the end of a movement; the fierce joy when your arms settled affectionately round two knees, your shoulder nestling comfortably into a thigh or a buttock and both bodies gliding through the air with the other player underneath.

It took two years before we blew up that bloody ball again.

Sex oozed from every pore.

He had pregnant women, engaged girls the night before their weddings, kids from high school, Sunday School teachers, anything with a hole in the right place and brush round it. His taste was all-embracing.

The way he put work on a new barmaid was shocking, and highly successful. He had a very convincing tongue.

He even had a hanger-on. Tom would hang round for the scraps. Sometimes a woman on the outer with the Great Lover would approach old Tom, who would promise to get her back into favour. On certain conditions. Tom had a tiny stubby one. He shaved the hairs from round it to make it look longer, but this itched and scratched so much he was always touching himself. And because he was always touching himself, he was always horny. I thought of him as the Shorthorn, but I didn't make a noise about it. They would have crucified him with a nickname like that. As it was, the publican once summed him up by saying, 'Bloody old Tom: says little, never thinks and does sweet fuckall.' Tom had worked two days in the cellar for him.

The thing about the Great Lover was that when you looked at him, you could see what women saw in him. A lot of blokes, you look at them and you wonder what even their mothers saw in them. Not him. He was alert, neatly built, had a sexy-looking head, a vigorous, adventurous smile, he could talk, and he never thought of anything but sex. Apart from the daily crossword, of course, and the gallopers. It was a pleasure to come in and see that cheeky head over the crossword.

When he got out of jail the thing he liked best was to drive a truck round. He worked for the dairy company for a bit as a mechanic first. One day the boss told him to drive a milk truck ten miles and deliver milk to a milk bar. He was a mechanic; this wasn't his job, but it was Saturday and the regular drivers didn't know, so off he went with the truck and twenty cans of milk and set up the proprietor's milk pump in the first drum. The pump was no good, couldn't get suction. The Great Lover had to heft the drums about six feet while the shopkeeper watched.

'What about giving us a hand?' he says.

'You the driver. You deliver the milk,' said the Greek.

'Your pump's dirty,' countered the Great Lover.

'So get the health inspector.'

'I might do that.'

'So I get the transport union.' And the Great Lover shut up. He was still wearing mechanic's overalls. After an hour he'd emptied six cans, and gave up in disgust. Back to the depot.

'You brought back fourteen?' said the boss. 'Christ, when I was a mechanic and they put that job on me I brought the lot back. That was six years ago. Has he still got that rotten pump?'

He left and got a job doing straight deliveries. He was so quick on his feet he'd be finished a whole day's run by one-thirty and worked at the bar—drinking middies—till four, which was knock-off time. When overtime was on, he'd work in the pub till five, then report back and clock off. The truck was discreetly hidden round the back of the pub. There were some big trees there.

The Great Lover had always been generous. Even when he was a kid.

One day he took a chick down to the beach, and took one of the boys with him.

'She had a real fair skin,' he says. 'I did her in the water, on the rocks, the sand, all over the place. And by this time me mate's going mad. I don't know what

I'm going to do with him. So I say to her, Give him one. She makes a fuss but in the end she says to me, Only for you. And she gives him one. Later she hawked the fork, but she still wanted to be in love with me. I told her, I don't care what you do in the daytime, just be there when I get home at night.'

When he got married to a girl that doted on him, and still does, he was down the pub so often she used to get mad, and round about half past nine one Saturday night, after he'd been there all day, she appears at the door with his pyjamas and throws them into the pub and yells out, 'You might as well sleep here.'

She had the sort of grim love for him you've seen on women determined to love their man, and determined their man will be on deck to be loved.

He bet on the horses, usually listening to the races over the pub loudspeaker with all the other devotees. The money he put into bookies' pockets wasn't funny. He went to the races in search of the golden fleece and came home shorn.

One day he came home drunk as a lord.

'I lob home, and next thing she's abusing Christ outa me. So I try to stand up straight at the kitchen table, and begin to peel out these dollar bills I won at Rosehill. She was still giving me the rounds of the kitchen when I came out with tens and fives and twos and by the time I reached forty she'd shut up, by fifty she was smiling, by sixty she was on my side and by the time I'd peeled off seventy she was kissing me and by the time I got to eighty she was jumping up and down, beside herself. I was RS by that time but she made me give her one before she'd let me go to sleep.'

He was seventeen years and ten months when he first went up.

'The bastards would keep 'em there eighteen months on remand often. They had no folks or lawyers. Fifteen months was nothing. When it sank in that I'd drawn two years I cried like a baby. I had two months to go till I was eighteen, so they waited two months and then gave me two years in the Bay. Now I'm a criminal and I never stole anything in me life. Christ it was cold at Long Bay. They moved me to Bathurst, where I really froze. When I got out it took me two months to thaw out. Then a bit after that I had a fight with Mick here, he give me a fractured cheekbone—here, see the line?— and I got six months for that. I wasn't supposed to be in the pub at all. One of the conditions.'

I never found out what he was inside for. I asked him if he knew any of the heavies.

'I know blokes you wouldn't want to even whisper their names.'

'You know Chewy Hughes?'

'Nice feller. In for twenty-two years, then out. The next week he put a broken bottle in someone's face, and he's in again for life.' His monster took over any old time, grog or no grog.

He'd been there talking to me for too long. His wife rang, he finished his beer and drove off in the truck to clock off and qualify for his overtime, and made his way home, where he discharged his obligations.

He played with us, sometimes on the wing, usually fullback. In the showers he used to sling off at my grey hairs. Despite his size, my old feller is surrounded by grey. Always worried about his next one. No other part of me is grey.

Mick got a job at Blacktown RSL.

'It's unbelievable,' he said to us when he had a free afternoon. 'There's a mile of it there. Long as you've got a nice white shirt on and your black bow tie and you're sober and speak nice, they're all over you.'

He patted his flat stomach.

'It helps too if you look fit, no beer gut and all.'

We wouldn't have argued if he did have a belly. He looked into the distance over the rim of his tilted glass. If his thickened eyebrow ridges allowed it, he would have had a smile on his face. You couldn't expect one round his mouth, he had his lips permanently pushed forward to cushion a sudden attack of king-hit, the main tribal and inter-tribal disease.

'Last night there was this singer. Beautiful. Not a bad singer too. When she's finished her act for the night, she comes out and there's a mob of officials, the Preso and Secretary and so on, all round her, wanting her to sit at their table. She looks round the whole place, doesn't miss a trick, and says no. They talk to her, tell her she's got to be looked after, but she still says no. She's carrying these bags, with her costumes in and whatever singers carry round.

'She lights on me, probably 'cause I figure the best place to be is right by the main door out to the foyer. She leaves their party, walks up to me and says Buy me a drink, big boy.'

Mick straightens up and nearly beams, face permitting.

'So I take her bags and sit her at a table with a mate of mine that I know won't go under my neck, and get permission from the official party to have a drink with her. They're dirty on me, but they have to agree 'cause she's such a success with the members and she's got a contract for more performances.

'OK. We're at the table and all she wants is one drink. Then she gets up. Carry my bags, she says. So I carry her bags out to the car, put 'em in the boot and she gives me the keys and says, You drive. Where? I say once I'm behind the wheel. Round a bit. So we drive round a bit, and I say, Where to now? And she says, Do I have to ask? Find a place, big boy. So I find a place, under some trees at the end of a street that goes nowhere, and we have a root in the car. And I tell you, she's beautiful. Then I take her back near the club, she takes the wheel and away she goes and I go back in the club and they ask me, Where the hell've you been? I tell 'em the truth and no one believes me.'

'That's the way it goes,' says Danny, who was more than half molo by that time. It was nearly five, after all.

Mick's thinking. We leave him think for a bit, then he comes out with it.

'I've had thousands of 'em. Easy ones. You know, the ones where you just have to strike up a bit of a conversation and look neat and speak nice to 'em and next thing you're in their pants.'

He paused and thought again.

'But,' he said. 'But I've never met—never had—one of 'em that you could call a decent root.'

'What do you mean, Mick?' I say. It's something that's often been on my mind. What I've found is that these ones that are hot for it, well they're hot for it all right, but they're just like a bloke when he wants it and just wants it alone and doesn't care who it is and how quick it's finished. They rip their pants off and crowd you in as if they're dying of starvation, then it's all over in two ups and they're on their way. They haven't done any particular thing you'll remember, they haven't made love in any sense at all, they've just had a root and that's all they want. Good bye. All you remember is a face, perhaps, and maybe a place. Like a lane, or under a bridge or in a car. You know, you might remember what model car it was.

'Well,' Mick says. 'I don't know. I don't know how to put it. Christ, I don't even know what I mean. All I know is, I've never had an easy one that was any good.'

We all put our heads down and thought a bit more, but no one had anything to add. Except Danny, who answered my thoughts.

'Shit, I can't even remember their faces.'

There was no action in the pub then and no one felt like playing pool. Young kids that had just graduated were on the tables.

Mick got to other things.

'My first day there, this American entertainer was playing. Winifred something. Well, it surprised me. I have to go to the dressing rooms with messages and to get autographs signed, and there's this big name entertainer shaking like a leaf.

'Would you mind? I say quietly as I can, and she signs a few, and I go out respectfully. Then when it's time for her act, her face is still down at the mouth, she looks really miserable. She walks along towards the stage, then a yard before the curtain she pulls her mouth open wide like this'—and Mick did the same, and though it wasn't entirely a broad flashing personality smile, we got the picture—'and goes over to the piano, and off she goes.

'You sort of get the idea they're always smiling, don't you. Yeah, and those autographs. Sometimes the members would give me two or three coasters to get signed, sometimes a dozen. But you can never tell. Once they went mad, it was a Saturday night and my pocket was out to here with 'em. And you wouldn't want to know, she was so down in the mouth I wasn't game to go in and ask her. So I sat down backstage and wrote Best Wishes and signed her name to forty-eight place-mats and gave 'em out to the members and they were happy as Larry. Next morning I see her name in the paper about something or other and I've spelt the name wrong. Two t's instead of one.'

He liked you to laugh if he felt he'd made a funny.

Friday night some of the boys take the casual barmaid up to the Lake. Actually it's only Dog Man takes her, the others go up in their cars to watch.

He finds a place in among the trees and goes to town, the others kill their lights and cut their motors and glide down near. Then they get out and creep over and look in the window of Dog Man's car while he's up her.

After a bit they hear him say Let's get out, there's more room outside. The boys creep back behind trees and he gets out with the barmaid, their backsides white in the dim light from the streetlights two hundred metres away.

They get stuck into it again. On a blanket, and his knees keep digging into bits of rock.

Suddenly there's a car round a corner over to the

right and another at the same time to the left. Very slow. Too slow.

The cars watch the ground for a bit, then douse their lights and men get out. The Great Lover's got his eyes peeled and a paddy waggon comes round the corner with its lights out.

'The feds!' he yells. And goes for his life.

'No. Can't be,' says someone else.

But it is. All run, including the barmaid. Some bad-minded citizen in one of the nearby houses has been minding other people's business.

Come Saturday morning and we get the Great Lover's story.

'I'm first away, off like a shot. Next thing they're firing guns at me. So I stop, hands up. Into the waggon I go. In the copshop this bull says to me, I've seen you before. Christ almighty, I thought I was gone. Two stretches before, now this. And I haven't done anything. I'd be up for eighteen months. I've seen you before, he says. OK, Dick Tracy, I say. But I'm not feeling cheeky. If I go up again I'll neck myself, for sure. So they leave me and I'm wondering how to kill myself, I think I'm gone. History. Then bugger me, this morning they let me go. No charge, nothing. Just the dollar.'

Dog Man fronted about eleven. He had grazes over his face, on his forehead, he was limping with a dirty great bandage round one knee and the other ankle wrapped in white rag and his foot in a soft slipper. He had red hair, it always stuck up and out, all over. And wild eyes.

'Well, pants man,' the Great Lover said. 'What's the strong of you?' Sibley was listening, for once, instead of talking.

'Bloody feds,' Dog Man says. 'Feds. Wouldn't feed 'em. If my dogs behaved like that I'd shoot 'em. There I am, rasping away and someone gives the alarm they've sprung us. Up I get, into my strides in half a second, and off. Went for me life. Over to the right I see you'—the Great Lover—'bail up, but I put me head down and keep going. And it's getting darker and darker the way I'm going. I bump into a few trees and go through plenty of bushes, prickles and all, and suddenly I'm flying. I've gone over this thirty foot cliff, legs still running in the air. Would have been better if I'd landed in the water, but oh no, I've got to land in a heap of rubbish where someone's shot branches and plants and Christ knows what. Did me ankle. But at least I got away. Didn't spend no night in boob.'

We talked the subject out until it was like a punctured balloon.

Someone asked about his dogs.

'No good,' he said. 'Shot three of 'em last week. When they won't run and don't bring me in anything, they're dead. Can't afford to feed 'em like kings and have 'em live like kings. Yeah, three last week. With a lousy twenty-two. That's all you need to kill 'em. I'd feel better if it took a twelve gauge shotgun, or a proper rifle to kill 'em. But they got no heart. Die without a murmur. Not even a kick. No heart at all.'

He shook his head. He looked very sad. I know for a fact he paid four hundred dollars for one of those greyhounds.

'How do you get rid of 'em?' I ask. 'The bodies, I mean.'

'Easy as shitting in bed,' he says. 'In the cemetery.'

And he stands there, lowering his beer—he drinks new beer—and keeping us waiting.

'Cemetery? You don't pay to bury 'em, do you?'

'Don't have to. Up Castle Hill where I go, they dig fresh graves in the cemetery for tomorrow's bods. OK? Now I'm not about to dig holes just to bury dead dogs. Far as I'm concerned Manual Labor is a Mexican bandit. So I just drop 'em in one of the holes, one to a hole I mean, sprinkle earth over 'em and that's it. Next day they bury some stiff on top of the dog. Plenty of bods up there on top of dogs. You know the place, off Showground Road.'

We knew the place.

I wondered, as I swallowed a mouthful of Resch's, what archaeologists of the future might say about twentieth century people buried with their animals.

Dog Man started to say something.

'This sheila invited us up to her flat. There was five of us,' then in the middle of the sentence he excused himself and went for a piss.

We didn't see him for eight months.

Into our world of the Southern Cross came a small sharp corner of another world.

A girl and a boy came in for a drink, early afternoon. It was a Thursday. They were nicely dressed, and clean, with shoes on.

'This haircut cost me three-ninety, actually.'

It wasn't a good haircut. His auburn hair fell to shoulder length, but it wasn't a patch on Noel's, or Bleachy's young brother. Theirs just grew, and they washed it; theirs shone so much that girls would look after them in the street and shake their heads and put a hand to their own hair in that gesture women have; theirs they cut with a pair of scissors and a mirror, for free.

It fell sort of straggly, thinned and not shiny. The girl looked at it without much expression. She'd lived with hair all her life.

'It costs me at least that,' she said. 'But there's a boy at work pays thirteen dollars for a haircut and styling. It doesn't look any different from yours. I don't think that's too much to pay,' she said supportively.

They finished their drinks and departed, walking busily to the boy's car. They didn't see us, didn't notice the cracked wall, they were the only inhabitants of the planet.

I leaned on the bar, looking out after them, thinking how many days thirteen dollars would keep me in schooners. Nearly three, if I only drank in the pub and didn't take any cans home.

A hair cut could last a few weeks, it wouldn't be over in three days.

Just the same, it was another world. I wondered what they did of an afternoon when work was finished. I mean, what sort of a tribe did they have. Did they drink? Did they fight? A fight now and then might stir them up to live, to have solid enjoyment, bright eyes, quick muscles and life on every face.

Maybe. Maybe they had those things, but if so, how? I only knew the way of *our* tribe.

The comfortable liberals with fine minds might shake out equality over us like salt over stew, but the lower middle class up the hill at the bowling club would make sure there was no equality in the suburbs.

And we were glad to help them.

Alone at the red bar, I looked at my fingertips. Those lines, forming loops and whorls on the ends of my fingers, reached inside me as if they were the ends of cables, keeping their pattern like Brighton Rock right through my insides.

Cut me in half and you'd find those patterns even in the tumbling rivers of my blood.

The rest of me was just insulation. The secret was somehow in the cables.

When I was with my darling I thought of this, and gave her something to hold, for the pleasure of seeing her little hand cupped, delicate as an eyelid.

From where I stood near the door I saw the pub dog, a large black individual with plenty of labrador, checking on various points and command posts round his territory.

He walked to the corner of the snack bar and sniffed the concrete edge. He nodded and grinned and walked calmly to the other end of the covered beer garden, sniffed again. This time he waved his tail. When he'd been right round the traps in his afternoon patrol, he settled back in his guard house, which was a niche in the wall out front near the bottle department. He hadn't quite worn away the patch of grass that formed his couch. It was very comfortable. If the sun had been hotter he would have taken up his post just inside the door of the bottle-oh, on the wooden floor.

Passing dogs in cars and trucks boasted to Blackie, Look how fast I can go. But he knew.

An old Airedale with a bad leg limped down the street. Blackie watched. The Airedale saw him a long way off but didn't falter; he was too proud to get off the path.

Blackie let him pass without getting to his feet. You don't fight a three-legged dog.

His muzzle was right down along his left forepaw when the brindle boxer came along. Now this boxer had a very real inferiority complex. He wasn't the right colour and his owner had impressed on him from the time he was a pup that he was worth next to nothing.

His body was nearly black instead of the right boxer tan, his nose badly formed—the part where his head joined the top of his nose wasn't the right shape. He was a mess as a boxer, he might as well have been a mongrel.

Sometimes he got very sad, and didn't go out. Other times, like today, he went round saying, Look, I haven't let these disadvantages get me down, I'm normal, well-balanced, friendly. And when he saw Blackie he wagged his stump, where the tail had been docked, to show his equable nature and friendly intentions, and avoided staring—a signal of aggressive intent—but glanced and let his eyes roll away as his head went from side to side, hardly ever looking directly at Blackie on his home ground.

His wagging stump didn't show, but Blackie knew what was what from the other language.

He got up hospitably, exchanged a few pleasantries with the boxer, took him round to show him the boundaries of his kingdom and showed him the view from each corner of the pub yard and let him look inside the pub door and round the back, in at the covered beer garden to see the humans he looked after, and the snack bar, which interested the boxer by the way it smelt, and finally took him to one of his far boundaries, well away from headquarters.

He looked at the newcomer, at the traffic, at his domain, then with more energy than he had yet displayed, went outside his boundary and had a businesslike pee. The visit was over.

His ears were up as far as he could elevate them, his tail too. His eyes were bright. He looked straight at the boxer. The boxer caught the straight look, took a step back.

Blackie walked straight at the stranger, so he either had to attack before he got to him, or get out of the way. The boxer turned and gave a little spurt of a run—he was light on his feet despite the wrong colouring and bad shape—stopped and turned to look. Blackie was still advancing.

The boxer turned and walked away up the street with great dignity, but not too slowly. Blackie followed him for perhaps twenty metres, seeing him off his spread, then turned and walked slowly home.

* * *

In the pub you saw the same piece of theatre. Down to the harmless look, the no staring, no frowning, the slight cough to indicate weakness and mortality, the shoulders unassumingly slumped, the eyebrows raised to accompany the favour of a beer received from the barmaid, the slow gestures, the looking away, when the locals turned to see who the stranger was in enemy territory, so they got a good look but no confronting examination.

And not a word spoken.

The little old man with the sack patrolled his own beat. I never saw *him* challenged for his territory. Maybe it was a big territory. I guess it has a boundary, too, and another old man with a sack recognises the boundary. Little men with sacks have cut up the land into their own private territories and no one but them knows where the boundaries are.

Mick came in later, worried. He looked round for someone to play pool with, or Flash to talk to. No one. His eyes found me.

'Just saw me mate off.'

'The jug?'

'Nothing like that. New Guinea. Got a job there for two years. It all started when I had some time on me hands six months back. I got in this pub one day at Dulwich Hill and was pleasant to the girl behind the bar, and she had a bit of time on her hands. One thing led to another. She was married, and she came right out and said she played round a bit, she and her old man. Well, the upshot was I said, What time'll I meet you? She said ten-thirty. At ten-forty-five, she came out, very careful, looking in all directions. She gets in the car and off we go to Cook's River. I didn't want to be trapped anywhere near where her old man might be looking for her.

'OK. So far so good. I get into it and I have one. Give me another, she says. I can't, I'm dying, I say. You know, he's just about to go right down.'

I made a sympathetic noise, and Mick got on with it.

'Suddenly, without a word of warning, these muscles of hers grab me. Before he has a chance to go down. Hurt like buggery. Stopped the blood in the old feller. Before I know it he's hard again.

'What are you doing? I said. Just lie on me, she says, and keep still. So I keep still. Without a word of a lie, these muscles that she's got down there, they move back and forward on it, like a hand. I've never felt anything like it before or since. It was beautiful!'

I believed him.

'Well, I went out with her for five months. Did me job over her. What should happen but me mate gets her. He speaks better than I do, and I make the mistake of telling him about her. He starts chatting her up and soon she likes him, likes him a lot. That's what she told me, anyway.

'So I go along with it, and by that time I'm fixed up with another sheila.

'We get to this ball. Her old man's at work, but I told me mate not to have her out with him in public like that. He wouldn't be told. So what does he do but get set up for a group photograph. I warn him, but he's too far gone on those muscles of hers to listen to me. OK, so he lets 'em take the photo, I'm in it too, and that's that.'

He looked round quickly, as if someone might be behind him. No one was. His knee, against the tiles, brushed a few spatters of stale blood.

'Anyway, she must have shown the photograph round, like women do, or maybe left it round at home, but—you guessed it—her old man gets hold of it and next thing my mate knows, he's going out the front door of his house and just as he opens the door a bullet thuds into it beside him. Only a twenty-two, but it could make a mess of you, hollow point and all. He ducked and ran, and looked back to where the slug came from. Her husband was crouched in a tree in the paddock opposite and he'd been there for hours. He'd tied a piece of cotton to the door handle and run it across the road to signal him when someone pulled open the door. My mate's so scared he gets a job in New Guinea. And he's gone today.'

'I suppose you're hoping he doesn't come after you,' I said.

'Why me?'

'You were into her.'

'He doesn't know that.'

'He might have belted her. Women like to talk. When they spill, they spill.'

'Yeah,' he said, gloomily. 'Yeah, they talk.'

He began to look worried. I'd been a bit hard on him.

'How did she manage to grab you like that? With those muscles?'

'Oh, that. She told me she practised from the time she was sixteen, when she—well I suppose she was playing with herself and found she had muscles—found she could put a bit of pressure on her finger, or something.'

A BB thudded on the glass door then. We both ducked automatically. Didn't even look outside.

I caught Alky Jack laughing in his corner one morning after he'd done his sweeping and made his little fire of papers and cartons. His few teeth gleamed crazily in his red-pink mouth. His tongue was coated with white and the shine of spit on the mucous surface of his mouth was somehow sinister, even while it looked surprisingly healthy. He had the profile you ought to see on coins, but don't. Wise, experienced, corrupt. The sort of thing that gives you confidence in a leader.

'Money is shit,' he said. 'Piled up, it stinks. Spread out, it's good fertiliser. The rich hoard it up, they're at their richest when they die.' He chuckled.

'An illustration of the neatness principle. The two lines of the graph, their increasing piles of goods and decreasing bodily powers, meet at that point. Subtract the cost of the funeral and the tax on death, and they pass on their net value to their heirs.'

In a way it didn't matter that it was me who was there to listen to him, he was thinking aloud most of the time. The others wouldn't stand still once the subject got away from races, football, the latest murders or direct quotes from the papers. They got suspicious if something sounded like an opinion that didn't have the backing of what was on public show.

'The hoarders never feel emergencies, yet emergency is with them all the time. Emergency, or the coming shortage, is the word for death. When they lay up tinned food or money or possessions or land or companies or insurance against the evil times, they're counting on the sureness of death. These here—' he waved a hand at the regulars—'they never think of it. They lift the glass and banish it from their minds.

'The rich never hoard smiles or sharing or honesty or love or generosity. They hoard more and more employees, more machines. For them, not even death and taxes. They hide from the penalties of life and death by forming companies. Evade tax, evade death duties—since a company can't die. They can play both sides in a war and not be hanged. Or even called to account.'

Even I began to get uneasy. It was just a lecture.

'It's all been said before, but no one learns, no one remembers. The land's in mortal danger when the nation's richer and the people just as poor. Rich men grow like mushrooms overnight and overnight die. But once a strong, independent lower class decays, they can't be resurrected. Their absence cuts the country's legs from under it, because they are the muscles of the country, they do the work and they do the consuming.' Then he returned to his pet theme.

'If you could maybe sometime tell me why the whole damn thing, here and elsewhere—now that we've destroyed the Australians who shared everything with each other—why the whole economy depends for its existence on competition instead of generosity, remembering that we're manipulating goods and resources that are not ours, but are on loan from the planet.'

I couldn't tell him why. Instead, I lifted my glass, which contained the golden river, and let the torrent flow over my tongue. Which became the red of the river, a river leading through dark underground tunnels, entering bubbling caves, uniting with dark streams.

At least Alky Jack was pushing himself, trying to be taller than when he was born, even if only in talk and thinking. Trying to work something out, something about how men should live. We stayed the same, did nothing. It was a bit poor, somehow.

His latest boss had a confidential habit. Ernie was a bit shy about letting it out to us, but we finally got his guts.

'He's got you in his office there and he gets you to look over his shoulder at some figures. He keeps moving the paper so you have to stay pretty close in order to focus, then he does it.'

'Does what?' says the Great Lover, looking up from the crossword in that morning's Tele.

Ernie was so long answering that we guessed.

'Dirty bastard,' said the Great Lover virtuously.

'He's a flip,' said the Darkfella, grinning.

'A dead set vagina,' said Mick, who thought this was a clever thing to say.

'Have you read a book this year?' said Sibley. 'Do you buy medicines? Do you attend church?'

'Piss off, Sibley,' said the Great Lover.

'Do you believe in God or the Bible?' persisted Sibley.

Mick turned to him.

'Out.'

Sibley out.

'Why don't you do it to *him*?' I suggested to Ernie.

'He's the boss,' Ernie said. 'Sometimes he even says Excuse Me before he does it. He's rotten, I tell you. And there's a girl just come to work there, trying to get my job. Making a play for the boss, but so far he hasn't given her a tumble.'

'That's what he's told you,' said old Hugh, who'd just come in for his rum and beer chaser.

'Well, he waits till she's about to come in his office and he lets one go, then when she comes in he moves a bit away from me, and smiles at her then catches the scent of it again and looks at me with a frown and back at her with a smile. He doesn't need to point, the way he does it. He might just as well tell her it was me that farted.'

'She might know it's him, but just goes along with it because he's the boss,' the Darkfella said helpfully.

'Next time he does it, roar out That's wet at the edges! So the rest of the office can hear. That'll put his weights up,' said the Great Lover, who didn't understand that someone wouldn't be game to dob the boss.

149

We were no help to Ernie.

'Why don't you just run out of the room when he does it, and hold your nose?' said Tom, who'd got wind that the Great Lover was in the pub.

Old Hugh hit the nail on the head.

'Get friendly with this sheila, if she wants your job. Take her out to a dance or something. Does she like dancing?'

'Yeah,' said Ernie. 'Loves it.'

'Most of the bitches do,' old Hugh said sourly. 'Then get her to a dance and show her you like her. You'll learn a lot about her. Study her. Then if you're smart enough you'll get a line on how she thinks. If any of 'em think. Then you might stand a chance of keeping your job.'

No one thought this was a good idea, but a week later I found Ernie had done just that. The girl had gone with him, probably to find his weaknesses so she could undercut him. She was well on in her cost accountancy course, whatever that was, and Ernie started to have nightmares about her not only getting his job but getting the boss's job too. In which case he'd have to learn dancing.

He was standing at the red bar one Saturday afternoon and sneaking salt on to his hand to lick off when the bar manager came along and tapped him on the shoulder.

'Phone,' he said. Ernie gulped guiltily at his palm,

looked round and saw we all noticed his little aid to thirst, and made off to take the call. He stuck one finger in the offside ear to blot out the pub roar, and craned his head forward to listen. I noticed his head rear up and Ernie say something that looked like What?

Then he came away from the red phone back to the red bar. He didn't look at us, just went towards his glass. When he got to it he didn't see it. He turned blindly away, went towards the front door, stopped, shook his head, turned round and went the other way out towards the car park. He wasn't so much walking as propping on stiff legs and this gave him an appearance of lurching.

'What's up him?' Flash asked. No one knew. We looked away, and went on talking about this and that.

It wasn't much later that we heard a commotion outside. It was no effort to turn round and wonder what it was all about.

Someone called, 'It's Ernie!'

We couldn't see Ernie. We went out. Maybe a car had backed over him.

When we got there, a ring of spectators surrounded someone on the dirt. I got closer and there was Ernie, lying full-length, drumming on the ground with his fists and feet. There was dust all over him, he was raising a cloud all round. We moved back a bit out of the dust.

He didn't stop. Maybe he was having a fit. Some moved back a bit further in case it *was* a fit. I pushed in, bent down and grabbed his shoulder, trying not to breathe the dust in.

'Ernie! What the bloody hell's the matter?' I shouted. He was making a sort of moaning sound, like a retarded person that gets excited but can't speak actual words.

'Shut up!' I yelled, and he slowed down a bit. 'What's up?'

'Mum,' he said. 'Me Mum.' And began the noise again.

'What about your Mum?' I said, more quietly.

'Dead,' he said. And as he got the word out his voice rose in a shrill scream. It startled me, I moved back a bit myself. Then it settled down to a lower noise, still not making any actual word. Each time his breath ran out he sucked in more and began again, going up high, then lower. After a bit, when he regained his breath, he didn't go up high, but started low and got up to the previous steady note and held it. This was worse than the scream.

I didn't know what to do. The spectators had moved well back.

'His Mum's just died,' I said to them when a suitable break came in Ernie's sound.

No one said anything for a while. Then they began to leave. I heard someone say, 'My Mum's dead too. I didn't go on like that.'

When the mob had gone, one individual hadn't moved.

Blackie sat there. As the last of them left, he turned his head a bit and back at me and said, They're only humans, they don't understand.

Ernie stopped his noise, but continued the drumming with his hands. His legs stopped just after he stopped the noise.

Blackie looked back to Ernie, with his head slightly on one side. The head came back to straight after a while and changed over to slightly on the other side. His eyebrows were up in a funny way; down at the outside but up in the middle. He wasn't a spaniel, but that's how his eyebrows were, like a spaniel. He wasn't anything, really, apart from the labrador in his past. But I suppose most of *us* are pretty well mixed, too.

He was sitting on his rump and his back legs curled round on the bare dirt. He took a sort of half-slide, half-step towards Ernie. His tongue went inside his mouth, his mouth shut and he took a big swallow.

His mouth stayed shut for a bit as he watched Ernie, who was getting tired by now. Blackie looked down at the ground for a few seconds, extended his arms and put his head down on his hands looking at Ernie. I guess he could feel Ernie's sorrow drumming on the gravel.

He took another big swallow and gave a very quiet, restrained moan. You couldn't call it a howl. A sort of groan.

Then he got up, turned his body away with his

head still looking back at Ernie, and his mouth still closed. One more swallow and he walked away quietly, looking back.

It wasn't till he got out of sight round the corner of the pub and to his headquarters near the bottle department that he allowed his mouth to come open and his long pink tongue to come out and loll in the sunlight as he breathed.

As if he knew that an open mouth and lolling tongue near Ernie's sorrow looked too much like a grin. His eyebrows stayed up in the middle, but you'd never mistake him for a spaniel. He stayed there a long time, thinking about Ernie.

Blackie didn't have time to get to know *his* mother: he was taken from her when he was very small.

We didn't hear much from Ernie for a while. Some said he was off the grog, others said he was drinking in a pub with carpet on the floor. He was caught in the clutches of this girl at the office, trying to keep near her, trying to learn to dance, even starting to imagine himself in love with her.

I'm prepared to believe he knew as much about being in love as I know about micro-biology. Anyway, as the saying goes, he did his nuts over her. I know, I took the trouble to go after him and find out.

I watched them together. They say love is blind, but she knew exactly what she was doing. I saw the way she looked at him. In his case it was blind. But he didn't look at her enough. He didn't watch her.

There he was, walking along, and when he spoke to her he didn't look and when she spoke to him he'd answer the words, but not the look in her eyes, or the little grin that made her mouth mobile. He looked straight ahead, like some idea of man that he had, as a hunter that looked for dangers and left details to women.

He should have watched her.

If she made those faces at what I said, I'd have known.

She sucked him in properly, and all the time he was going to dancing lessons she was out with Ernie's boss, which grew to four times a week. She had to stay home with her mother on Saturday and Sunday because her old man was drunk all the weekend and her younger brothers and sisters needed their older sister to keep them steady and to be an example, and to do the housework because her mother took turns.

That's what she told Ernie. He swallowed it.

People like Ernie go along for years, masculinely looking straight ahead, blind to the dalliance at their sides and under their noses. Tunnel vision, they call it.

One Monday morning Ernie was late getting off to work. As he rounded the corner at the top of the hill in Parramatta, there they were, they'd just put their bags in the car and she was closing the door of the motel room. Laughing.

Ernie got to work first. The girl had her mother sick in bed, she said. She came in a few minutes after the boss and explained to him why she was late. She looked happy and alive, and Ernie did notice one thing. As she turned to talk to him, her face shed the happy look and put out this sincere, quiet, wide-eyed look. Ernie was blind to the spiritual meaning of it, all he saw was the contrast with the previous expression.

The following Saturday he went to her house. It was dark already. Her brothers and sisters were not there, her old man wasn't there, her mother was just going out, and the girl getting ready to go. He waited for the old girl to depart, then walked in the door.

The girl was making bathroom noises. On the way through the kitchen he picked up the handiest thing, which was a jaffle iron. You know, the thing with two metal halves like soup plates in which you put the sandwich then close the other half over it, slip the catch at the end of the two handles, and hold it over the gas to toast.

He crept up to the bathroom. She was naked, bent over, drying her legs and feet, one of which was up on the side of the bath. He hit her on the head with the edge of the iron and she dropped like a stone, hitting her face on the side of the bath on the way down.

Having her limp like that turned him on, but he stuck to his guns. He hauled her into the kitchen and looked round for something to fix her with.

Maybe one of her brothers was a camper, for high on a ledge over the room-divider was a hammer and several iron pegs.

With a tea towel round the peg, he positioned it a little forward and above her left ear as her head lay on its side on the linoleum. He hoped it was a wood floor.

He made a heavy blow with the hammer and was sickened at how easily the peg went through the temple and plunged through the brain. He lifted the head. No, it hadn't come out the other side. Two more blows and it did. Then came the hard work. Try as he might, he couldn't get the spike through the floor. He lifted the lino at the seam, found a crack in the floorboards and hammered the spike through the crack.

Why he wanted to have her head nailed down was a mystery he couldn't explain. Perhaps he'd read it in a book once. Or in the Bible.

They didn't catch him straight away. He started coming to the pub every day, staying till ten and staggering home. It made a big mystery in the papers, and they all had a great time with it.

Luckily, the boss had an alibi. He was at home waiting for the girl to drive to his place, where they'd get into his car and go on from there. He waited and waited, and since she wasn't on the phone, he took his wife out.

It took the police till next Friday to get around to Ernie. He hadn't even left a fingerprint in the girl's place. But at eight o'clock when he saw a car pull up in the car park, and two plainclothes men walk in the pub, he ran.

That was the end of Ernie.

At the trial they asked him why. It wasn't her two-timing him, it was because he was convinced she already had his job.

Next time anyone saw him was one busy weekend— for the coppers—when they had so many fighters and drunks and over-the-limit drivers in the cells at the police station that they put the overflow into maximum security Parramatta.

Danny was our representative.

'They had a special lounge room ready for me along the corridor past all these cells with little windows and placards out front with the crim's name and what he'd done, like murder, and how long he was in for. Maybe the information was for the visitors. Anyway, it was a fluke. I saw Ernie's card. The old brain acted quick. I dropped my handkerchief, which they let me keep, to the floor. I bent to pick it up and as I was straightening I took a quick look in the little window. He had a room to himself, he was sitting on his little bunk, looking at nothing.

'I call out, Hey, Ernie! It's me, Danny, and the screw with me hauls me away to my room, which I share with eight others, the scruffiest looking lot you ever see. Drunk, sick, nasty. I wasn't game to go to sleep. Ernie didn't answer.'

Danny went around telling everyone the good news that Ernie was still in the land of the living, but after an hour you couldn't understand what he was saying.

I could see the jail corridor of time inhabited not just by Ernie, but by Danny and Alky Jack and all the rest of us, with each a step forward and each year another cell and each cell smaller until at the end solitary confinement with no room to move your shoulders or lift up your knee or your glass or throw a punch.

Just lying flat on your back.

When I got to Fortress Australia an owl was sitting on the front fence. As I shut the car door she flew away flapping like washing in the wind.

I looked out into the dark a long time.

Life was a lot of little days, of little short days, all strung together like a woman's beads, arranged in a circle, with a mouth swallowing its own tail.

The next Wednesday I was in the Southern Cross right after work, about half past two—I start at five-thirty in spring and autumn, and five in summer—and old Hugh came in just as I was near the end of the first, and best, schooner of the day. He got his rum and middy of beer and sat down near the door with a ray of sunlight across his face. The sun shone on his perfect tooth, the only one in his head.

I wouldn't tell her this, though if I did I know she'd understand without me having to waste one word in explanation, but old Hugh's perfect tooth reminds me of my darling's teeth shining when she opens her mouth to smile or talk.

She talks a lot, actually, and I like it. I guess I like the sound of her voice, which is bright and bubbly.

I swallowed the rest of the schooner and lit out for where she works. There was a red phone nearby so I ring her up and get this song at the other end. You know by now it wasn't an actual song, it was her answering the phone.

She'd interrupt anything if you wanted her. It only took her seven minutes to get ready and come down.

'What kept you?' I demanded.

'I came as soon as I could,' she says, anxious to please. Her mouth didn't know whether to go down.

'Did you ever stop to think I might not be there some day if you keep me waiting like this?'

'Oh, you wouldn't, would you? Oh no, don't do that. If you'd rather I didn't go and freshen up—'

I couldn't let her go on. I grabbed her there in the street and lifted her up in a big hug and swung her round so her feet were off the ground. Round and round, like a carousel. People drew back so as not to get their clothes dusty from her shoes; some smiled, some looked superior.

When we got to the car she bent down and kissed the back bumper. When you think about it, and the love that includes a man's car, you couldn't feel awkward. It's just that—well—it was my car, and if she loved the old car that much, well.

She looks back up at me and says, 'You know how I feel about good old CLY, don't you?' CLY is the prefix part of my car's registration.

In the car it's all I can do to get her into the seat belt. She's got this habit of suddenly grabbing me round the neck or the head and pulling me over to be kissed. With the seat belt on she can't move far.

I've spoken to her about it often. Safety angle and all that.

You can imagine how much difference that makes.

Coming late at night out of the city over bridges, the white moon competes across the water with the golden lights of wharves. I usually award a draw.

It was late one night in a strange city that first she took my mind.

Thinking about her in the car I knew the human race would survive. The grog wouldn't touch us, pollution wouldn't kill us, war wouldn't wipe us out. Doom didn't belong in the same world as my darling.

Thursday. There's been rain a few days before and we've got up all the debris that comes in over the course from the gutters. I told you we're at the bottom of a depression, with the land rising away on all four sides. Plastic toys and bottles, papers, all sorts of rubbish come out of those gutters and make a mess of the fairways.

All *that's* done and the greens are still too wet to mow, so Wal and I go up the high side of the fourth fairway and work on a blocked drain.

I tell you, this is the best job I've had. To have grass all round, and trees.

Especially trees. The soil's poor, anything you plant has to be nursed. I always keep my eye open for anything that looks thirsty, and work round to it before the leaves start to go.

This drain. Wal and I work on it for an hour or two and the old twelve inch pipes under the ground are the sort that are laid in halves. All you do is dig round them and under, sling a chain round and lift with the front-end loader, lay them to one side and get them apart in your own time.

Wal had seen willow roots like this before, so we didn't chop them, we used the tow bar of the tractor to extract them from the pipes. If you've never seen a fourteen foot length of solid tangled willow roots, you'll have to imagine it. It fills the pipes completely and takes their inside shape, so it comes out smooth and round, with a diminishing tail.

We left it there on the edge of the rough to dry. I put two white stones up front for eyes and slit it horizontally to make a mouth. Thursday was Ladies Day.

We replaced the pipes and put the spoil back and it wasn't till half an hour later that we saw the first encounter between our monster and one of the old biddies. It was her third shot off the tee and it went past a small grove of new poplars—just sticks at that stage—and into the willow tree. When she left her buggy on the fairway edge and trudged into the rough, seven iron at the ready, she almost trod on the monster lying in foot-high grass.

She was a spunky old girl, and instead of continuing to scream—the first scream only went two seconds— she whaled into it with the seven iron. Mostly about the head. The first thing to go were its eyes, but she didn't stop.

Wal grinned from his seat on the front-end loader. He wasn't one to waste a perfectly good laugh on the fresh air. He waited till lunch, which we had in a sort of dungeon under the clubhouse, and retailed his story to the other boys before going off into fits and roars and gales.

'The longest root I ever saw in me life!' he raved. And took a look after lunch to see if she was still killing it.

Some of the boys decided to have a Saturday night at King's Cross. I had things to do earlier in the city so I stayed there in the afternoon and was to meet them at night. With a bit of food in me I walked down to the water at Rushcutters Bay, watched the sailing boats, the moored cruisers. It was early March and junior teams were playing football trials on the oval.

I didn't often leave the Mead, so every time I saw lights like this I had to go slow and look and think about it. The bay spread round in a lazy half-circle, the yachts, the strolling people, the parked cars, rich houses. I had to try to assimilate the peace, the wealth, the calm luxury of pleasant surroundings. The Mead had nothing like this, all we had was the car sale yards for colour, the factories, the jail, and houses. And the six-lane stream of cars flowing all day.

166

* * *

There were even a few kids playing marbles on a dirt patch under shady fig trees where grass wouldn't grow. It was years since I'd seen a game of marbles. They even said the old words.

'Stop fudging!'

'That's my dib.'

'Mine's the blood alley.'

'No it's not, yours is the connie agate.'

'Come on, there's nothing in it.'

'Dibs in.'

'For keeps.'

'No takings.'

'Bags first shot.'

'Rolls on!'

'Come on, knuckle down.'

'No slogs!'

'Fudge! No fudges.'

'Knuckle down! Look! No fudges.'

I went up the hill to look round a bit before I met the boys. They reckon you're liable to see funny things there, like cats being walked, collars and leads and all. I saw people being walked, collars and leads. I saw four girls tied together and a guy sitting on a little five-ply platform on their shoulders. They were carrying him along, and when they got a bit slow he'd either lean

167

over and give them a lick of his ice-cream or tap them with a switch, a long twig of willow.

I sat in the little park to wait for the boys. Upstairs, the moon floated transparent as a jellyfish in the day sky. I began to have a dream. I was in this room in a building I'd never seen before. There was no name on the outside, nothing to show what it was. A cat was with me. I like cats a lot and I liked this one, but he started to get bigger. His body got longer, he got fatter, everything about him got bigger including his mouth, though he didn't turn on me when he got bigger than I was. I tried to get behind him and push him out the door while he could still get through, but he wouldn't move. Then he was far too big to go through the door.

Still he didn't turn on me, though his mouth was bigger than a lion's. He expanded quicker then, so that he pushed me against the side of the room, squeezing the life out of me. His breath stank like the tigers at the Zoo.

I woke up in a sweat, arms thrashing about and yelling. Just in time to see two coppers change directions at the footpath and come towards me. When I was clear that I wasn't going to be suffocated, I got my breath and sat up straight and wiped the sweat away with a handkerchief.

The coppers looked at my eyes, rolled up both sleeves for needle marks and so on, got me to stand in case I was drunk. They went, but didn't look satisfied.

The place was quiet. The gambling joints up the street had too much protection to crack down on, they were looking for those who had no protection. Cops will be cops.

When the boys found somewhere to park, they went straight to get a drink or two. No stupid dreams for them. Mick used a name he knew and got us in to a club where all sorts gathered. People were drinking and having some entertainment and after two hours we started to wonder if that's all there was to the joint. We needn't have worried. The guards on the doors made sure no one could come in and we all settled down to watch the Oyster Derby.

If this is not your style of thing, skip this paragraph. They got five of the girls—they operated the derby in heats and semi-finals right the way up to the play-off and the grand final—to strip below the waist and lie down with their legs open towards the other end of the room. Each one had an oyster placed inside, and the boys lined up at the other end of the room for each heat.

Skip two paragraphs. On the word Go the boys raced up to the girls, got down on hands and knees and with their teeth extracted the oysters and ran back up the other end of the room to deposit the oyster on a plate. By that time the next heat of boys were lined up, a fresh round of oysters in position, and they set sail for the oysters. And so on.

Make it three paragraphs. After eleven heats the novelty was beginning to wear thin. The semis and the finals only brought the best competitors together, and believe me they were really quick. But the idea was the same even if they took their time. I would have liked it better, myself.

The regulars cheered their mates as if they did this every week, which they did. The onlookers and the failed competitors got a real kick out of the finalists polishing off the plates of oysters at the finish.

When the party got a little rough after midnight, I was all for going. But the boys couldn't get enough of this stuff. When three girls did handstands and the boss of the place and his special guests ate strawberry, chocolate and coffee ice-cream from similar places, it found me yawning.

The boys were pretty drunk, and what with not being used to much in the way of extras from their girlfriends, they wanted to stay.

Even Mick got sick of looking at the same thing all night, so he and I pressured the others into taking a walk.

We cautioned them to walk steady, the cops late at night were pretty sudden on drunks, it looked bad for tourists, and we didn't feel like a chase through back alleys.

On the way home we went south through places where there were no police in the streets, but dark buildings and few streetlights, natural places for spring locks, steel sheets over doors; chains, spy-holes and weapons.

The Mead, our tribal suburb, was home to us, and safe by comparison. But any time, a natural disaster such as a new expressway could mow them and us off the face of the earth and leave it neat and clean with concrete and bitumen and a pretty grass verge.

In the meantime it was night, and the different classes equal in sleep.

WOULD I?

On Sunday I went to see my sunny girl. She was waiting for me sitting on the stone ledge outside her house, not looking a bit like a business executive.

She loved the sun, and sat in it every chance she got. The way she sat there, face up to the sun, arms supporting her on the stone slab and bent inwards at the elbow in that way girls have, legs relaxed and toes pointed as if someone posed her, I thought to myself Would I ever forget the way she looked at that moment?

I told myself no.

Next time I saw Sibley alone I asked him how his investigations were going.

'I'm finding all sorts of things,' he said cheerfully. 'This is another dimension here,' looking round the Southern Cross.

'Questioning non-drinkers, too. Do you know, Lance, how many non-drinkers have never held a social conversation with a drinker? Or know no drinkers by name. Or have never visited a drinker's home, or have no drinkers among their personal friends. Do you know the percentage of non-drinkers that belong to an organisation for the assimilation of drinkers?'

'No, Sibley. You've got me there. But what do you mean, assimilation?'

'That's my aim, the aim of the thesis. To investigate means of assimilating the drinker into the main body of society.'

I thought a bit. 'Sibley, maybe you shouldn't say too much about this. The guys round here are likely to be pretty sensitive about thinking of themselves as another race, or having to be assimilated into the rest of society. I reckon they feel they *are* our society, and the thought of having educated people stooping to lift them up, well, they might take it hard.'

'Don't worry, Lance. History is on my side. Research and quantitative analysis will bring a solution to their problems.'

I shook my head. His eyes followed the crack up the back wall where it pointed to the clock. It had spread a bit.

'My opinion at the moment is that drinkers should be encouraged to join local organisations, be part of the community.' He fished in his pocket and brought out papers.

'These are opinions from non-drinkers. I'll read a few to you. Eighty-seven per cent said they'd feel uncomfortable if a drinker sat next to them in public transport or a theatre. Similar percentages said they have nothing personal against drinkers, but they could never be friendly with one and they thought their appearance was unattractive. Similar numbers said drinkers try to get more for nothing than non-drinkers, that there's always trouble when you let drinkers into a nice neighbourhood—they give it a drinking atmosphere. And here's some hard figures. Drinkers are pretty much alike: ninety per cent. There should be restrictions on them to protect others from drinkers' lack of responsibility: ninety-four per cent. The two cultures can never merge: ninety-four. Drinkers probably prefer not to mix with non-drinkers: ninety-nine per cent.'

'Where did you get these figures, Sibley?'

'Round here, in the Mead. Oh, I see what you're getting at. Yes, over on the North Shore, where there's no chance of drinkers buying land or houses or keeping up with the rates, the percentages are low; they're on the drinkers' side in droves. Very liberal, very humane.'

'Very remote.'

'Exactly,' he said pleasantly. 'People can't act outside their own frames.'

Sibley and I chatted on a bit and this time he put a few down him. Some of the other guys must have watched us for a while, and got interested. They'd been telling Sibley to piss off lately, never mind his free beer. I guess they wanted to ask *him* a few questions.

'What's the strength of you, Sibley,' the Great Lover said. 'Why study us? What's it all about? Who's going to see all those answers?'

'It's his thesis,' I said.

'His whatsis?' said Mick.

'My thesis,' said Sibley proudly. 'For my PhD.'

'What's that when it's at home?' said Serge. He didn't usually ask questions, unless you thought a brief 'Outside' was a question.

175

'His doctor's degree,' I explained. But Sibley wanted the floor.

'The study of drinkers,' he orated, 'is the study of a dying race.' He'd had too much to drink. 'Hopefully, the results of my surveys and questions and calculations will illustrate the dimensions of the drinking problem. And I mean hopefully. It is entirely possible that all drinkers can be helped from total reliance on alcohol to independence of the drug. For it *is* a drug problem. Society has a good number of well-educated, well-qualified, well-disposed humanitarian people who will be prepared to give time to help, to raise up those who can't kick the habit by themselves, to reform the drinker, to absorb him into the main body of society, to integrate and assimilate him into the mainstream of Australian culture.' Digging his grave with his tongue.

'What's so crook about grog?' said the Great Lover. Love of alcohol oozed from every pore.

'Alcohol oppresses you all. It ties you in to this way of life.' Sibley waved a thin arm round to indicate the slopped red bar, the decrepit chairs that so often doubled for weapons, the punched door, broken glass, the cracked glass doors at the back of the pub, the hills and hollows in the pub yard, the browned paint on the rafters and high ceiling of the saloon bar, the sight of Alky Jack bent over his glass and Danny playing football in some corner of his head that still worked.

'What will your whatsit do?' asked Mick politely.

'It might be published,' Sibley answered. 'My analysis of you could be read everywhere.'

'Yeah, but what will it do to us?'

This was Sibley's chance. Never before had they shown so much interest in what he was doing. Perhaps he was getting through. If he could have this effect on them while he was a beginner, then when he had his doctorate and he worked on other social evils, he might find he had powers, personal powers, that made his choice of vocation more than just chance. It might be his destiny to change men's lives. Abetted by the beer he saw himself a public figure, the sort of guru who is asked to pronounce on society's ills by all the media.

He decided to try out these powers. He would persuade them, help them to see a better way, show concern, lift them up.

'If I am successful,' he said, his eyes glowing with persuasive intentness, 'and others join me to help drinkers all over the country—all over the world—then the whole way of life of drinkers will be changed. Changed for the better, changed irrevocably.'

He watched their faces. The King was looking away, maybe through the windows, no expression on his face. Maybe Sibley had got him looking already at his way of life. Serge looked at a spot at the side of Sibley's jaw, Mick at his chest and slight shoulders like a butcher guessing the dressed weight of a carcass.

'You won't even look at your beer, won't even stop at the pub on the way home—'

177

'Won't look at a beer!' said the Great Lover incredulously.

'Won't look at the stuff,' Sibley said firmly. 'You'll never have to congregate in surroundings like this, you won't have to listen to that racket—' the races weren't on, but Sibley's eyes went up to the loudspeakers. 'My effect will be to take you away from gambling, from wasted time, wasted lives, from poverty, to constructive pursuits, educational interests, work that is for the benefit of all, to helping the unfortunate and oppressed of other lands.'

Sibley paused for breath, and Mick asked me, 'Any chance of this happening, Meat?'

'Well,' I said. 'I don't know. If he's right and he gets a lot of other people interested, he might make an effect. These things sort of grow, maybe if he gets governments interested, they might make things tough for drinkers. Maybe. I don't know.'

Sibley knew. 'I can do it, I tell you. You can't go on living like this. Putting effort into things that are a waste of time and money and all your abilities. If I get the support I hope for, then a certain amount of compulsion may be necessary.' He smiled a tolerant smile. 'I hope it won't be necessary, of course. But when you try to do things for people, things for their own good, you sometimes have to *make* them see that what you have in mind is right. If drinkers could be raised up to the standard of life of those more fortunate, if these conditions and ways of life could be blotted out, poverty and oppression could be replaced by happiness, prosperity, solid goals in life, worthwhile things that give life a quality drinkers never dream of. I'm not alone, you know,' he said defiantly. 'There are great numbers of enlightened men and women of all professions, able and willing to give time and help to the assimilation of the drinker. All he needs to know, to get him on the right track, is that there are well-disposed people who feel for him and want to help and want to see him raised up to the level of the rest of society.'

Sibley was good for another fifteen minutes of this, but he had no audience. Without a word, the other guys turned and walked away back to their places at the bar.

I heard a voice say something like '. . . I'll give the cunt well-disposed.' In a very cold tone, it was. Might have been Serge. Or Mick. Or the King, who hadn't said anything before.

I persuaded Sibley to stuff his papers back in his pocket and go home. 'Write up your findings, do something, but get out of here.'

He didn't understand, but he'd had enough and the beer had reduced his statistical ability. He went.

I hadn't seen Sibley for a while and no one mentioned his name.

I don't know why I mention him now though I miss having him round, him and his coloured pens and bits of paper. Maybe he's living-in at the university, working his test results up into a book.

The publican came round asking if we'd seen one of his beer barrels. You know, the stainless steel kegs the breweries lovingly send with our nourishing brew tightly enclosed.

'Was it full?'

'No. Nothing like that. Just an empty. But I'm one short. Have you seen it, Danny?'

'I might have emptied it. After that I've got no use for it. Long as she keeps coming through the pipes.' He went on talking, but it wasn't to us.

'Where'd you leave it?' Mick said.

'Out the yard, with the rest.'

'Some kid's pinched it and sailed it down the creek.'

Kids rode canoes down as far as the first weir.

After that, they took no notice.

Sibley should have been on somebody's stocklist. They'd have missed him, too.

Tuesday I was back on the golf course sitting on the International, thinking of this and that, my darling, and how the arm of the radiogram or the insides of it knows the record that's on it is just that wide. I tried to trick it with a twelve inch record then a nine inch and a six inch. I was wasting my time. The machine knew. Every time the needle came down in the right place, just on the edge.

When I brought up the subject of records and things, no one ever mentioned how clever the machine was. I used to say something like that sometimes, but no one ever took any notice. Either they didn't realise, or they knew the machine was clever.

I decided they didn't realise.

After work I went to see my darling. She dropped what

she was doing, though I told her to be sure not to interrupt anything important, and ran out to where I was with the car.

I got out to meet her, but before I could reach her she reached the car and kissed his eyes, his front lights.

Once upon a time this used to embarrass me. Now it doesn't.

When I felt like pulling her leg I'd threaten to sell him.

'You'd never sell good old CLY. Please,' she said. Half was command, the other half question. A third half pleading.

Selling him was not on. He was ten and I wanted to keep him while he ran, and after he gave up the ghost I had ideas of putting a new motor in him or a transmission or whatever was necessary to give him as much immortality as I could. The dents and spots and creases he acquired over the years made his personality shine out. The new front wing I'd picked up in an alley from a guy who said he was a wrecker, wasn't quite the same colour as the original one, and this gave an extra character to his front. As did the chrome piece in the bumper that had snapped off in a collision with a post that wasn't there.

I always felt sorry for the toe on each foot—in both cases the third toe if you count toes as you count fingers—that was bent.

'When I was a baby the doctor said they should be broken to make them straight. Then they would have been nice to look at.'

She hid them underneath her when she sat on the bed.

This made me feel pretty special towards those toes, as you can imagine. The thought of a little baby having its toes broken by some doctor.

Next day out on the course with the dew seducing me into getting down off the tractor and standing with the sun behind my head so the light shone into the heart of the dewdrops and rayed out emeralds and blinding golds, I thought of her again. And the little bent toes.

It was a day for mowing the rough. In and out the trees, raising a bit of dust later when the dew disappeared, skirting the base of the trees to cut up to the trunks and not hurt the bark and the tree-flesh beneath. To get seventeen hundred revs you had to go back to second. You needed seventeen hundred for the blade speed or you didn't cut cleanly, just bruised and slashed.

And the smell of cut grass rising up all round.

I don't get my kicks out of loud noises—whether it's sound equipment or the scream of turbines—so I always plug in.

I have these little white earplugs, and no matter if the motor's in second, as soon as you plug in peace comes.

You still hear the birds, though, and voices. Just that everything's a long way off. A real long way.

I like that.

Did you know that on a golf course the ladies hit off from different tees, closer to the hole? They haven't protested yet at the inequality.

I suppose I only mention mowing because I remembered just then that most of that day the grass was short and it made you feel a bit brutal to be going round cutting wisps of grass that was dead.

There's nothing like ploughing through long grass, smelling the rich green, knowing the grass grows stronger and thicker for the cut you're making.

I suppose if you put your ear down and listened you might hear the noise grass makes when it's cut, but I don't know that it'd be a cry of pain.

DEATH OF THE DARKFELLA

The Darkfella collected a broken collarbone in the game against Christian Brothers Old Boys, and it set with a lump like an egg an inch or two from where the clavicle meets the top of the rib cage.

It was only a week since he'd been sent off the field for a head tackle. Which was crazy.

The Darkfella was good-natured, spindly and by turns alert and very vague. He was probably in one of his switched-off states when he noticed this winger making for his spot near the sideline and threw out a long arm when the winger ducked inside him. The ref should have used his head, the Darkfella meant no harm and did none. His sleeve got in the winger's eye, and he rubbed his eyes with his sleeve. The ref thought he was blinded or concussed.

The Darkfella was embarrassed and went off grinning, not sure if he was a villain. But when the team cheered him off, calling out things like Killer and Mangler and 'Take his name, Sir,' he held his head higher and increased the length of his stride, which was long enough already, and loose, so you were never sure where the advancing foot was going to land. He wasn't, either.

I try never to have words with referees. In prison you have to call the warders Sir; in school too; same on the football field.

The Darkfella healed up with this egg near his collar. Maybe it had something to do with him taking the bandages off and wiggling the arm round to show us the way the two ends of bone moved. And he played on with us, usually on the wing. Hoping he didn't get the ball.

His wife left him about this time and went to live with another guy a mile away, leaving the Darkfella's little boy with him to look after. The Darkfella was up the bush one weekend and met a quiet, fair girl, tall as he was, and brought her back to Sydney to live with him while his other wife got a divorce.

After they settled down a bit, the Darkfella got to feeling pretty happy, sometimes even getting full at the Southern Cross. He drank new beer.

The Darkfella had a kerp like no one else. It was fairly long and very thin. When its mind was on nothing in particular, he could tie a knot in it. Often used to do it in the shower after the game.

One Saturday morning during the season when we had a bye, he was full by about midday, overturned his car at the bend at the bridge end of O'Brien's Road, had enough sense to get out and run like hell to Parramatta Hospital, taking a good short cut through the park. He beat the cops to the hospital and was in bed by the time they dashed in with their breathalyser.

'What I can't understand,' he said for the hundred and thirty-eighth time, 'is how they came to get a reading of sober. They said I was sober as a judge. When they asked me where the keys of the car were, I said they'd fallen out. One of them pretended to be sorry for me and put an arm on my shoulder, but I saw his other hand feeling under my pillow for the keys. I had 'em between my legs. Put 'em there soon as I saw the cops walk in up the other end of the ward.'

Next thing I heard, just after the end of the season—we got into the finals, but Clovelly beat us 9-8 at Chatswood—was that the Darkfella was in a coma.

He'd been making a delivery on Captain Cook Drive when a car on the wrong side of the road pinned him to the front of his van. Fifteen days in a coma, and at the end of it pneumonia and death. They always seem to die when they get pneumonia. You'd think they'd be able to pump out their lungs, or something.

His wife that left him stepped in, on good advice, and claimed his body, gave him a funeral and got custody of his little boy. Suddenly found she wanted to look after him.

His coffin lid was open when I saw him last. There was some nice satin, white and shining, and some petal pink stuff—decorations or flowers—and we all followed in the cortege with our lights on right to the crematorium. It was pleasant at the crematorium, with trees and shrubs and flowers, and pools for the fish. And a fountain. You'd never want to leave there. The road in was so straight, there were no gates, no barriers, everything neat and in its place. It was a great place to be dead.

At his benefit night we arranged a few kegs—eighteens—because we were all pretty sad about the Darkfella, and there was roulette and crown and anchor and other gambling games to raise money to send his tall wife back home to the bush.

We made a mess of the eighteens, what with the sadness and the fights that broke out—it was windy weather: the guys fight more in windy weather—but it's only fair to say that the eighteens made a mess of us. Even Serge had beer when the Bacardi ran out.

Alky Jack sat talking to himself. I walked over a bit behind him. Yes, still at the benefit party. Out here the dark was much closer. Only a few strung bulbs to keep it at bay.

'We will go then, you and I, where the pelican shits its nest.'

He'd seen me coming.

'How's Jack?' sitting on the grass beside him.

'This world's rapidly giving me the tom-tits.'

'I'll never believe that, Jack. You love the place. It'll be all they can do at closing time to get you out.'

'Drink your beer.' He paused to look round at the party. Bodies were all over the grass, the tents set up for roulette, crown and anchor, pontoon.

I look sideways at him, he's looking gloomily into his beer. The whole world's at the bottom of that glass.

'Reminds me of the twenties and thirties. The economy's falling to pieces, so they clamp down on obscenity, pornography, dissent, loud voices. All they want is populations with their heads down and their mouths shut, so they can patch up a mess that's getting worse all the time. So they want to clean up the population's morals, instead of making a new system and disturbing the owners of the present one. They pick at symptoms instead of healing the sick body. They find the smell offensive and want to deodorise it instead of burying it.

'And the people they're doing this to won't resist. They've had proved to them lately that the effectiveness of military power is limited, the economy shows them the shortcomings of romantic free enterprise, and the polluted water, earth and sky tells them there are no more frontiers: we've come to a brick wall. The end of the line. As far as this system's going to take us.

'Newspapers tell us the social fabric is falling apart, there's anxiety and terror, lawlessness in the streets, in the institutions that overlook the streets. Work is empty, living pointless. No one created this mess and no one wants it, but we can't escape it. They want to crush the groans and cries that come from it.

'And the older among us know no resistance is possible. We're the stoned age, Meat.' And he grinned at me and got to his feet. He wasn't all that steady, but with the skill of that portion of his brain not eaten out

191

by alcohol, that kept him moving in search of another drink, he arrived at the keg and brought me back a drink as well without splashing any.

'We are at the mercy of the best traditions of modern discourse: argument by assertion. I do it myself, I get angry. I predict a return to magic. Only in guesses and superstitions and blind hope can we get comfort.

'The modern cult of violence and animalism,'—he looked down at his trousers, but said nothing. I looked too, but there was no sign there of violence or animal-ism—'is an admission of defeat. We can't be men and resist or overthrow the monster that rides us, this way of doing things, this economy with its roots in feudalism, so let us go the other way and be barbaric. And since we can't free ourselves from the past, let us use educated words for our defeat: alienation, cult of absurdity, realism, the beauty of the irrational, cult of cruelty.

'But'—he looked at me sadly—'the emperor has no clothes. It's no wonder men come to prefer ugliness, the nasty things of life, the bizarre, the grossly sensual, the degrading. At least ugliness is honest. The monster on our backs pretends to be kindness and goodness and justice and beauty and freedom. And all the time we see its arse, which is ugliness unredeemed, cruelty. Absurd, gross, degrading.'

He was silent for a bit. I didn't butt in with junior comments. When I looked back at him his face was strange and worked up.

One day the dancing light on the globes of his eyes would be gone; the sun still would shine on the round earth, but Jack would be missing. My old man died in Korea, but Jack fitted all my requirements for a father: you always knew where he'd be, what he liked, and what he thought. If you didn't feel like talking to him, all you had to do was move away.

He started to shout, if you can imagine the beginning of a shouted nothing. It wasn't actually a whole word. Just the steam blowing off his heated mind.

He did it again. I thought maybe he's choking. No, he was OK. While he tried to get it out I thought a bit. We wore our freedom like a shirt, ready to change it for a daily wage to buy freedom again at the bottom of a glass. And after however many glasses it took, the glass got bigger and bigger, we stepped into the glass and claimed our freedom to float away.

Alky Jack started several more times.

'Tell 'em—!' he roared. Then he caught himself and stopped. As if his mind moved about in a strange house and brushed against unfamiliar furniture and he snagged himself on an edge. Leaving him with a splinter of doubt. He rubbed his arm, then plunged ahead, splinter or no splinter.

'Tell 'em, Meat!'

'Tell 'em what, Jack?'

'Tell 'em they're people!' he shouted. 'Humans!'

That shut me up. Did he know I was thinking of writing the Southern Cross on to paper? I looked at him. He was looking at the bottom of his glass, which was empty, as if he knew death was waiting for him not far off. And he still had so much to say. So many sentences not finished. And he knew he would never finish them.

I remembered the woman next door to Fortress Australia, a patient mother, who waited every night for her children to come home from their foolish games. I shivered. It was getting cool.

'I'll get two more beers, Jack,' I said, scrambling to my feet.

OVERHANG

The morning after, I was feeling sad. Gentleness was indicated.

Gently I got to my feet and gently I lifted both hands to my head. There's a lot to be said for levelling-out the blood pressure by lying down, but times come when the upright stance is better. Reduces the pressure at the top of the vessel. What I needed.

Some dew on the grass, not much. I looked up. Sun dived at me, tried to crash-tackle my head through two glassy openings in front. I prudently shut them, felt forward with a foot to look for balance.

Several empty bottles of pilsner tumbled over on their sides with a suicide shriek and bashed together like one of those new concussion bombs.

I tried to open my eyes. No. That was a nowhere nothing.

I felt round blind in my pockets for paper and some means of inscribing my will. No paper.

I bent my knees slowly and after three months reached down near the ground. A bottle with a long slopey neck nuzzled my hand like a death adder. I was interested to find my skin so sensitive.

Something swept round in an arc until I was off balance. I steadied and let it move another few inches. I think it was an arm. If it was an arm I'm pretty sure it belonged to me, or someone close to me. Wetness encountered the outer covering of my arm nerves and the awkward thing on the end of my arm. Another bottle made of glass.

The beer label came off, courtesy of wetness.

I walked a few miles further along the grass and came to a body. Prodigal of time, I spent a lot getting down far enough to search the body for a pen. I still couldn't open my eyes, the sun was waiting for foolish moves like that.

The sick man inside me could stand it no longer. Squatting down, I mean. I straightened, slowly, like one of those trees on the movies, or demolished chimneys, that pick themselves up and come straight again like before they fell. The last bit very slowly.

Getting my top half upright I put both hands on both hips. One hip each. In doing this, I found my own pen. It was in two pieces. I took out the refill, and used that, throwing the broken bits away. The next question was how to get it out. You might think this is no easy thing, and you are dead right. First, which hand?

To make a short story shorter, I wrote out my will on the back of the beer bottle label. The sun dried it while I was thinking.

To whom it may concern. Last will and testament. Being of sound mind.

I had to get another label then, that one was full.

I don't smoke, which is a rare affliction at the Mead. The same body I tried to rob before had a packet of cigarettes. Which I split open, allowing the coffin nails to escape on the grass. They didn't make much noise, but I guess that's because they didn't want anyone to know they were free.

I opened out the empty packet and wrote the rest of my will on the white cardboard. Why is the inside of cigarette packets always white? I asked the question then and I'm asking it now.

No one answered me then, either.

I wish I had a lot of things, I wrote. I'd enjoy giving a lot of things to people. I'd make my darling rich, for a start, so she wouldn't have to worry about anything.

I was really drunk.

Things were not what she wanted; she could do without things. I never saw a less thingy person, man or woman. Only animals are less thingy than she is.

There was no thing I could give her. She just wanted me.

And I was near death. I wrote quickly: Dear world, you are all I know. I like you. Take the lot.

The last bit wasn't much chop. I crossed it out with my dying effort and wrote: I give you all I've got.

Before I collapsed, I got the two bits of paper and folded them together and stuck them in a buttonhole in the front of my shirt and slowly lowered myself to the earth to die.

'Beer makes the world go round,' I said in farewell.

My eyes were already shut, but as soon as I hit the earth a steel curtain behind my eyes came down and I passed away. Goodbye, I said. My mouth stayed open, but did I care?

That afternoon around three I was jumping out of my skin. I have this lucky digestive system, I can be dying in the morning and right as rain by lunch. Usually I don't get crook at all. I found out later some of the boys played a little joke on me.

I can drink a good deal, and until I hit the night air I don't show it. Even walk straight. But when I go, I go. Out like a light. No headaches, just sometimes a little uneasy in the belly. But when you get fed spirits in your beer, you lose your timing. You pass out at entirely the wrong time.

Anyway, last night was last night. I'd missed some day, it was up to me to make the most of what was left.

My little pet car got me to the back of the pub into a nice shady spot by three. Blackie was standing guard, watching us come to drink when we weren't thirsty. Yet he never made a snide remark. There was an old toilet block out the back of the Southern Cross. It was brick, and looked OK painted white. It was the sort of old outhouse that you'd whitewash years before they put the plastic in the kalsomine. It was hardly ever used.

It was further to go past the bar for a pee, then come back, so I went for a pee in there.

There was a man hanging in the darkness. He'd stopped swinging, so I knew he must be dead. There was no hurry.

I had my pee. I even turned round and gave the little bloke a look—his first look—at a dead man.

I felt sorry for the man hanging. His face looked resigned, but that could be my imagination, or the relaxation of death. I felt sorry for his tongue, too. There was a fly on it.

Relaxation. That might be why he wanted to die. Plenty of people are dying to relax. I guess that isn't funny to people who care more about dying than we do, in our tribe.

I put the little bloke away and patted the dead man's pockets. He had money. Why would a man with money neck himself? He could have drunk his money out first. A comb, a letter, some keys, and shoes. Imported. The trousers tailored. A good knitted shirt. With short sleeves, and the points of both elbows worn down smooth and whitened and powdery. A desk worker. On his wrist one of those watches where you can see the guts, wheels turning and things ticking. The sort of thing where they don't even have the price on the ads.

I guess things have as much pull on me as they have on my little darling. I lifted out the letter. It wasn't new.

There was no light there to read by, so out I went and in to the bar. Sharon gave me a schooner. I took it over to a chair.

It was addressed to a woman. Inside, it said 'Dear Elissa', then a comma.

I haven't had a day's sickness since I last saw you. Remember all the little things I used to get wrong with me? A chill, a temperature, pains in the back or the chest, and I used to be ashamed of them. Now they're gone. And I've found what my sickness really was. Loving was my sickness. I recovered from that and my body is better. The person I loved above everything ignored me. Now I'm where I can't feel her ignoring me, and I don't have to get something wrong with me to attract her attention, which was usually irritated and tight-lipped with impatience.

Loving was the main thing in living. I never bothered to take ego trips at work or among friends. I found it easy to work for others and take orders and knuckle under to discipline. But now I've got rid from inside myself of dependence on an employer—I'm out on my own—and I won't take orders from anyone. I do as I like and people lap it up.

I'm well thought of now, where before they didn't know I was there. People listen to me. Money comes easily and bigger orders are automatic when I simply say I want bigger orders. All because I won't listen to anyone. I had no idea people were so simple and so stupid.

I make love when I feel like it and with whom, and treat them all as if I'm going to throw them over tomorrow. The result? They're hanging all over me, begging me never to leave. Offering everything.

And what of the person I loved above everything? I know that whatever she says, she's same as the rest. With the addition of tears. Can't be happy without me. I know it.

She used to say it was ridiculous to expect the fever and anguish and passion of love to survive the first months or years. It never abated for me. And I felt humiliated that I didn't have this toughness that could look calmly on the death of love.

Now I care for nobody and they all want me. And she. She finds—I know she finds—the fever and the anguish unendurable.

As I said, I haven't had a day's sickness since. All that's happened is I've died.

Vivian.

I'd have felt easier if he smelt of grog. But he'd done it because he wanted to die. He'd been wrong about Elissa.

I went out to the car, pretending to get something. On the way back I went in to the old toilet to put the letter back. I stuffed it into Vivian's hip pocket and went back to the door. What would I do?

I walked to the bar and told Sharon. 'There's a stiff in the old shouse.'

'Yeah,' she said, not looking up. Waiting for the crack. I waited, too. At last she'd poured the beers and one for me and looked up as she passed it over and took the money.

'You joking?'

'Not this time. Not that sort of stiff. This sort.' I made a hand sign at my throat. She stood there watching me. I didn't look away. She shrugged with her eyebrows and pushed her lips upward and went towards the manager. She stopped, turned. 'Not kidding?'

'Not kidding.'

'Okay,' she called back.

The bar manager lumbered out and I walked behind. He didn't send Sharon back.

They both took in the sight of Vivian.

'Is he dead?' said Sharon.

'He's stopped swinging,' I said, but she didn't get it.

'How did you come to find it,' said the bar manager.

'Came in for a piss.'

'Better call the police,' he said.

Vivian's socks were down, there were the scars of boils on his ankles. And from his shanks a few pathetic hairs spread down towards bald ankle bones.

In a place like the Southern Cross you can't descend on an old toilet in a body and have nobody notice. Footsteps on cracked concrete announced spectators.

They crowded in and round Vivian. He started to swing again. And that's how he became the property of the Southern Cross.

Up in the corner of the eaves I noticed the skeleton of a small bird. Maybe it just didn't have the energy left after its time of panic and bewilderment.

'Better cut him down,' someone said.

'He's doing no harm up there.'

'Where'd he get the rope?'

'Hey. That looks like a bit of my rope.' A man dashed out to his ute. He was a builder. In he came, shark-eyed.

'That's my rope. Don't you bastards cut it. I'll undo the knot when you want him down.'

'Aren't we going to take him down?'

'Where'll we put him?'

'On the bar?'

'Cut it out. I want to sell beer on that bar.'

'So? He'll be star of the bar.'

With appropriate ceremony he was borne into the manager's office and sat on some newspapers in an easy chair. The builder got his rope back, undamaged. He marked where the neck had been, and the knot, to show his kids.

The photographers came, then the police. By night-fall Vivian was a celebrity. I made sure the boys from the press got the letter first. Man swings for love, and all that.

I once saw a funeral take off from the Old Men's Home, the box carried on a dray, just a horse and cart. No mourners, just a driver. They shot the box in on the floor of the dray: Bang! and at the graveside shot it in again: Bang! to the bottom of the hole in the ground. I was a little kid then, it impressed me.

Vivian's was a pauper burial too. We'd whipped round and got plenty of flowers, but we didn't think of the style of service and stuff like that. We assumed he had plenty of brass. We hadn't contributed to that. Whoever his relatives were, if he had any, they tied everything up so it worked out the dead man had nought.

Not that he needed it. A hole in the ground is a hole in the ground, however much it costs, however many words are said from the top looking down.

No one turned up at the paddock but us from the pub. It was a rainy day, none of the press or TV came. Even the minister, hired for the occasion and not scoring much out of it, wanted to stand fifty yards away on the paved part of the road. The ground was wet and soggy and bad for shoes. He wanted two dry feet, didn't care who else got wet, long as he didn't. He was prepared to say the words from there, while we stood round in the mud.

Not for long. Serge put a hand under his collar and lifted him off the bitumen, his arm swung like a crane and the man of the cloth was deposited on wet soil.

'Over there, mate. That's you. Not fifty yards away 'cause you're frightened of getting your bloody feet wet.'

The parson did as he was told and said the words by the hole in the ground. Someone held an umbrella over the coffin so the raindrops only splashed on the foot end.

As far as we could see, the words did nothing for the cells that died, the circuits that failed. But who knows?

No strange women turned up, no Elissa. Old Viv had been dead wrong about her. Much he knew. She didn't give a stuff.

When we got back home to the pub, a shiny steel beer keg stood in the corner of the covered area. You could get in there, round the back of the pub, without breaking and entering. All you had to do was open a wire gate.

'Someone's brought back his keg,' I remarked to Alky Jack.

'Yeah,' he said and went on looking down his glass.

When the publican came round later he saw it.

'Some cunt's finished with that keg I lost,' he said.

'Christ, it's heavy,' when he tried to lift it. 'Hey! Some cunt's welded the bung in!' he yelled. Then, 'Some cunt's cut the whole top out and welded it back.'

Some cunt had indeed been busy. He shook it. It didn't rattle and it didn't slop, as it would if there was beer in it.

'Bugger it. I've put it in as lost. It can do for a doorstop. Give us a hand.'

The door near the pool tables was always banging. We used the heavy keg to keep it open. When guys kicked its steel sides hoping for a hollow boom, all they got was a flat knock. Didn't even rock. They'd look at their thongs, toes, elastic-sided boots or five dollar Italian pub specials, shake their heads, look at the keg again and pass by.

'What's in that bloody keg?' they'd say.

No one knew or cared. It was a doorstop. Fair enough.

The wind that blew up from the south and east brought rubber from Goodyear and the warm smell of bitumen from Shell. Sackcloth and ashes spread over the suburbs from elegant chimneys tall as minarets.

Dogs yapped in the distance a continual yap-yap, playing their fierce games, machine guns firing over open ground. Maybe in their games men fell.

After ten we all went home to imitate the dead.

The Southern Cross is a book without pages.

It is a whale on its side in an uneven sea, listening to ocean music; in its belly is a tribe of Jonahs.

The Southern Cross is an old, battered, experienced flower, that opens six mornings and closes six nights a week, and on the seventh day rests.

It is a deflated football that ought to be blown up.

The Southern Cross at night is a light in the darkness, a kind of music borrowed from the sun.

It is driftwood. Bars, chairs, buildings, all are gathered on the shore where the tide left them.

The Cross is the past pretending to promise the future.

It is sharp and nervous as the hearing of the blind.

The Cross is a place where you cannot see your self.

It does not contain the future: that is up the street somewhere, over the hill, around the corner, in the brains of young children, in a pattern of words and objects that no one has recognised yet.

No one knew who did him over, and when he got out of hospital he didn't know either. He'd always been an annoying bastard, now he was still annoying, but it was understandable. An ordinary guy acting stupid is hard to take, but anyone can put up with a crazy man.

The queer fella came back with one arm held funny, sort of limp from the wrist. His left leg dragged and pointed inwards as if the ankle stiffened in a broken position. A big scar over his right eye gave his face a lopsided look, I think the bones had been pushed in that side of his forehead. If it wasn't a car hit him—and left him for dead—someone must have picked him up, say by leg and neck, and hurled him against something.

There was another scar in his hair, but you could only see that if he bent.

His injuries never made the papers or anything. Someone just found him, put him in hospital, and let him go when he was patched up.

Some days he'd suddenly run round outside the pub brandishing a big stick in his good hand, yelling, 'I'll get the lot of you! Come out and fight, you bastards! Come on, I'm game!' Flailing like a madman fighting the sea.

No one went. While it was a novelty they'd watch, sipping, from the doors, then after a while when it became a regular performance, they'd say, 'There goes that silly bastard. Gone off again.' And forget about it.

He'd come in looking more settled and confident. I guess in his head he always won the fight.

Some nights he'd camp out in the grass at the back of the pub. When the police came after ten, looking for drinkers on the premises, they'd miss him. The grass was long.

He was guarding the place, though he was asleep. For breakfast he'd chew a piece of gravel, moving it round in his mouth. The snack bar woman gave him end bits of bread that no one would buy. He'd rat the rubbish for more substantial tucker. For liquid he had a choice of abandoned beer glasses left out overnight by people drinking in their cars; there was a tap at the back of the pub for fresh water.

Other times he was normal and hunched over the bar like the rest of us, like the thirsty round a well.

(I climbed up in the struts supporting the roof members one night to get an old guy's coat someone had thrown up there for a joke, and when I looked down they all looked like round animals attached to a rectangular, many-titted mother.)

Then maybe he'd rouse himself and become a would-be publican, going round talking to groups of guys, buying drinks—drinking sevens, like a publican—giving advice to the barmaids, even going behind the bar to count the glasses, looking at the latest amount rung up on the registers. They were Nationals, if it matters.

'Takings are down,' he'd say. 'You've all got your hands in the till.'

'That's enough of that. Piss off,' Sharon said.

He thought, for some reason, all four registers should show the same amount.

'Someone's made a blue,' he'd accuse them. 'Happens all the time.'

I guess he was lucky he could still talk.

If it was a quiet day, he'd start making motor noises in the bar, beginning with the sound of cars starting up and getting on to a steady top gear sound. Then, glass in hand, he'd go out in the car park, examining the vehicles that happened to be there. I don't know what

213

he saw or what he thought, maybe to him it was a yard of used cars.

Saturday after the New Year, he drank his third beer in a hurry and marched out the back of the pub where the side wall is low, climbed up on the roof and we heard him tramping over the iron of the roof, then lost the sound when he reached the tiles.

I thought I'd better go out and catch him if he fell off, and seeing me go, a few others came. By the time we got there he was perched on top of the Southern Cross sign, driving the pub. We heard the noise of his motor clearly, despite the traffic, and we yelled at him to come down. He didn't look at us, he had his eyes on the road.

He was riding the body of the sign, legs straddling it. Then he started to pull sideways at the top mounting of the sign.

'What's the stupid bastard up to?' someone said.

We watched a bit longer. His efforts were stronger, he tore frantically to pull the sign to the left. His feet came up and smashed the Southern part of the neon sign, making it read THE CROSS. Still he wrenched at it.

'He's trying to make a left turn,' I said. 'He's driving it. Trying to turn the wheel. He's trying to drive the pub on the road. Out into the traffic.'

When he couldn't turn the wheel, and saw it was hopeless, he stopped making engine noise and came down. We helped him off the roof, he didn't thank us. He went straight in and bought another beer, set it before him and thought and thought.

That day ended up, too, with the queer fella outside brandishing his stick, challenging the pub.

'Come on! Out! Someone pinched the key to the steering lock! Who did it? Come on, out!'

We never saw him hide it, but he put that stick away in a special place. It was always the same stick. There was a darker mark on it where he held it in his good hand.

Storms excited him. During a beauty, drinkers leaned at the red bar looking enviously out at the fury of the weather.

No doubt old people, fit for dying, lay awake grateful for this symphonic accompaniment to their last significant action, imagining themselves at the eye of the storm.

Lightning flashes lit the set faces at the red bar. Thunders roaring echoes in their single hearts.

'Go it, God!' shouted the queer fella. 'Give it to 'em! Stick it right up 'em!'

And he clapped his hands delightedly at the next thunderclap right overhead.

BETTER THAN A WORLD FULL
OF NONGS

It was around this time some guys dressed in sharp
suits came round and asked us when we'd seen young
Sibley last.

'A month ago,' I said. I think it was a month.

They asked around a bit more and went away.
They didn't tell us who they were and we didn't ask.
Young guys are always going missing.

A week later some of Sibley's papers turned up, part
of his findings. Someone's young brother found them
in the empty yard behind the welding shed attached
to the compressor hiring place. This open space was
a dead-set destination for a parking area, but at that
time was a haven for dock, wort, Parramatta grass,
paspalum and that aniseed weed that stinks on your

hands for hours and takes over whole paddocks for its lush contamination.

The papers were single sheets stapled together in sections. I hoped Sibley had made better copies and that these were roughs. Some of the guys took a look at them, turned over pages, but there were too many words. They might have read more if they'd had the authority of print. They ended up passing them over to me.

'You know more about this sort of junk,' Mick said. 'Besides, you got on with him OK.'

That seemed a good enough reason for everyone. I took the sheets, got a fresh schooner and began to read Sibley's mind.

'Decision making is individual, group and hierarchical.

General feeling: drinkers are part of nature, victims of nature.

Present-oriented: the past gone, future non-existent.

All made the same choice as most chosen value orientation, except in area of new beer, old, or Resch's.

Drinkers have no drives or motivations, exc. towards Southern Cross.'

This must have been early stuff. The next sheet had some general observations, probably for his own use.

'NB. They don't live in the apparent world alone, nor in the world of social activity, but are constantly at the mercy of their language. Language is not incidental. Their real world is built on the language habits of the group.'

There followed a bit on word sequences. Young Sibley had really listened to the pearls that fell from our frothed lips.

'Word sequences most used:
I'm going to
That's a
I want a
I got
Is a
He's a
I'll bloody
It's a
She's a
He's going to
I don't know
Look at
Buggered if
Come outside.'

Then a set of what he called Further Remarks.

'Drinkers seem inferior to non-drinkers in the same apparent degree as they lack contact with non-drinker groups.

There is need for more adequate grasp of Drinkers' concepts and conceptual styles if educational programmes are to start in a known framework rather than on an untested set of assumptions.

Classificatory ability poor, exc. with local natural objects such as schooner, middy or seven. Some have seen a champagne glass, but port, sherry, etc glasses showed low recognition. Wineglass gained 50% recognition, but evidence points to beerglasses or water tumblers being generally used for wine.'

Maybe if I'd kept on at school and gone to University I'd have been able to write a thesis. But why bother? My name was on the board for pool and I partnered the Great Lover in the weekly tournament. I folded the papers and got Sharon to mind them for me. She had a plastic bag.

As we tossed for the break I hoped Sibley would turn up. One more PhD in the world wasn't going to matter. Even if he failed and swept streets, hefted garbage tins or filled cars with juice, it seemed better to fill the world with educated people, no matter what job they did.

On the Sunday I got home early from the club and for some reason angry. I felt angry with that mother next door still waiting for her kids to come home to sleep.

'Let 'em stay out a bit longer,' I called to her.

'It's getting dark. Time they came home,' was all she said. Not even upset that I chipped her.

Later I heard them come home, noisy and laughing and playing and fighting. Real kids. I looked out—my front door's always open—and she kissed each one lightly.

After that kiss they all fell silent and walked in her little house like zombies.

SHORTY

He was a pleasant little guy. Never made much fuss round the pub, kept his blues for other places, which helped the cause of peace and quiet in the Cross. And he only had one eye. That is, he had two but one was glass. He lost one to a BB shot before he was eighteen.

I was there when this big girl took a fancy to him. He'd peeled off from a group and was on his way for a pee. She stepped out in front of him and bumped his chest with one enormous lung. He sank into her some distance, then the pneumatic effect pushed him back in a slow motion rebound.

'Sorry,' he said.

'Sorry,' she said a fraction later, waiting for the sight of her to register. His eyes were just above the lung that fended him off.

221

He was about to duck past, but she stepped to that side.

'Sorry,' he said, dying for his pee.

'What religion are you?' she said, fixing him with her eyes.

'Heathen,' Shorty said immediately.

'Pardon.'

'Heathen.'

'What's that?'

'Heathen.'

'Oh.'

That stopped her. She exhibited doubt, her reactions slowed, he slipped past.

The day he got back from a week away fishing at Ulladulla she was there again, watching him over the bar. I say over, because she was humped in a little metal chair over by the wall, and he was standing over the other side of the bar. Her eyes just skidded over the red bar and hit his face.

He looked away. And told us about the lump over his left eye, while he ate his chocolate. He always ate chocolate with beer.

'I was in this pub, I mean we were but the others pissed off up the street for some fish and chips—the counter lunch there was lousy—and I was on my own. Some big bloke kept pushing me down the bar, a bit, then another bit. I look up at him.'

'Git outa here,' he says.

'What did you say?' I say.

'Git outa here, wog. This is a white man's pub.'

'So I go whack. And knock this big bloke arse over head.'

'Outside,' he says. So we go outside and get stuck into it. Things end up much the same way out there. I collect this lump over the eye and I end up flattening this big bastard. That's all right. The others turn up with the fish and chips and we sit outside at a table and polish 'em off. We're drinking there for quite a while, it was just after Gunsynd got beaten and some locals were talking near us and after a bit I realised they were talking about me beating this bloke. Turns out he was the golden boy of the district. They went on about it, but right at the death this one that had seen it—he didn't seem to know I was sitting right at his elbow—he says, "By Christ, you should have seen that little wog bloke hit him".'

He waited, looking from one to the other of us. We said nothing.

'He said I was a little wog bloke.'

'We heard.'

'You bastards,' he said. 'I'm no wog.'

We looked at him, said nothing.

'I know I'm dark—'

'Dark? We have to bring you in to the light to see who it is.'

223

'Bastards,' he said. 'Useless bastards. You can all get stuffed.'

And turned away from us to pretend to drink alone. This brought him face to face with the big girl.

'Christ,' he said. 'She won't take her eyes off me.'

'Likes wogs,' someone said. We laughed. Shorty had a great sense of humour. He'd make his good eye go round in circles while the glassy one stared at you. For a moment you didn't want to laugh because you thought it could see you.

A month later he was living with her.

Some weeks after that we thought we'd have a bit of a joke with old Shorty, so we went round to the boarding house where he stayed. It was half past eight in the morning, and a Saturday, so we had till ten before the pub opened.

We listened outside their window, which we found by identifying Shorty's voice. He'd woken up dying for one. He worked hard during the week and though we'd last seen him late the night before we had no reason to doubt that it had been anything else but a good root that put him off to sleep.

But here and now was a different story. We could hear him after her, trying to catch hold of her, touching her, making little whispers like Come on, Love, and Aw, Open Up, Love, and Let's Get on the Bed And I'll Show you Something.

'Get away,' she said. And her voice was only a few tones deeper than old Hugh's after his rum chaser.

He came back like a terrier, worrying at her from all sides. She belted him a backhander with one of her forearms that weighed as much as both his legs. She was strong as a horse.

Back he came, she belted him again and repeated her advice to get away.

This went on for an hour. It was at least ten minutes. I studied a straying mantis that bobbed and swayed when I got near him and tried putting my finger near his triangular jaws, but he refused to bite.

There was a sudden silence from the bedroom. Perhaps thirty minutes silence, then she started to grunt. Sounded fearsome, but there were no sounds of her hitting him. I'll swear the grunts went on for an hour. The Cross would be open, the first beers getting poured.

The grunts got faster. And faster and faster until they merged into one awful long oooooooooooooo! which rose near the end to a sharp scream, then cut off like a knife. Silence.

I couldn't help it. I thought of the bar, I thought of what was going on inside. I gave them a minute to get their breaths back and yelled in at the window, 'Why don't you pick on a man your own size?'

More silence as they came up for air. You could hear them puffing. Time stood still.

225

A voice came from the room, a voice dripping with sweat, heavy with spent effort.

'I never found one my size.'

It seemed reasonable.

We lit out for the pub, where we belonged.

The big girl got too much for him. There were fights, cuts and bruises. And a broken rib where she fell on him.

He went to a football function up at the bowling club with the boys, but somehow she got in. He danced with some bird he'd never seen before, put the hard word on her in the middle of the dance floor and got his face slapped. Twice: the big girl had to be in the act.

When he didn't come home to tea at all for a week, she came in to the pub at eight o'clock one night and let him have his tea, plate and all. All over him. Gravy and chops, dabs of mashed potato and squashy pumpkin and a spattering of beans, the whole mess highlighted by a generous helping of tomato sauce.

The whole pub was on it. Naturally, because before she let fly she yelled, 'Here's your dinner, Shorty!' And there was Shorty, wearing plate and food together. With a final gesture she tossed him a knife and fork, which fell clattering to the floor. He couldn't catch them: tucker was all over his face, blinding him.

The pub roared.

Not outfaced, Shorty's tongue came out, did a circuit round his mouth—the beer hadn't left his hand and he didn't spill a drop—tasted a bit and yelled back at her. 'You stupid big slut. How many times I told you I like 'em well done? On the burnt side. Another thing, there's no taste in the gravy. Bet you forgot the bloody salt.'

That was all right. He ate what he could salvage of his dinner, wiped his face on a Daily Telegraph left over from the morning, and asked for another beer. But it finished him with the big girl.

He couldn't go and drink at another pub, that wasn't done round the Mead. He had to get out altogether. He just couldn't shake her off his tail.

He left.

We saw him next a year later. He came back brown as a berry from Queensland and was having his first drink of Cross beer on a Friday afternoon when I'd got off a bit early from the course as a result of a deluge. Couldn't take the tractors anywhere near the fairways for fear of damaging the grass.

'I just got in,' he said. 'Where's the rest of the boys?'

'Bit early yet.'

'Been up north,' he says. 'Banana land.' And slipped a milk chocolate into his mouth.

'On the coast?' I say. It's good to see Shorty again.

227

'In to Isa,' says Shorty. 'Got a job at the trade.' He was a carpenter occasionally. 'Put in these shelves for shops for a bit, then went out further for nine rotten months.'

'What kept you there?'

'The brass. Good brass. White men won't work out there. Only six months, then they get out.'

'On the stations?'

'On the stations. Went down to seven stone two from twelve and a half stone.'

Shorty had always been a bit of a hard doer, and I didn't know whether to believe him. He looked poor on it, anyway.

'I started to feel tired all the time, and got sores that wouldn't heal. Next time I was in town I go along to this quack and he says Get back to the surf and get some green vegetables into you. Tinned stuff'll keep you alive for a while, but you can't work hard on it.

'She was a pretty hard town, Mount Isa. There was a cop hit a bloke with his baton, a bloke that knifed someone, and you wouldn't want to know, the bloke died. It took two plane loads of cops in from Brisbane to quiet the town. They could only walk round in twos and threes. And then not right in the town. People spat on 'em. Real worked up, they were.

'In the pub where I was, there was a boxing ring out the back. When you had a blue, it was all out the back. Rules and all. Referee.

'Murders every now and again. One bloke with a job at the mine blew himself and his shop up with gelignite that he used at the mine. He blew the lot to the shithouse, himself, her and three of his kids.'

He scratched his head. 'I'll never know why they always take the kids with 'em. You'd think they could send 'em away to grandma's or something. Or up the shop for a lolly, and then do it. The only one to escape was his eldest daughter, and he'd been doing her and the wife found out, and the town. Why he didn't take her with him beats me, too. Anyway, let's get on to more cheerful stuff.'

'Was it a good town to drink in?' I say.

'I tell you, one thing impressed me. A lot of the ringers, on the stations, were black. These black ringers would come in at the weekend, say once a month. Cowboy hats and all. Say one had around two-seventy dollars. They'd put their names up on this big blackboard, there'd be maybe sixty names up. Start with two-seventy on Friday, and cut it out by Monday. The station owner, or manager, would send a taxi in for 'em—they're too valuable to muck around with, the good ones—and the publican would give 'em a dozen bottles of plonk and the taxi waiting at the door. Beat it, see you next time.'

'They wouldn't short change 'em?'

'Not game. Christ, they looked poor on it. Thin? Poor as piss. Yet they'd jog thirty miles in the sun and not notice it. White man couldn't do it. Couldn't do their work either. Once they're on those cattle ponies there's nothing'll touch 'em. Beautiful to see 'em work.

'Came south and in the Walgett Oasis I met a guy I hadn't seen since school, David Parks. He was all for going in to the bar where the blacks drink. Watch out, I tell him. I know all about them, he says, so in I go with him, you know, sort of keep an eye on him. Stop him doing anything too stupid. Well, he goes in and the first thing he pulls out of his kick is a twenty-dollar bill. Kid there weren't fifty pairs of eyes see that money inside half a second.

'In two ups he was drinking with four of the biggest blacks you've ever seen. I shifted my notes to an inside pocket and just left some silver in my pants pocket. David Parks spent twelve dollars and had two beers. He started to get worried about where the brass was going, so he pretends he's running short. What about you? The blacks ask me. You got money. I whipped out the silver from my kick and slapped it on the counter. There y'are, I said. If you can get twelve beers out of that, tell *me* how, I want to know. Or else lend us a quid.

'They took no notice of me after that. I drank my silver and left Parks with 'em. Hour and a half he was there by himself, playing pool with 'em, too scared to leave, and for that last hour and a half the big ones

230

were gone and he was still too scared to leave. Until the full twenty bucks had gone.

'Picked up two on the road.'

'Two who?'

'Two jokers. When I asked where they wanted to go they said Doesn't matter, where you're headed for. Gilgandra, I said. That's the place, they said. They got in.

'Well, without a word of a lie I was scared. Scared I was going to bring my heart up. I was nearly vomiting. You wouldn't believe it. I tried opening windows. No good. They complained of the draught. I tried smoking. No good. They smoked a packet of mine in the first fifty miles. I got panicky. It was another two hundred miles to Gilgandra. One-eighty, to be exact. So I thought, I'll shift you. I opened her out. The Ford was in good nick and the road wasn't that bad. Eighty most of the time, round bends and all, and up near the ton where I could.

'Thank Christ it was too much for 'em. They got scared. I could see 'em looking at me sideways. Must've thought I was off my head. This next town coming up, they said, We get off here. Sure? I said. This is our stop, they said. OK, off they got.

'Do you know I had the seats out, upholstery sprayed, Aerosol in that car, under it, through it. Out in the sun with the doors open for weeks, but it never left the car. Sold it in the end.'

231

'What did you say to the buyer?'

'Told him some kids pinched it and taken it joyriding and left it like that. It'd go away in a week, and that was why I'd knocked two hundred off the price.'

'You're exaggerating,' I said, grinning at him as he took an extra large swallow.

'I kid you not. Soap and water they did not know.'

'Any other hitch-hikers?'

'Yeah, coming back. In Tamworth I picked up this guy by the road with a pack and all. Real hitcher. Bugger me if he doesn't come from Windsor. He's clean, speaks real nice, got good manners and we get on real well. The first place I stop he says, Let me buy you a beer. So he buys me a beer. I never drink much on the road. He tells me he's a professor. He's just spent seven days in the bush to find out how hitchhikers see the country. And we go on from there. So I decide I'll take him all the way, tell him I'm on the way to Sydney, and Bob's your uncle. He talks most of the way, but he seems to know when to stop. You know?

'Sort of natural gentleman. Doesn't try to push his opinions, always gives me plenty of chance to say something if I want to, but doesn't let the pause go on too long, you know, if I can't think of anything to say and he feels I might get embarrassed. Not being as brainy as he is. But he never talked to me as if I was stupid or something.'

'You were wrapped in this bloke, Shorty.'

'Suppose I was, at that. Took him in to the RSL at Windsor and bought him a beer and told him I'd enjoyed having him on the trip. Then I took him all the way to his joint, big two-storey place painted white, two car garage, all the trimmings.'

I couldn't resist it. 'All very clean, kept nice, and all the rest?' I said while he stuffed two bits of chocolate into his mouth.

'Beautiful. That professoring must be a bloody good lurk. Taught me something, anyway.'

'What was that?'

'A bloke doesn't have to be a prick just because he's got a good education.'

When I got Sibley's mind back from Sharon I sat out in the sun and read the printout.

> 'Evidence suggests fighting tendencies precede indulgence in drinking. Also evidence that indulgence releases and accentuates the same proclivities for aggressiveness. Cycle accelerated by habituating effect of being a drinker.'

Sibley had been watching the little dialogues that found expression in knuckle, knee and slipper. The next gobbet of wisdom told me

> 'The habit of drinking and fighting develops a compulsive quality.

Drinkers seem aware of this, without avoiding
   either.
The habit is characterised by free-ranging hostility,
   perhaps caused by:

Territorial uncertainty and disruption, e.g.
   foreclosure of mortgages, non-payment of hire-
   purchase commitments, threat of new housing
   development and higher rents than they can
   afford.
Overcrowding.
Socio-cultural change. (Transition from cottage to
   high-rise environment.)
Financial difficulty following disruption of family
   relationships.
Percept monotony.
Underproductivity.
Subordinate status.
Effect of social fragmentation; belonging to a group
   alienated from other groups.
Environmental monotony.
Powerlessness in face of incomprehensible forces of
   government, business and education.'

I was looking for some sign from Sibley that we might
have liked being drinkers, and might have enjoyed the
occasional biff. Or even needed it. Maybe if we didn't
push each other away with fists we might get so close

we'd end up being a warm jelly mass, no guy able to tell where he ended and others began.

> 'Their hostility has no specific object and often turns inward to group- and self-destructiveness.
>
> NB. Suggestion for a Ministry of Subcultural Research.
>
> Expected benefits: fresh approaches to problems of society e.g. Study of drinkers can reflect conflicts of the larger whole. Drinkers tend to cohere into a subculture which acts out problems bequeathed by the past.'

That was enough for the moment. For some reason I felt extra thirsty, so when I folded the papers I gave them back to Sharon and took my rightful place at the bar. I didn't mind that both elbows rested in a cool pool. I even felt a bit dirty on all the laughing, and the cracked jokes flying around: there had to be some place in the world that was kept safe for pugnacity. I drank for two hours hoping for some sort of stoush, before the mood passed. I blamed Sibley. He was getting at me.

THIS BIT DOESN'T NEED A TITLE

Next time I saw my darling I burst in on her at her place—she's got this crazy habit of not locking her door—just as she was trying on her swimming gear.

Sometimes I go for a swim, and once in a while I go with her. She swims a lot. She has dozens of swim-suits, all colours. Her skin goes this golden colour and it's great to be walking down to the water with her because everyone looks at her like they look at the other three or four girls with spectacular shapes that you might see in one day. It's very pleasant walking with that sort of girl, I can tell you.

She's unconscious of her looks, sometimes.

For instance, she's got this golden hair under her arms that she never cuts. Just a little tuft under each, not a massive bush. And she'll never shave her legs.

I think she never looks at them. The rest of the population takes care of that.

What I'm on about is a line of hairs that stick out a little way under the bottom leg of the swimsuits. Just fine hairs.

When she's in a two-piece, or anyrate when she's got the bottom half on, there's this thin line of hairs climbing up from the triangle to her navel. It's a deep navel, you can't see bottom, and it's only a fine line of hairs. Curly, like the ones lower.

I mention this because it was the first thing to hit me when I burst in on her.

'Hullo,' she says, smiling all over and whipping off this blue thing at the same time. Never before or since have I seen a girl, woman, child, man, pup or any living thing welcome you the way she did.

I must have been hypnotised, looking her all over. She was smiling at me.

'Bursting with sex, you are,' she said.

SHE DIDN'T EVEN STOP TO THINK

At the course we got out on the greens first thing in the morning. We knew shortly the big sit-on machines would be there for one of us to ride round on, but in the meantime it was three one-man machines dividing up the eighteen greens every second or third morning.

The dew marked the edge of your cut, and made the job easy. It wasn't so easy on mornings with no dew. It's hard to see a three millimetre cut from two metres in the air with the sun behind you.

I spent the time thinking of the radiogram and the spindle. The difference was, I'd been silly enough to mention it to my darling the night before. Sunday night.

She had a player and we'd sat on the carpet playing her music on it. I don't have any music. As for carpet.

'I wonder what,' I said, and left the words there. She picked them up a minute or two later, it was that sort of evening. We'd made love on and off during the day, though to describe it better, when you were with her, everything was making love.

Even watching her. Even talking to her and watching the little expressions on her face as different words pleased her.

'What do you wonder?'

I should have left it there. But no, I had to go and tell her. It was one of those moments you come to, where if you go one way: that's it. There's no going the other way, and no going back where you started.

'How the machine knows.'

'Knows what?' She had her legs tucked up under her, the way girls do. I tried it, but I can only do it for a minute or two. Her blood system or muscles or something must be different. I have to move, or better still, get up on two feet.

'How wide the record is, and that there's two of them on the spindle so it lets down only the one and keeps the others up above that edge there?'

I pointed to it, as men do. As other men do, pointing to a mountain, or a car smash. I see them doing it and I always think: stupid bastard! She's got eyes, she's probably a damn sight smarter than you and she probably saw whatever it is when you were still scratching your balls. But I couldn't help it. I pointed, just like the rest.

'That little edge there.'

She didn't even stop to think.

'That's easy.' My bottom jaw fell. Just like Mum's when she finally stopped breathing.

'Why do you look like that? I thought you wanted to know. There you are, see when the record goes down, under here, that edge hits this little plastic knob— that's how it knows the width. It's either a twelve or a nine or a very small one. So according whether it hits the knob or goes there, so the arm knows where to come down.'

She told me how the thing knew there's more to come on the spindle. I didn't hear. I didn't want to know. I hadn't ever wanted to know.

Modern technology she had reduced to common-sense and observation, seeing how it worked and what happened when.

I wanted magic. I wanted to admire the people who thought it up and the people who made it. Just like you look up at the stars and one of them, like Sirius, has a surface temperature of twelve thousand degrees and another is dead and shrinking to a pinpoint. Or that there's millions of them that make our sun look like a flea on a dog's back.

If it's just commonsense and one step after the other, how is it a whole world full of people goes off at sparrow fart each morning to work for it and be part of it? For a lifetime.

241

How can they give—yes, give—their lives to some stupid little thing anyone can understand?

Looking at stars or through electron microscopes has got to be different.

Maybe I'm jumping the gun and all those little jobs have wonder and magic in them and things you go home in awe about and sometimes think about at night when the power of them suddenly hits you. I don't mean to be all that intolerant, though I'm not altogether against intolerance, and if those jobs I call little have some things in them I haven't seen, then I'm sorry.

But I can tell you something that has awe and majesty and something so close to magic that I bet no one can put it into all the words needed to describe it.

And that's when Danny's on the burst and swerves just before taking a pass from the half, and that swerve takes him past a stiff-arm the ref didn't see and wouldn't have seen, and then he takes three strides towards the inside centre—not away, towards—and this wrong-foots the inside centre so his tackle misses Danny by a whisker after Danny's sidestep. So how is Danny, who works on the council waving flags and Stop and Go signs to traffic, how is Danny's brain able to do these things, and his arms and legs and speed and balance and eyes, all in the space of one second, tell him that another four strides towards the fullback aiming slightly to the fullback's right, which Danny

242

saw early in the game was his favourite side to tackle, will convince the fullback that he has Danny dead to rights, and how is it Danny knows that if his own centre is caught by the opposing winger who has come in, that he'll still have time to reverse the ball to his lock coming up the middle four metres behind him and about three to his right and this would be the better pass because the lock's not covered, and finally passes, all before the fullback drives his shoulder into a hip made of air because Danny sidesteps again at the last moment. How is it?

And to see him in the pub, you wouldn't think he could piss straight.

But if it's sheer power you want, take my job.

What would you find to wonder at on a golf course? I'll tell you. It's all round you, whether you're on a tractor or on foot following a mower.

Grass.

Doesn't sound much like magic, does it? But I'm cutting it all year round and it's magic all right. Did you ever wonder how many blades of grass there are on a golf course? Count how many in a square foot.

Each of those blades, in good spring and summer weather, pushes up something like four inches a week, sometimes an inch a day. Can you imagine just what length of grass there is pushing up out of the ground every day? Every minute?

What does it? I don't know. It's just grass. Growing in dirt.

53560 square feet there are in an acre, and there were around five hundred acres. Around twenty-two million square feet. Take your own number of blades of grass for a square foot. Two hundred, at an inch a day would make over five metres of grass-blade. Five metres multiplied by twenty-two million? Work it out for yourself. I make it a hundred and ten thousand kilometres of grass a day. That's power. Just grass. Growing in dirt.

What does it? Nearly three times round the earth, in one golf course. Some blade of grass. Let's know if I've worked it out wrong. I might have exaggerated the four inches or under-estimated the two hundred blades.

It's something I can't grasp. The power in the bits of sand and dirt, and the water we give it, I can't understand how it goes on churning out magic day after day, and me there cutting it fast as it grows.

Sometimes when I'm hypnotised by the straight lines I'm drawing with the edge of the cutters on the fairways, I think: what if with some other magic, some additive, we could eat grass? Fast-growing, hardy, needs no care, just dirt and water.

I get carried away for a bit then look up and see I'm heading straight for a tee where some joker's hitting off. You can't cut fairways crooked, so you can't swerve. If the ball's coming straight at you, all you can do is cut

the motor and go to ground. Taking care you don't lose
a leg in the cutters on the way down.

She only looked at it for a second and she knew. I wish
I hadn't asked her.

LIZ THE LARGE

Elizabeth Large was her name, but so many people called her Big Betty that when she moved up the hill on the Mead, she told everyone her name was Liz. Better she should have christened herself afresh, but she stuck with her parent's choice.

They called her Liz the Large. She had a big mole, brown as a scab, on her cheek, and one single hair poking up out of it.

She wasn't always a big woman. Twenty-five years ago she had been fifteen and she and her girl friends had nothing better to do on weekends than follow the football round. When young girls follow football they get to have some liking for footballers.

Johnny Bickel—he later played second row in grade, but never made it to representative teams—

thought she'd be an easy root and began to take notice of her, and she responded to what seemed to be the new world opening before her. The other girls had to watch from a distance and eye off other boys when Johnny let Liz go with him to the games and sit there waiting for him to shower and come to take her out after he'd had a few beers with the team.

Johnny was pleased at the prospect of a whole new girl opening before him, too. However, that's not the way it happened.

In later years, when she was drunk, which was five times a week, she'd come out with her story, and everyone would pretend it couldn't possibly be true. Just to keep her going.

'Don't come that sorta bullshit with me,' they'd say. 'There never was a time you were like that.'

Sometimes when she insisted and they kept on at her, she'd squeeze out a few tears. It wasn't easy. She was a big horse and hard as nails. Two years before, I hit her on the arse with an airgun slug and she didn't even twitch.

'You believe me, don't you?' she said to me.

'Course I do, Liz. Believe what?'

'You know, about me and Johnny.'

'Johnny who?'

'You don't really know?'

'Not yet.' I took a swallow, put the glass down and listened.

'I was only fifteen. Not fat like now. A skinny kid. Johnny was a footballer.'

'Johnny who?'

'Bickel,' and her voice had a shade of alcoholic reverence.

The name rang a bell. There was a real estate agent called Bickel, his name plastered all over the place, vacant blocks, houses. You know the thing: Sold By, etc.

'He wouldn't believe I was a virgin. But I was. He took me down by the river, you know where the bridge is in Parramatta Park, where the willow trees come down near the water. It wasn't a car park then, it was all grass down to the water. I wanted it to be nice for him, but he couldn't get it in.'

'Couldn't?'

'Couldn't. Something about the way I was made, or just being so young. He got the tip of it in, but for a long while he couldn't get the rest. He got it out and put spit on it and kept trying. At last he got me to put my legs up against two trees—I was hurting in the back from the ground and little stones, but he kept trying—and with the tip in he sort of drew back and set himself and dug his feet into the ground and drove. Later he said it was how he was supposed to push in the scrum, but he wasn't laughing then. He looked very grim. It was hurting him, too, poor Johnny. But he got it in. When it went in, it went so fast he knocked all the breath out of me. And kid I didn't need all the breath I had.

'But you should have heard him. He was quiet for a second, then this look came over his face and his hands dug into me and he started real low: Ooooooooorrrr, and he didn't stop till he was yelling.'

'Sort of a victory yell?' I suggested.

'Don't give us the shits, Meat. He pulled it out as slow as he could, it was hurting something dreadful, and when it was out I looked and the skin was peeled right back from the tip like a banana.'

'Tough,' I commented. 'What did you do?'

'Do?' she almost yelled. 'You shoulda seen me! When he pulled out, there was blood everywhere!'

'Poor Johnny.'

'Poor bloody me! I was all torn inside.'

I looked at her stupidly. It had always been part of our boys' culture that as soon as girls were big enough they were old enough and when they were old enough they were big enough. It had no place to accommodate this bit of body news. Big enough to drive a team of horses through, big as a horse's collar, yes, that was the extent of our caring. But torn?

Poor bitch.

She didn't want to say any more, maybe because then the bloke came in that she was living with. For years she was cocking it up for all and sundry, but now she lived with a bloke.

All the time she was cocking it up she was married, but that was different. He was only her old man. She lived with this new bloke in a station waggon parked near her husband's place. When they weren't there, they'd be at the Cross.

They'd been there so long, the milko delivered milk to the car.

As I said, she wasn't a skinny kid now, she was big and fat. And sometimes she liked to pretend she was being bullied.

I was going past the station waggon one night around tea-time, taking Danny up the hill to his place—his pains were bad, too bad to keep drinking—and I passed the car which was the home of Large Liz.

'If you wanta sleep with me tonight,' she shouted, with a laugh in her voice, 'You'll have to sleep in the bath.'

It was a hot night, there was no bath, and sleeping with her would be like sleeping in a bath anytime.

In the pub she had a habit of getting her drinks when it was her turn to shout, and backing away from the bar stern first. That was OK, but instead of sort of sliding sideways and back, she'd charge backwards out into the main stream and rarely did she miss backing into some poor bastard with a beer, or since it was near the taps, more likely three or four schooners in his hands.

'Hey!' the bloke would say, surveying the damage and looking at her.

'Sorry,' she'd say.

A man would have felt bound to replace the spilt beer, but that sort of equality hadn't reached Liz. The man would see it was a female, shake his head and say lamely, 'That's all right, love.'

Next time she got a beer she'd do it again. Never seemed to make the connection between this time and last.

Funny thing. About three weeks after she told me the story of Johnny's getting peeled, she was passing me to get a drink and said out of the blue, 'I had to go to a specialist with it. But they could never fix it up. Not the way it was before. Johnny opened it right up.'

The guy with me gaped, but when I didn't say anything he didn't ask.

Poor Liz. We heard only a while ago something was the matter with her. Her attendance at the pub had been a bit erratic; when she came in she didn't have the same old bounce, and she went down from schooners to middies.

One day, a bit curious—besides, she wasn't a bad poor bugger—I drove up to the station waggon and parked opposite, putting the bonnet up and fiddling with the hose clips. A doctor was with her. They'd called him from the glass-sided public phone up the street, and she lay in the back of the station waggon. The doctor opened the side curtains to get a good look at her, and he was hunched up on the floor of the waggon trying to examine her.

There were sounds of arguing.

'Look,' he was saying. 'I'll tell you when you're dead. I'm the doctor, not you. I'm an expert and the instruments say you're dead. You've got no pulse for a start.' She was so massive, her pulse was miles under the surface.

'But I'm here talking to you.'

'So there's life after death.' He was a young doctor.

'How could I talk if I was dead?'

'Any more lip out of you and I'll sign the death certificate now.'

He folded his arms, looking down on her from where he knelt on the waggon floor. There was very little room, but he managed to look imposing.

She began to yell a bit weakly, Help, Help, and the like.

I walked over, rubbing my fingers on a piece of scrap rag.

'I'll show you up! You'll never get the better of me!'

She saw my face round the end of the vehicle.

'You're my witness, Meat. He's making out I'm dead. You can see I'm not dead, can't you?'

She didn't sound too sure herself. But I can tell movement and the sounds of sensible speech.

'You'll never die, Liz,' I said. She cheered up.

'Yeah, wouldn't be dead for a million bucks,' she said defiantly.

The doctor was uneasy with a third person present, and I was about to chip him about the way he treated people. Then I remembered I might have an accident or something one day when I was full. He might come to my accident and treat me, as they say, conservatively. You know, just leave you. Do nothing. I decided not to offend him.

What? What was I thinking of? Bugger him. 'I heard what you said,' I told him. 'You do what you can for her.'

She sort of recovered for a while and went back to schooners but she always looked peculiar. Then she went down and down over the next two months, to middies, then to sevens, and finally got so low they moved her to hospital over her protests.

She didn't know and the doctor didn't know, but when the ward sister saw her after they'd bathed her, she moved her to Maternity.

'What's all this?' Liz wanted to know. 'Come on, what's the strength of you mob? What am I doin' here?'

The other ladies with big bellies in the ward, and nice coloured tops over their nighties, sitting up in bed reading magazines and sniffing the big bunches of flowers that were all round the place, smiled at Liz the Large.

'Just rest, dear,' they said. 'Sit back and rest. There'll be a cup of tea along in a minute.'

'Rest be buggered,' says Liz, undaunted by the prevailing kindness. 'I'm crook and they go and stick me in here. It's unreal. Me, in the pudding club! They're bloody mad.'

'When is it due?' asked one young lady in a nice voice.

'Due?' she choked, although her voice sounded, they tell me, as if the volume had been turned down quite a bit. 'Due? I'm not due. Nothing's due. I'm not having any kid. Jesus Christ, this can't be happening to me!' And she turned her face away. In the other direction, actually, but there was another woman with a fat belly smiling at her. Liz groaned and looked away.

'Will you all stop grinning at me? You give me the pip.'

The day before she would have said shits. They were wearing her down already.

And she could feel it. When they brought her some pink night wear—Liz didn't have any to bring to hospital, she always slept rough—she made a fuss, but in the end the young nurses got her into it and combed her hair and fluffed it up a bit around the sides—Liz always had it drawn back tight out of the way so it wouldn't get in her beer—she looked a lot less like the old Liz and a lot more like the rest of the ladies waiting for their babies.

At first she resented this. Why did they have to doll her up like the others? She didn't feel right. But by next morning, after the best sleep she'd had since she was a little girl in pigtails, it somehow didn't matter so much that she was different.

When the night nurse hovered near her, she woke instantly—she always slept light in the station waggon, all sorts of characters got up near the Lake—and was just about to tell her to get to buggery, when her eye caught sight of the other beds and several of the bellies that were facing up, what with their owners sleeping on their backs.

Instead, she said, 'You don't have to worry about me. I'm all right.'

The nurses told stories to each other when they had their tea break about difficult patients they'd had. It wouldn't have done Liz any good to know she didn't even get a mention.

The next two weeks were a new life, even though both kidneys were failing and they were trying to keep her alive till the baby came.

As she sank lower, she still didn't believe there was a baby. Not even when it was kicking. She'd always had a full belly, and the little thing inside her didn't take up enough room to swell her out any more than she already was.

Word got around and we made sure the boys gave her a visit. Sharon was always on duty in visiting hours, so we fixed it with the publican for her to take an hour off in a slack time. When he looked a bit doubtful, we pulled all the boys out of the pub and showed him how slack business could get and he agreed right away.

Most of them said later they never knew Liz the Large would come up so well with a bit of care and soap and looking after.

In a fortnight she sank as far as she was going to, then fell right through the world. As she seemed to go, one of the women noticed—it was ten in the morning, opening time at the Cross—and called the sister. They got screens round in a hurry, saw they couldn't do anything for Liz and then remembered the baby. They looked at each other. What now?

There was no doctor around, so they pulled the blanket down and Liz's nightie up, spread her legs wide, lifted her knees high and had a look.

The top of a little head—only a square inch of it—was on show. They smiled then, and spoke to Liz. Quietly, but close to her ear so she'd hear if she was still conscious.

'It's your baby, Liz. He's coming now. Just a little squeeze now. Bear down, love. Bear down. Can you hear, sweetheart? Just a bit of effort. Come on now, help us. You can do it. We'll see it gets looked after.'

She must have heard, because the muscles in the big thighs tensed and the huge stomach moved and the little head slid out. It was covered with short, but very dark hair. Liz had black hair.

'Bit more now, love,' they said. 'Better if *you* do it. Come on, don't go away. Liz! Another effort. Push now. Bear down. Come on, one more time.'

The stomach moved again, very slowly, but it was enough. The baby slithered out into waiting hands. They upended him quick and got him to yell and clear his throat.

The sound made Liz open her eyes. They held him up on the cord so she could see.

Her lips moved. Very softly she said, 'Well, bugger me!' And rested. They waited, still holding him up.

'Is he all there?' she said.

They held him closer, turned him round, showed her the face and ears, the arms and legs—right number of fingers and toes—and his little prick and balls.

The slowest smile moved the corners of her mouth and the puffy skin under her eyes.

She said no more words, but the smile stayed until her bottom jaw dropped. By that time the cord was cut, the little fellow washed all over and wrapped up and put in one of those cots with the wheels on in a big room with about sixty other newcomers to the world.

They cremated her and gave the ashes to the bloke she lived with in the station waggon, but he thought they might get lost or something and gave them to her husband to put on the mantelpiece.

The husband took the boy and got his married daughter to live in and look after him along with her own three.

They had a big party up at the house to wet the baby's head and everyone went. So many went that the publican—who knew about it the required number of days in advance—told his casuals not to come in, and helped in the bar himself.

There were four fights and the police came around three o'clock. One stranger wandered over towards the Lake and got himself drowned in one of the eighty-foot holes, but the party was for the baby and Liz the Large, and no one took much notice of this event.

ANAL PASSIVE, EFFEMINATE, BORN LOSER

Sharon kept Sibley's mind under the bar for me till I asked for it. The next page in the pile was 'Attitudes of Drinkers'.

'People in authority exploit them, are distrusted and held in contempt. Success and achievement felt to be beyond their control.

Chance—lotteries and gambling—take their place.

Activity leading to long-range goals is futile. Short-term gratification only.

Physical labour acceptable to gain present needs; no value in itself except for sportsmen in training.

Upward mobility by any member amounts to rejection of the group.'

I skipped the figures and graphs and test results. The last pages contained Sibley's conclusions. I took a quick look, wondering if the other guys had read much of it before they brought it home to the pub. I was certain they were his rough copies; he'd gone off somewhere with better copies to work it into proper shape for his thesis.

'Drinkers: Conclusions.

High incidence of educational retardation.

Deceitful, suspicious, intolerant.

Marked tendency to be aggressive, quarrelsome, provocative and disobedient to rules of society.

Tendency of weaker status drinkers to be timid, fearful.

Weaker drinkers show disproportionate number of specific psychogenic disorders.

No cases of severe mental deficiency apart from physical damage. Some disorders referable to degree of emotional deprivation, few cases of affectionless psychopathy.

Few disorders with overt psycho-neurotic symptoms.

Few individuals with well-evolved obsessive-compulsive, phobic or dissociative syndromes or free-ranging anxiety states, apart from thirst for drink.

N.B. These observations require further testing.'

There was a last page headed 'General Speculations'.

'In my opinion drinkers cannot be raised to our level
   of civilisation in a single generation.
Drinkers are a relic of the oldest type of man.
Perhaps they should be confined to their drinking
   areas and left alone.'

I read it all and was folding it ready to give to Sharon
to keep in case anyone asked for it, when a small bit
of paper fluttered out, unattached. It was hard to tell,
but the ink looked newer than the rest. It said, 'Their
customs and language may be more complex than I
imagined. They well may be a wasted minority with
valuable potential.'

An afterthought, I suppose. I wonder what made
him change his mind.

I hoped Sibley was tucked away somewhere trying
to make head or tail of us. I looked up and there was
Mick watching me. And the King, over his shoulder.
In another group Serge's round face was turned slightly
towards me. They watched my face for a bit, looked
down at the papers, then back to the guys they were
with.

Something came into my head. Some words. One
of Sibley's papers had words—words like 'anal passive,
effeminate, born loser'. I hoped they'd given me *all*
the papers. I hoped they didn't find *that* bit of paper.
Hoped real hard.

FORTY-THREE MINUTES
AND BLOOD

On the course a woman caught me fair on the breast-bone with a low ball from the first tee. My breastbone is fairly solid, I think, and although I felt it a bit and there was a lump under the skin, no bruise came out and nothing was broken. She didn't apologise, just swore at me for getting in the road.

It was one of those balls that you see coming, they curve and you move to one side, but they follow you and it seems inevitable that you'll get hit. And you do.

The ball bounced off my chest into the end of the stormwater drain there, which is about three metres deep. The pipes are underground most of the way, but at their far mouth, water gets round the end pipe and scoops away the earth.

It was a horrible lie for a ball. She'd made a lousy start to her round.

'Why didn't you get out of the way?' she asked me. 'Now look what you've done.' She was about forty, with a strong chin like a man. It was Ladies Day. She didn't ask where it hit or whether it hurt.

'I suppose you'll go crying to the committee now,' she said. 'There's no complainers like men. Always think they're hurt when they're not.'

I hadn't said a word. Wasn't even rubbing the spot.

Just for the sake of it, I watched her play the ball. I knew she'd pick it up and put it higher and not penalise herself for the hazard, so I kept watching. She hit it and by some fluke the ball bounced off a rock and went straight up the fairway. She looked round in a superior way. As if I'd think she was a good player.

Four hours later I'd knocked off and had a shower and was getting in the car, off towards the Cross of the South.

I heard the sound of studded golf shoes on the bitumen and there she was.

'Does it hurt?' she asked, and her voice wasn't raucous.

'Forgotten all about it,' I said.

'I'll rub it for you if you like.'

'Rub it?' I said foolishly.

'I'm a physiotherapist. Come on, follow my car, but park a few houses further on.'

Why not? I followed her. It wasn't far.

Why does the car go faster just because you put more gas in? Why doesn't it just give louder bangs? Anyway.

In her bedroom she wouldn't let me touch anything. Not her breasts, not her hair. No kisses to warm her up.

'You don't know,' she said. 'You men don't know how to make love.'

Eventually in I get and the natural thing starts to happen. As soon as she detects that I'm on the way she goes whack! right on the nuts. Talk about hurt.

'You just wait for *me*. You don't know how to make love. The more I see of men the more I like golf.'

The pain didn't go for about another ten minutes. I know, I caught sight of the time on my watch, on a chair near the bed.

There I stuck, rasping away. And I mean rasping. Every now and then I'd take a side look at the watch. It got to forty-three minutes before she arrived.

When she came she really went off, screaming, kicking and scratching, her hands gouging deep scratches in my back till I grabbed them both and held them behind her back, trying to stay in the saddle.

When she subsided, she said, 'Well?' Still puffing.

I said, 'You're different.' It was all I could think to say.

'They all say that,' she said derisively.

Poor bastards, whoever they were. I was in a mess. The old feller was red raw, with two long cuts on top. I don't know what was inside, but it must have been two sharp lumps of gristle hanging down. They dug channels into him and I went home to drink at the Cross with my tail well and truly between my legs.

Forty-three minutes. Christ, I needed a physiotherapist to fix up the damage. She'd rubbed it for me all right. Ladies Day.

When I rang my darling I put off seeing her long enough for him to heal up.

'You won't forget?' she said.

'No, I won't forget,' I said. I felt rotten putting her off. She never put me off. She was always breaking other arrangements to fit me in.

'Are you sure *you* won't forget?' I added.

Weak, wasn't it?

'No, I won't forget. It's in my little book.'

'You might overlook it.'

'I've underlined it. I won't forget it if I've underlined it.'

I knew she wouldn't forget. I went back to my beer.

It wasn't a happy day. I don't think the other guys would know why more fuel makes the engine go faster, instead of just causing bigger explosions, but I wasn't going to ask. It *must* have made bigger explosions, maybe that was the key. And the bigger bangs pushed the shaft faster and the next one faster still. So the effect multiplied, everything went faster.

That was it. I'd worked the bastard out. The day was worse than ever. Another mystery gone. I picked up the underneath pages of the Great Lover's paper without disturbing his crossword. Miracle Operation, it said. Bone marrow replaced. They'd fixed up some sick kid that had bad blood.

Blood? Yes, it was made in the marrow and the marrow was in the bones. But how did the blood get out? I've seen all sorts of bones, and eaten plenty of marrow, but the bones were sealed at both ends, weren't they? How did the blood get out?

I gave him back his paper. Maybe it wasn't such a bad day.

For generations back, guys competed for the body and shape that you took into your heart and had in your mind when you were in her and even when you were miles away. The shape of her in you that warmed your insides whatever the weather. For generations back, guys clobbered each other. And it was good.

If I didn't feel so alive on the field and in the Cross on the alert for a sudden swing, maybe I wouldn't feel so alive when I caught sight of my darling in the distance with her body full of life in shape and movement.

Maybe without the itch of healing cuts and the halo of bruises round the eye sockets no one would get the dry mouth of desire for his darling. Just thinking about her I felt alive and strong and nearly brought the schooner glass down on the red bar to smash it for the sheer joy of the feeling flooding through bones and blood. I had to stop myself bashing my fist against the bar. A broken hand is a drawback.

I even had to stop myself going up to the boys and saying Let's clear the pub.

Calm down boy, I told me. Calm down, monster.

I put my free hand in my pocket and looked outside at the world, away from the inviting faces that could easily wear blood and swelling.

The birds weren't flying for fun and swooping for joy; they were dead scared to stay in one place for long. Big bastard birds were waiting in the sky to tear them to pieces. And the little birds had to pounce on their own dinner in their spare time from guarding their backs.

In the street, at the lights, men were rotting in their cars, fighting nothing, only fearing: fearing crashes, fearing cops. Their blood whitened in fear and got thin. In weariness they rested their heads on women who wished them far away, preferably to a battle-field, where chance could take them off. Chance could provide another diversion.

The smell of uneasy peace hung over the world. The stale stink of peace hovered over the country's industries and business and workers when by rights they should have been at each others' throats as the system decreed they should.

The same stink floated under the barnlike roof of the pub and across from side to side of the red bar. I was thirsty, but not for water. And for more than beer.

It would be a great day for a fight. Milling round the red bar up to the ankles in red blood.

Let's get off the subject.

I can't.

Don't tell me Christ didn't work all his life for the moment when they put the crown of thorns on him and blood ran down his face. The blood made him what he was and what he became. Blood was his motto. The violence of the authorities simply co-operated in his plans.

He could have let well enough alone. He could have gone along with the status quo. But no, he had to stir things up, cause division in the community, set brother against brother. He chose the violent way to push peace.

Why? Because there's no other way. His intrusion into public life was violence. (Who elected him? Who elected me to write our tribe?) Same as any action has its violent angle. Think about it. Whatever takes place, someone or some thing suffers. It may be good or bad, but that's opinion. It's unavoidable, and that's how it is.

The Good Shepherd? Why do you think he saved the lost sheep? For the pot, of course, and let a poor old wolf and his family go hungry. It boiled down to who would get to eat that sheep, that's all. Kindness?

Out at the juniors' game that Saturday afternoon there was something of a disagreement between us and them.

When something like this came about, there was no audience: all were actors.

The ref gave eleven penalties to our two. That was enough. They were our kids, we were responsible. We couldn't let our kids go down the drain and nothing done. The opposition support thought otherwise.

It was a strange ground, we were on a hill and decided to descend to press our point of view. We descended.

'Stop!' someone cried.

Stop be buggered. Bodies hurled themselves down the slope. Not just leaping over the white fence. Diving.

Just before the clash of the two sides a peculiar sound rose from the ranks of the guys closing in on each other. It was like a wail, but it was no wail. It was like a howl, but more than a howl. It rose. It rose more. By the time contact was made it was one solid wall of sound, a battering ram of yell, a vast engine aimed in at the centre. Then the roar stopped abruptly.

As if it had never been, and the whole mass settled down to action. Grunts, squashy punches, the brittle sound of nose bones. The creak of fence posts ripped out, nails and all. These took over.

Blood ran fast and red and healthy. Satisfaction warmed me like a blanket.

Turning the other cheek made no sense here. It would make an impression for sure; it could become a joke that would never die. But win, lose: who cares? The fight's the thing.

Once I heard a voice calling Meat, Meat, above the tumult and the shouting, but there was no way I could answer.

I got some spatters of red, then a spurt of someone's blood in both eyes. I put my hands up to wipe it away. Several fists came to visit. I side-stepped, saw another movement, and ducked. But the movement was only a shadow. I ducked straight into two uppercuts.

My lights failed; left, then right. I wanted to see, but the eyes refused to open. The lid muscles weren't strong enough to lift all that swelling; under the skin, blood filled both sockets.

I couldn't see to see. Out of action. I stumbled out of the fight looking for a fence to guide me back to the gate, like a blind man in the dark looking for something that wasn't there. The swelling took three days to go down. I didn't even see who clobbered me.

The day wasn't entirely wasted. In the taxi I began to laugh, which made the driver sneer. I laughed so much I nearly burst and told him to have a beer with the change.

Blackie welcomed me, so did Alky Jack. I held my eyelids open with both hands to see where I was going.

'What's the other bloke look like?' said Jack.

'Didn't clap eyes on him, Jack,' I said and Sharon brought me my beer—my food and drink, and at the end of every day, my sleep.

The blood mood had passed. All I wanted now was to get pissed.

'I think I'll iron myself out, Jack,' I said to him. 'Are you going to get drunk with me?'

'Going to!' he roared. 'What do you think I've been doing here all day? Going to!' He was very derisive. 'I don't go round wasting my time fighting. The day's for drinking. When I can no longer talk all day, think all day, drink all day—that will be it. Finish.' He had the hide to sound angry as well as righteous. 'Until then—all day every day—me.'

I stood there, wondering who I'd get drunk with. I not only wanted to be drunk myself, but the cause of drunkenness in others.

In a quieter voice, Alky Jack added, 'Well. Maybe at the end.' And paused. 'At the end, maybe I'd even trade the beer for another few minutes.'

E H

He was a Queenslander and though this is an interesting fact about any man, some get over it. Eh never did.

Eh is pronounced 'ay' as in day. It was a question at the end of every sentence. That was the way up north Queensland.

He was a short, thick fair-haired guy, and when the boys got tired of calling him Eh they called him Guy, to stir him.

'Bloody Kings Cross Yanks,' he'd growl. 'What's up with "blokes", eh? Or fellers? Guy, for Christ sake, it'd make you sick, eh?'

He worked for the council on night shift, and this was Thursday afternoon. The night before, his work was enlivened by an accident to the clumsy yellow street-sweeping machine with the flashing lights that goes into action round Parramatta in the early hours.

A drunk in a long American car fell asleep at the wheel and took the back wheel off the big machine—it has only one back wheel—and pushed the whole thing into the window of a butcher's shop.

Eh wanted to go back there in the morning to see the butcher's face.

'I like looking at blokes to see the way they take things, eh?'

Eh lived with a woman a bit more than twice his age. This lady was the Great Lover's Mum, a handsome woman who acted more like a mother to Eh than a girl friend. I guess a mother was what he wanted.

I first got to know him at the Cross when he was talking of his early life in Queensland, before he came to Sydney. When they sneaked in to poultry farms up there they grabbed the birds by the throat. In New South you grab them by the legs. When you grab their legs they never let out a single squark.

'No, mate, eh? Up there it's round the throat. Although I must confess one time I broke into a big farm, full of real grouse poultry, eh? I'm a bit slow grabbing this bird and the next thing there's forty thousand chooks roaring their heads off. I went through that chicken wire head first, eh? They had automatic lights and shotguns and I was lucky to get away, eh?'

He'd had a hard time just existing when he'd been out of work in the country for three months. He'd stolen

274

from fish shops and nicked off, snatched a woman's purse once and got twenty-five cents. After that he decided it was a lousy way to live, so he went to Brisbane and lived on the cats.

He could look like a little boy, sort of sad and vulnerable with big grey eyes, and after dark in city streets the lonely old cats would see him and ask him directions or whatever it is they do to sound out boys. Once he found he could do it, he came to Sydney and lived five months with a cat of about fifty-five in his pretty little flat at Potts Point. That was his longest stay with any one cat.

He'd been married once. Kids, too.

'I went to leave home once, the kids hanging on round me crying Daddy don't go, but the missus knew I wasn't going, eh?'

'How?' I said, since he waited for it.

''Cause I took the dog with me, eh?'

He didn't want to tell me how he finally came to leave.

All he said was he'd never get clear of the tangle of his life, that was how he put it. Tangle.

'Several times I've stopped the cracks in the room, you know, with paper and stuff and turned the gas on, eh? Never done it. No guts, eh?'

I knew a dozen young guys no more than twenty-five, had done the same thing. It was a common confession. I've never given it a thought.

I wouldn't neck myself, I might miss something. Besides, there's no grog in the grave.

While I'd been in that gas-filled boarding house room in my head, he was back up north. Hungry.

'So I ate mangoes. The first night I ate four dozen mangoes and my tongue swole up, eh? One night I was hiding in the bush and first thing in the morning a bloke scared shit out of me bursting out of thick brush, no tracks, eh? Chased by this cassowary. I ducked, I was in this little hollow, with branches over the top and bits of bark and grass to keep the dew off, eh? And when I was hungry I circled round near a property where I knew the people—too bloody proud to go ask for a feed, never liked handouts—and this dam they had, with barbed wire round it to keep out the sheep and animals, there was a kangaroo bogged in it, eh? I'm so bloody hungry I'll eat the bastard alive. So I take my clothes off, to keep 'em dry, eh? And crawl under the wire in this mud and what do I do but get bogged too, eh? Down on my hands and knees.

'Before I know it, something's up me. I look round and there's this sheepdog, going to town on me. I can't move and he gets in, slips in on the sweat and all, like an expert, eh? Which he is. I know the dog, and all round the town everyone'll tell you he'll fuck anything, eh? Zot! Up me like a flash. My hands were stuck, I had to wear it. I tried to move and gradually got a hand

276

free and went forward under the wire, eh? Tore all my back on the barbed wire and got forward under the wire, but not before he blew, eh?'

He looked at me sort of up from under his eyebrows and continued.

'I got away from him, chased him, grabbed a horse from the paddock and chased that bloody dog for miles on horseback, still naked, eh? I'd have killed him if I found him. And when I gave up I was hungrier than ever, eh?'

For the younger boys the most interesting thing about Eh was the seven tattoos on his stalk.

When it was out straight the seven tattoos were clear. Four were girls and you could read their names. He said the figures were pretty much like the photos he gave the tattoo artist.

Also there was Mother, a sea snake, and a clock-face.

I asked him why no sheepdog, but he only muttered.

I should have asked him why the clockface.

When it was down they just looked like dirty marks.

Eh played breakaway, when he was selected. When he wasn't, he didn't complain, just quietly got the shits. I should have asked him how he kept it extended while the tattooman worked on it with his needle.

Serge met his match one day amongst the various strangers he picked fights with when he played pool with a few of the kids one Thursday.

A scrawny little man, middle aged, in old trousers and a blue working singlet, potted the black while he was on another colour.

Serge had been off with the 'flu and spent most of the day getting well on Bacardi, and by this time he was well and truly. Despite his large capacity.

'That's game,' he announces. And by local rules it is. When you're on the black you mustn't miss it and you mustn't pot another colour.

But the little man wasn't having any. He'd bet two dollars on that game and didn't like to lose. He was forty-nine and only three days out of jail. Tough little rooster.

'Outside,' said Serge, and tipped his thumb in that direction. The monster looked out of his eyes, but the monster was drunk.

Never mind, Serge had this guy fucked and burnt.

They didn't get there. The little man got in three king hits before they got to the door, and closed both his eyes. Serge couldn't see. His face bled like a pig. The little bloke didn't stop there. While Serge was flailing round trying blindly to connect, he cut him to pieces. Hitting Serge in the body was a waste of time, his solar plexus was a foot or two underneath the flesh, but around the head he bled like anyone else. Every time he breathed out he spattered hundreds of red drops over his opponent.

The little bloke departed. Serge was a mess. When he'd got to a tap and cold water had helped stop the bleeding, he found the only benefit he received from this brief encounter was he'd sobered up slightly.

It was a lesson to the young guys. You could see them look round speculatively at the eight or nine middle-aged guys that always sat under the windows on the street side of the red bar. They'd been there since they were boys.

They never got up when there was a fight. When there was action coming and you saw the furtive gleam of pink as men whipped out their teeth and shoved them deep in their pockets, they hardly even turned their heads.

Don't worry about Serge. Whatever cuts and gashes he got healed up without scars. Like flesh-coloured porridge, or water closing after you pull your hand out.

MAYBE

Alky Jack wasn't impressed. He'd seen it all before.

He started talking before I got to where he was leaning over the red bar, one elbow in an odd pool of dry amongst the slops.

'The population must be kept passive,' I heard him say. 'This is done by myth. These myths are put in your cornflakes every morning. The kids are given them on a spoon at school. Their pop songs are heavy with them. The telly is rotten with myths. At present they're American myths because we cop so much of their stuff; later it'll be our own myths. But it's all the same.'

'What do you mean, Jack?' I said. I knew he'd tell me. He'd keep on talking whether I was there or not. I'd been thinking about something I read in a magazine, and wondering how light can go at the same speed no matter what speed the thing is going that shoots out the light. It felt good, knowing no one was going to tell me why.

'That it's a free society, you can work where you like, human rights are respected, anyone can become a boss and an enterpriser, education is a universal right, we're all equal, the elite is generous and just and the best people to be in charge and they only want the good of the rest of us, rebellion is a sin against God and religion, private property is sanctified and necessary to humanity; that our bosses work like buggery and the mob is lazy, they're honest and we're dishonest, they're superior and we're inferior. That's the myth.

'And because we live in compartments and the compartments have nothing to do with each other, all the bullshit about communication doesn't have one atom of effect. There's in every country a class of people that only see other people with Daimlers or Lincolns, and never see the hungry. And all down the scale there's different strata of people who only ever mix with their own lot; at work, at the club, at church. And this lot here, who do we mix with? Ourselves. That's why none of you mob ever thinks you're badly off. You see nothing else.'

I'm not bothered about what other people have, whether I see it or not. But I knew Alky Jack would have a good answer to this: probably that circumstances acclimatised me to what I know.

He'd be right. But the trouble with me is I really have no wants, except be with the guys and have a beer now and then. You can always get a place to sleep.

And with a bit of luck, one good meal a day. But what makes the light shoot out anyway? Why does it have to go anywhere?

'The word Human is the beginning of metaphysics,' Alky Jack went on after a minute. 'And yet,' he went on, his voice sinking and the words coming spaced and slow, 'and yet, a human is a tool as an animal is, as a tree or a lump of rock is; a human is a thing used. Everything's used. Nothing exists for itself.'

He seemed on the brink of some lighting-up inside his head.

'Perhaps there *is* no specially human thing apart from being used. Or using yourself. Perhaps all us animals are machines. Perhaps that's what we're trying to do all the time with new making and inventing—duplicate ourselves and other animals. Duplicate their movements like in machines, their interior workings like in refineries and processing, their mental workings like in computers and data banks, duplicate their behaviour like in social systems.'

His hand wandered round looking for his drink. I moved it towards the open part of his hand—he couldn't see anything for looking into his own head—taking care to touch the glass near the bottom and not tip it.

283

'So maybe all we do comes from within ourselves. And maybe we break down and get crook when we don't act like the machines we ought to be.'

He leaned forward over the bar. Sharon gave him a glance, saw he was thinking, and went on working.

'If it all comes from inside us, then neither Hitler nor JC was mad. Loving others and dying for others looks like a mistake, but if it comes from inside. . . .

'In that case hating, destroying and killing are quite understandable. After all, I hate the bastards that tell the man on the jackhammer that he's not working hard enough and his machine's too noisy, when he's working at the bottom of a hundred foot hole in winter at six in the morning, building shiny air-conditioned offices for the critic that says he's superior because he earns more.'

He looked at me.

'You don't understand. Look at you. On the way to being an alcoholic like me. Not Alky Jack: Alky Meat.'

He wasn't usually sarcastic. Usually he never had a bad word for anyone.

'I mean really hate 'em. I could line the bastards up. You know. Rapid fire. Mow the cunts down.'

I didn't believe him. Couldn't have done it in a million years. But he thought he could at that moment.

'Jack,' I said. 'Maybe the ones that keep the mob passive with little myths, maybe their urge to be the

284

boss comes from inside, and maybe the ones that believe the myths, maybe their urge to believe comes from inside, and maybe their urge not to do anything about it even if they know they're being handled, maybe that comes from inside. So we're where we've always been. Maybe?'

He looked at me again. Really looked. His eyes had a sort of cutting edge.

'Do you imagine you've disposed of the human race in a few well-chosen words?'

'No, Jack.' I always liked to give him his name. It was the only way I could say I liked him.

'No, Jack, all I mean is whichever lot a guy belongs to—you know, by the composition inside, like you said—what he has to do is what he digs out of himself. And what the whole lot of us has to do is keep digging inside and keep making things that get their idea from inside, so what they are and what they do stay sort of in line.'

'Stop it,' he said. 'I don't want to hear it. I know what you're saying comes from what I was getting to, but I don't like where it's getting to. I don't want to come to that conclusion. I want to stay thinking that with some effort we can change.'

'Maybe we can,' I said helpfully.

'You young bastard. You don't care. Whichever way it comes out, you don't give a stuff.'

He was right.

'No,' he said manfully. 'I don't care if arguing gets me pointed in that direction, I don't want to go there. I think if a thing's wrong and unjust it should be changed. And can be changed.'

'I hope you're right, Jack,' I said. I meant it. It meant a lot to him.

But light *does* travel, they've proved it. So what makes it travel? What pushes it? It goes so fast it's sort of like an explosion.

The Great Lover took to sitting on the doorstop, resting his glass on a cross-member of the floor-to-ceiling glass partitions that lined the back of the pub. It was only a few weeks after we'd found the newly heavy keg that it began to change shape.

'I think that keg's getting shorter,' Flash said to him.

'It would with his arse sitting on it,' Danny said.

'Yeah,' Mick said, showing an interest. 'Look how it's bowed out in the guts of it. Hey, King. Take a look at the heavy keg.'

The King looked at the keg and at Mick. He said, 'He's collapsing it, the heat of his bum's melting the steel.'

'It's allowed,' Mick said.

'He's let a few go, that's what's doing it,' Flash put in.

'Shut up, you cunts,' the Great Lover said mildly, looking up from the morning's crossword. 'What's a four-letter word denoting labour?'

'Kids,' Mick said promptly, proud of his wit.

'Look, Meat,' Flash said. 'Look what he's done.'

'It looks shorter,' I told him.

'Maybe it's getting fatter,' I added.

'How can a stainless steel keg get fat?' said Flash. 'I think Meat's been thumping the mutton.'

'Meat's got some to thump,' Mick said.

'That's allowed too,' said the King.

'It can't be shorter,' the Great Lover said. He stood up. 'There. It was up to my knee yesterday, it's up to my knee today.'

'You were pissed then, you're pissed now,' Flash said.

I was convinced it was the same height. Next day the recessed top was puffed up. The thing was getting fatter from all angles.

Saturday, during the fifth race everyone with a bet on was over near the other door, the one furthest from the pool tables. The gallopers were eight hundred metres from the finish of a two thousand four hundred metre Invitation Stakes, no one was near the fat keg when it went off like a bomb. We were deafened for the finish of the race and guys were going round frantically saying 'What won? Didja hear?' It might have been the last trump for all the notice they took.

It took a few minutes for the smell to percolate through the red bar. The publican was at the races, the explosion brought the bar manager out of the woodwork, the smell brought him to the ruptured keg. The weld round the top was intact, the split was half an inch from it, running along parallel. The steel had almost gone back to its original shape.

'I can't see what's in it,' he said, peering at the crack. 'But something's rotten.' His face was screwed up, the smell hurt.

Mick stood near and said, 'Those kids that pinched it must have put a cat in it or something and welded it back up.'

The smell was like slimy, strong tentacles reaching out of that keg and gripping you. When you took a sniff you felt weak, like an open grave was breathing up at you.

'Listen, fellers,' the bar manager said, 'let's get this out of here,' and Mick and the King grabbed hold of it without a word and took it outside, smell and all. The bar manager had things to do and disappeared after picking up a few glasses. Mick and the King were gone till the start of the sixth.

Sunday when I drove past to the club around ten in the morning, there it was, perched on top of the neon sign of the Cross. It was stayed there with rope, lashed tight.

For the sake of neighbouring noses, I hoped the crack was well open and the smell venting high in the air.

We forgot about the keg after we got used to seeing it up there. No one round the place was strong enough to lift it down and it wasn't doing any harm. The publican asked Mick if it was secure and Mick said nothing would shift it.

'I'll get it down for you when the stink's gone,' Mick said.

'Fair enough,' the publican said, and that was that. In the next months you could see a thin line going up the outside wall of the pub where the ants made a highway. The keg was black with them on the side of the crack.

It was another Saturday months later. The publican was off to the races again watching his share of a syndicate-owned galloper come second. Mick and the King were in the pub together.

'What do you think?' Mick said.

'Well, I reckon,' agreed the King.

'Fair enough,' Mick said. They both downed their beer and went outside. Mick shinned up the wall on to the roof and pulled the King up after him. Mick was taller, he got his nose up near the crack of the keg and sniffed. There were no ants there anymore, so they were pretty safe.

They put it in the King's ute and took it away.

Monday the keg was back where it was before, holding back the banging door. It was no longer swollen, no longer cracked. A new weld had appeared alongside the earlier one.

Whoever was drinking near the door sat on it and waited for a game or just talked or watched. It had lost its extra weight, it was just an empty keg again. Guys in from the car park kicked it when no one sat on it, and were rewarded with a good hollow boom.

Apart from the welds, the only difference from an ordinary keg was that it rattled. Whatever was dead inside it had left bones. Ants had no use for bones.

Guys that wanted to show their strength would lift it up when the music from the juke-box was on, and shake it in time to the music. Made a horrible racket. Those bones *had* to be bigger than cats' bones.

A DIFFERENT SORT OF CHAPTER

In the Cross of the South we sat in beerchairs, at beer-glass tables and trod on concrete, enemy of all that was glass, enemy of human skin and of the fragile skull.

In Fortress Australia, I sat at a typewriter of glass—made from melted beerglasses—with red keys like the Red Bar, typing on this beerglass paper in letters of amber.

In my darling's bed I said, 'Once upon a time we weren't here, but that was going to end. Someday, again, we won't be here. And it'll be forever.'

In my sprawling Sydney, each Cross had its Alky Jack and its Danny and the rest; and each bed had its Meat Man and his darling.

They were my pub, my house, my darling, my town and my people. All beautiful.

RONNY

Next time I saw him he asked me to do him a favour.

Why not? It was a Sunday, my darling had had to go somewhere with some study group or something—I never ask questions: I suppose she takes that as a sign of no interest—and I didn't feel like going to the Leagues Club, so I said OK.

Ronny drove. He went in close to the city to a street where the houses are all touching, each with a foot thick wall between the ones on either side.

'Remember, once you touch her, she's yours.'

'Touch who?'

'You'll see. It only takes the slightest touch. A finger. And she's yours.'

'Come on, who is it?'

'She's this crim's missus, and he told me to look after her while he's inside. You know, see she gets a bit.

293

He doesn't want everyone in the district through her. He knows I'm clean.'

'Why me, then?'

'I'm bloody sick of her. Trouble is, now she's used to me, she wants me. As I say, all you have to do is touch her. Arm, hand, anywhere.'

We get there early, I've had nothing to eat, he brings out some bottles, introduces me and says how about a beer for breakfast. She's stuck on him, you can see that. She looks only at him, hardly at me, just nods hullo, then turns back to him and the lights go on behind the eyes.

He talks a bit and she's hovering round trying to get near him, but he keeps talking, sitting at the kitchen table and filling her glass and pushing it towards her every time she makes a move. She tries to touch his soft pink hand, but he keeps it out of the way.

'I better get some cigarettes,' he says suddenly and bolts for the door. On the way past me he says Go for your life, Meat, so she can't hear it. The little kids have nappies on and the place stinks of them and they're running round dirty and yelling, but she takes no notice. I make sure the nappies don't brush my gear.

When he's gone I try to make some talk with her and it's very hard going. She's polite and when I get up to rinse my glass with water—a habit I have when I drink bottled beer—she shrinks away from me even though I'm two metres away. I stay on my feet and try all sorts of indirect movements to get a little nearer.

By and by, like a horse, she gets used to me being there, and doesn't move so far away. I pour her another beer, she shoots the glass out, gets her hand away from it and leaves it till I fill it, then brings her hand back to get the glass.

Several times I get up for one reason or another, and she flattens against the wall when I pass. I stop and face her and she still shrinks. All the time I keep my voice down, real low, just like when you're calming an animal that finds you strange.

In the end I trapped her in a corner of the kitchen, just worked her into the corner bit by bit and got closer to her.

I pretended to have an itch on my leg and my hand whipped down suddenly to scratch, she reared back but there was nowhere to go. Her arm hit the wall and bounced outwards and my hand came up from scratching at the same time. The back of my hand touched the inside of her forearm, which was bare.

She was against me in a flash, pressed up tight. Every bit of her, feet and legs and thighs and belly and chest and shoulders, pressed against me. And her face. I had to move my face to one side when her hair got in my mouth.

Her tongue—I got a sight of it just before, all coated with white—rammed into my mouth and round like a propeller.

She dragged me to the bed and tore the clothes off me. All she had to do was undo a couple of buttons and all she had on fell off.

While I was rooting her, the kids roamed round and several times patted me on the bare bum. With sticky fingers. Their nappies were full, the smell was strong enough to beat you black and blue. I hope that was Vegemite on their hands, or Golden Syrup. Peanut butter, even.

I'd drunk the better part of three bottles of beer and the one place I hadn't been to was the dunny. I was busting for a piss. I went to get off her, but she grabbed me tight, pulling me back in again. He hadn't gone down yet, especially with half of him being a piss-horn.

'Look,' I said. 'I need a piss. Gotta have one.'

'Never mind that,' she said.

'That's all right about you,' I said. 'I'm the one busting.'

She kept on holding me in to her and I tell you she was the strongest woman I've ever met. In this way, at least. Usually it's not that hard to get away from them.

Suddenly she looked me in the eyes and said, 'Do me a favour.' As if she was asking something very solemn, like when a person particularly wants to be buried rather than burned and gets someone to promise that it'll be done the way he wants it.

'Sure, anything. But let me up for a piss. For Christ sake.'

'Promise me.'

'Promise what? Let me up. I promise.'

'No, I'll let you up a little way, if you promise.'

'I promise. Now let me up.' I reckoned if she let me up a little way I could get my arms in against her and push her off.

'Do a bit on me,' she said sort of softly.

'What?'

'Do some on me. I'd like it. On me.'

'Cut it out, I couldn't do that.'

There I am, looking round for some way to get off, but she's strong as a lion. She lets me get him out and up a bit, but the power in her arms frightens me. There's no way I can escape.

'I'm just not used to the idea,' I said. 'I've been brought up to do it in the can.'

'You can't get there, can you? So let it go.'

'But the bed?' I said desperately. It was coming.

'Forget the bed.'

I did it. A little flow at first, then it poured. Must've been half a gallon. She let me up a bit more and grabbed the old feller and swished him round, playing the stream on her face, in her hair, on her stomach. It was everywhere, all over the bed and her, down her legs, everything.

The funny thing was, the way she did this to my water, as if it was something great, made me horny again so I got in and did it again, lying on her all covered in my own piss. The ups and downs of a white bum attracted a few more sticky pats. All very friendly.

When it's all over, she bursts into tears.

'You'll think I'm awful,' she said. And went on crying. I tried to pacify her as much as I could, but I was dying to have a shower and get the smell of her off me. And the smell of me.

'Tell me you think I'm not awful.'

'You're not awful,' I said. She stank. 'Everyone has things they like. Not everyone's the same.' I tried to get more conviction into it. 'If we were all the same, where'd the fun be?'

She sounded a bit calmer and looked at me to see how I was taking it. I hoped those kids had clean hands; every time they came round they patted me. They sure had a thing for bare bums.

'Get up on your hands and knees,' she said suddenly. 'I want to do something for you.'

Why not, after that? I got up on the wet bed on hands and knees. And I tell you what, it was OK. A bit embarrassing at first, but she did it so thoroughly and so enthusiastically that I soon got used to it and started to get quite a taste for it. I didn't realise she could get her tongue in so far.

Ronny got back a lot later. As we were driving through the Sunday traffic I wondered why she hadn't commented on the old chap. Most of them are alarmed or pleased, and mention him.

Perhaps they only do it to please me. Maybe there's plenty as big.

I enjoyed playing second-row with Ronny. No team ever pushed our pack off the ball while we were there. After he left the team I took the left side. Had trouble with my right shoulder. Still have a lump where the collarbone nestles in to the shoulder bone.

I haven't seen him for a long while.

She drove in to the yard behind the Cross one Monday and every day except Wednesdays after that for four months. That's how long she worked behind the red bar.

The moment the Great Lover lobbed he put work on her and never let up for one minute of those four months, but he didn't come within coo-ee of getting it. After the first week he was so amazed he began calling her the Untouchable. He couldn't understand it.

Her car was a mess, she wore the same clothes every day, and long boots to hide legs that didn't have much calf, but there was something about her. Her face was pale, not interesting-pale, sort of ashen-pale. You couldn't work out, under the bar light, if it was because of a thick coating of powder or just bad living.

She had wide cheekbones, slightly out of line as if someone had once lifted her off her feet with a right hook and the cheekbone had never come back into shape. She talked out of the side of her mouth, and it didn't look affected.

Nothing the boys said or did surprised her and she seemed to suffer no alarm at the frequent disturbances to good order that were normal near the Cross.

One day someone saw her at the trots with some of the trotting men who were really well in, and she was regarded with awe ever after. They were a race of gods, to the tribe. Then someone saw her at the races with a man who'd been a king at the prison where he'd spent years, one of those heavies whose names the other ex-prisoners never allowed themselves to even whisper outside.

Someone saw her at the baccarat just up the street from Darlinghurst cop shop. After that, even the Great Lover backed off a little. Not that he stopped putting work on her. With the Great Lover every sentence was sexual.

Her husband was dead and often her little boy was in the car with her on her day off.

'Into it yet?' I asked the Great Lover after three weeks.

'Still trying,' he said.

'Lost your touch.'

'Not me. No way, Meat. OK with me, whatever happens. If she does she does. If she doesn't, she's still apples.'

* * *

One day I was early at the red bar and Sharon had her day off, which was Tuesday, and Prue was alone in the bar. The pool cues were neatly laid out on the three tables, ready for the first game of the day. The red bar top was clean and dry, the racks of empty glasses under the bar were full.

'All set to go,' I commented when she'd given me my schooner.

She looked at me for a long time and said nothing.

I felt my face.

'I shaved,' I said.

'It's not that,' she said.

'Leprosy?' It didn't matter what I said, she didn't insult easy in the bar, her sense of humour was the same as a man's. I didn't have to talk nice to her. Matter of fact, she was one of those women that look down on you if you do.

'Is it really that big?' she said.

Christ, they'd told her. She'd probably seen thousands. Why did they have to mention me? Big stalk in a little garden.

I didn't say anything, sucking in beer while I wondered what I *would* say.

'I've always been partial to the organ,' she said with unchanged expression.

'Let's you and me go to a party,' she said. It wasn't so much an invitation.

302

'My sister will bring a friend. Tonight. I'll pick you up here. I go off at seven. I'll be back at eight. We'll go in my car.'

A sort of royal command performance. I said OK as if this was everyday stuff, but didn't say anything to the boys. It might not come off. Actually I decided I wouldn't say anything to the boys whatever happened. She might turn funny later. I didn't like that word heavies.

I drank the same as usual, then when she was going off at seven she said to me out of the side of her mouth, 'Don't you bloody forget or I'll cut half it off and cook it for breakfast.'

We got to her sister's place. Her sister was a cheap prostitute in the pub where she worked—you know, a quick dip upstairs, then minutes later she'd be down serving beer in the bar—but she was keen on this guy I was about to meet.

I hardly met him. We had a quick drink and whipped straight into adjoining bedrooms.

Prudence was out of her gear in about three seconds and was helping me with my belt while I was still untying my shoes. All she did was get trousers mixed up with shoes. She pushed me over on the bed, still getting in the way.

When she saw him, she said, 'I've seen three as big.' And I was glad of that, I didn't want to get mixed up with her just because she had some hang-up over big ones. Just the same I wished it was a full metre. What am I saying? There've been times he was ten metres. With legs, to slither across the floor and up their legs like a python.

She paid a lot of attention to him, though, and mucked round quite a long time before he was given his head.

When she was ready she flung herself down on her back and said, 'Watch it, boy. I've got very big piss flaps. There's a pox hole on one side and a melanoma the other. If you give any cheek I'll button 'em over your face like a balaclava.'

It gave me a slightly bitter taste, though. All the flesh, all the opportunity, no real sweat. Lashings of bare flesh. I thought: born naked, loving naked, and naked dead. But we weren't dead, and we weren't loving.

We finished first—she made a hell of a racket when she came—and she said, 'Let's have some fun.'

We crept naked to the door of the next room, peered round the door jamb. They were going to town well and truly so Prue waits till he's just short of the vinegar stroke then races into the room and jumps on the guy's back yelling, 'Wheeeeeeeeee!' Riding him like a racehorse ten metres from the post in a tight finish.

* * *

Once a week she gave me the royal command and I obliged. But it was never the same as the first time. Each time later she would twist round to make me understand she wanted it in the back. The mini-door with the ballroom beyond.

About her sister she said, 'She won't be in that again, with the guy you saw. She does it regular the first time, like I do, but her real kick is wanting it on her tongue. After the first time, if he does it in her, he won't see her for weeks. She has it the regular way in the course of the day's work, she wants it to be different for the guy that turns her on.'

It seemed reasonable.

Strange thing about Prudence. She never had a smell about her; no perfume, no sweat, not even a period smell. One thing she had, though, was a patch of darkish hairs down the middle of her chest, at the bottom of the cleavage.

And another thing. Three hairs round the edge of her left nipple. One at two o'clock, one at six o'clock, the third at ten.

Symmetrical. I used to tickle them, but she couldn't feel it. Just this ashen face looking at me, no expression, saying, 'Get on with it.'

One day she said to me, 'That's it, Meat. It's been a ball. I've got a friend if you want her.'

'I've got a friend too, Prue.'

305

'Sure you have.' She looked at me with the familiar absence of expression. 'This one's got dark skin,' she added, half trying to persuade me.

'I'm right, Prue. I'm fixed up.'

'She's so dark, actually, you'd need a miner's lamp to go down on it.'

'No sweat. I'm fixed up. Believe it.'

'The man who's never gone down on it is a vegetarian,' she went on.

'Sure, Prue.' I didn't mind one way or the other. 'It's been a ball for me too.'

'Schooner?'

'Schooner.'

The boys saw me talking to her and wanted to know what about, but I never told about Prue. Those guys talked their heads off when they got on to something interesting.

It was hardly a sexual farewell. On the other hand, I preferred the beer.

UNDERWATER SHOTS

I got to see my darling as soon as I could after she got back from wherever she'd been. When I got to her place she had just arrived back with her brother. I didn't know she had a brother.

Usually she comes on very generous, but for some reason she was snotty with him.

'You'll have to take a taxi back,' she told him. She wanted to see me, of course. 'It's my car, not his,' she said to me. 'I never let him drive it.'

She was so different from herself, the self I knew, that I felt a bit sorry for her brother. Actually, I'd got there earlier than I expected. The thought of seeing her again after missing her for so long made me cut short a five-game pool competition to two games.

'Can I give you a lift?' I asked the guy.

'No, you can't,' she said. 'Off you go, Roger. There's a taxi stand on the corner two blocks up.'

Roger shrugged. He didn't seem all that put out. He grinned at me and grabbed a bag from the back seat of her car and said Chow and off.

'I wouldn't have minded,' I started to say, but my darling ran at me, threw her arms round me and began kissing all round my face right there in the street. From the corner of my eye—she had me in such a tight grip I could hardly turn my neck—I saw Roger look back then resume his walk up the street. I guess he was used to the way his sister behaved.

She didn't want to go into her place just then.

'Let's go to the beach,' she said. 'I'd love to be near the water.'

Anything she wanted was OK with me. We parked her car and I drove her to the beach. The sea closed over me like those soft wet lips close over him when he's buried deep in her. She swam like she was washing off every bit of city dust and business worries. Then she wanted to go round the rock pools. We skipped over rocks and slipped on seaweed and made our way hand in hand on a headland where no other people come. I could see the devilment in her eye, but I didn't know what she had in mind till she got us both in this deep rock pool where you could see the bottom and the purple and gold and pink shells as clearly as if they were lit up.

'Take your shorts off,' she said happily. I took them off happily. 'Something I've always wanted to see.'

Under the clear water she got her two little hands— very narrow hands, fingers slim as pencils and the little fingers so tiny you'd think they'd fall off if she carried something heavy. And with these two little hands she worked on a friend of mine for a minute or two just to see what it looked like firing under water.

She thought it was cute. I thought they—the white shots—would have gone further. Out of the water they go quite a distance. I remember when I was fifteen, from a standing position I could reach six feet. Later, with a depressed angle of elevation—to constrict the bore—I could pass three metres. With the first and second shots, of course. The other seven or eight have less charge behind them.

Next day on the course I had to dig with the trench digger to lay PVC water pipes. A trench digger is a petrol-driven engine that has a steel belt like a chainsaw but much bigger teeth. It digs in and throws the earth back and to one side, leaving a clean trench about fifteen centimetres wide. You can adjust the depth.

I couldn't help it. I kept thinking of her and you should have seen that trench. If you go out to Carnarvon you'll see what I mean. It's from the southern bunker round the tenth green downhill to the water connection. The grass grows greener where you dig so you'll see it easily. My trench—the first one I'd ever dug, but that's no excuse—curved like a snake. Wal reckoned I had the shakes from being on the piss the night before, Laurie looked at it and shook his head, Bob laughed and said I ought to leave it alone or I'd go blind, and the boss said nothing. 'How's the fall?' he said. When it was clear that water actually flowed down the pipes, he let it go at that.

She'd never done anything like that before. She used to say she wanted it in her, to have it and keep it as long as nature and gravity allowed.

At her place I made love with her as if I couldn't be sure I'd ever make love again. As if I was dying tonight and she was going to die tomorrow.

Pat was as wide as he was tall, and had been in food for years. That's one way of putting it. You might say food had been in him for years.

Every six months or so he'd come back from parts west where he travelled round with shearers, cooking. They ate well.

He was at the Cross yesterday and handed me an old piece of paper with a shearer's name on, and a poem. The shearer, long dead, had left the game and died in Essendon. The paper was frayed, very fragile where the folds were, with marks from a fire.

Pat didn't say if the man died in the fire, just handed me the paper.

'You read a lot,' he said. 'Take a look at that.'

I read:

Even now I could shear them with the best
There's many a shed I've rung in the west
But I'm sick of the sight of a shearer's pen
And the piddling grievances of the men
So I decided as I've said before
That I will go and work no more
I'm having an easy time.

I've travelled the bush with a trap and pair
And a black boy to comb and brush my hair.
I've painted the towns red white and blue
Had big tallies out on the Paroo
I've taken my share in the small round yard
And found the ground was always hard.
Now I'm having an easy time.

I am a sensible sort of man
I won't work for a publican
I'll lounge about in the heat of the day
Chat with bagmen that come my way
And when the winter time comes round
Shooting roos in the hills I may be found
Having an easy time.

It was written in ink faded black, though the burn marks on the edges made me wonder.

Pat was a great reader. Burn marks are easy to make. How many times, when we were kids and it was winter and wet, had we made up messages in invisible ink—lemon juice or milk—and pretended to find treasure maps with judiciously burned edges? And Mum sniffing the air and yelling Who's playing with matches inside the house.

If the poem was really by an old shearer, it was sad. In the way that any man's sad that has delighted in a hard life and one day gets tired.

I didn't like the easy time he was giving the roos, though. Just stand there looking into the spotlight while you blow a hole through them. Not for me.

If they're on the run, well, maybe. Like the butterflies. But I don't shoot butterflies anymore.

Next time I see my darling she's washing her hair. You know the concentration birds get when they're doing something about themselves. They're in a world slightly to one side of the world you've just come from. Everything stops, the world sleeps while they pick clothes, paint nails or wash hair.

It was my bad luck she was expecting her cousin that day. He was in the rag trade, owned a clothing factory where they made women's dresses and things, and she had to go to a wedding in the family. He was the most convenient one to go with. And there was Aunt Yvonne to see—a sort of duty call so that she got round fairly regularly to see all the relatives—especially since her daughter, another cousin, had a new baby.

'You're not interested in that sort of thing, I know,' she said. And her eyes looked out at me from under

314

the wet hair and the towel. And the merry glinting of the coloured part of her eyes and the clear white as she looked at me had the usual effect.

You couldn't resist those eyes. They cracked your face open and you had to smile back, no matter what was on your mind.

As it turned out, she was in a hurry and didn't have time to dry her hair in the sun, she used an electric dryer. I held it for her, and it was hard to take my eyes off the white skin on her neck as it shaded to pink up near her cheeks and ears. From the side and back her head looked so small and finely made, you wondered at yourself for letting her go out in the street by herself.

The cousin turned up, a pale sort of guy with very expensive tailoring and gold cuff-links. Cars are for transport, they don't impress me. To me they're not a symbol. But I guess his white Mercedes sports was a satisfaction out on the open road when he put his foot down.

I didn't wait for them to go, I left. It wasn't my world, it was too far from the Cross of the South.

I made a point of turning up next day after work instead of going to the pub, but as usual I didn't bother to ring and let her know I was coming and this time she simply couldn't make the time to drop what she was doing. She had her accountant in and her tax return was late already.

My old car felt a bit sad, I think, driving away without her coming out and running up and giving him a big kiss on the forehead.

AIRBORNE

At the course we had a mixed day. Young Stan got the wind in his tail and began riding the little red Honda all over the place pretending to be taking tools to Laurie where he was working laying water pipes, but actually he was riding up the steeply banked greens —staying on the banks, of course—and peeling off like a hell driver.

He'd rev the motor, get into top, and come careering down the slope above the thirteenth tee. The thirteenth tee was newly grassed with kikuyu and made so there was a five foot drop at the end facing the fairway. He'd travel through the air about ten metres before the back wheel touched down. The suspension bottomed each time.

It was a slack day for golfers. He didn't get dobbed in.

I was lucky. The grass wasn't growing fast, and I got the job of planting trees. Couldn't have given me a better job. Nothing I planted there ever died on me except those willows the kids ripped up after school and tossed in the creek.

Even the truckloads of screaming pigs going past didn't bother me. I never eat bacon.

Once, when the sun was high, I looked up around me and wondered. From up there, what was I? A young guy that never thought of anything but his own concerns. Asking questions he didn't want answers to.

Not even bothering to tick off the days as they vanished behind me.

The blank moon flew like a kite among clouds. How big could the whole thing be? I mean, was it all *IN* something, the stars and galaxies and all that space? Was it all in a discarded cosmic soft drink bottle and was all our time contained in the time it will take to fall from a cosmic table? And were we such tiny specks that the world outside the bottle would never know our universe existed?

I struck some heavy clay and had to use the crowbar to loosen it up. That clay stopped my little gallop: I forgot about the size of the universe.

That afternoon in the Cross I felt pleasantly worked. The ground at the course was hard, you often had to use the bar to get down eighteen inches, and all in all it made the back and shoulders feel good. I never tire in the arms.

I was about an inch from the bottom of my second schooner, when who should lob but Dog Man. Eight months ago he'd gone for a pee in the middle of telling us about this sheila who invited five of them up to her flat.

The first words he said were, 'So the five of us were in it like rats up a drainpipe. She's laying there legs open and by the time it's Danny's turn he comes out blood all over the front of him, singlet and all. Mum'll think I cracked a maiden when she goes to wash this, he says. But when he's having another go I sneak round

on my hands and knees and tickle the sheila on the arse
and she gets going, bucking like a mule. Go, baby, go!
yells Danny and rides her like a cowboy. This time he
doesn't get thrown.'

'How did you go with your dogs,' I asked him.

'OK for a bit. Up Tweed Heads, managing for
owners. Took the caravan, wife and kids. Tell you what,
I was up there and got a temporary job in a club when
things were light on in the dog game, and this woman
latches on to me. Working there in the bar. Don't know
why, but she wanted *me*. You know me, she's sweet for
a month or so, but I couldn't get rid of her. She'd do
anything. One night I'd had three at her place by one
o'clock and fell asleep, dog tired. Five in the morning
I woke up to find her slurping on it. Chewing it. Tried
everything to get rid of her. Then I stayed late working.
At two I thought it was safe to go home, but there she
was up the road, waiting for me in the car. Don't you
want me, she says. For once I tell her the truth. The
magic's gone, I say. Next thing I know she's gone and
told the wife. I pack a bag at home and say to the wife,
OK, you got me. I'll go. But the wife wouldn't hear of
it. She said, No, that slut'll go. And she did.

'A month ago I see her in a pub at Tamworth, all
daggy. Gone to pieces. She saw me, came over and
threw a beer over me. The blokes I was talking to, one
of 'em was a copper and he says You want to charge
her? No, I said, I had it coming. And left it at that. I'll

never forget that bird. Talk about keen. Never met one like her before or since.'

He'd only been there the space of one schooner and he was putting work on the new barmaid. Sharon went on forever, but the casuals often only stayed a day or two.

'I'll wait for you,' he whispers across the bar.

Sure enough, next day I find he's waited for her till ten-fifteen and he's only in boots and shorts.

'I give her a few smoushes, ask her how she's getting home. No, she says, I'll be in nothing like that. Get out! she said when I had her in the car and tried to get the pants off. So I thought I'd better waste some of my cans on her. I fish under the seat and bring out two cans of draught. We'll have a beer instead, I say. So she has a beer. By the time she's finished two cans she says, Did you say instead? So I climb aboard and have three zots, three quickies—I don't want her drinking all the cans—and next day she doesn't want to know me. I walk up to the bar and say How was it last night? But she turns away and doesn't answer. Her old man's in boob,' he added.

Next day he comes in with that look about him that says he doesn't want to talk to anyone yet he's busting to talk to someone.

'Car's pranged. Thank Christ I haven't been down here zotting 'em down. Some idiot up the road came in from the left past a bus, it's peak hour and put the Torana into the Coach Inn.'

The Coach Inn was a tiny old stone house used since last century as a restaurant. I often used to go by and see candles flickering over the tables. It's gone now. They've put up one of those modern erections. Plenty of parking space, seventeenth century roof and all that.

His Torana was a write-off. It was the only dealings Dog Man ever had with the police that didn't end with him spending time in a cell. Apart from that drink at Tamworth.

While he was off the road he experimented with training a dingo he captured on a shooting trip.

'He's only a few months old. I wouldn't write off dingoes if I were you. It's not being a coward to keep out of range of rifles when there's cunts aiming at you: it's intelligence. And kid this dog isn't loaded with it. He won't do a thing you tell him.'

'Is that intelligence?' I asked. I knew it was the way I worked.

'I'll say it is. You know the sort of bloke that follows orders and does everything he's told. You get your first taste of that when you start work and someone sends you over to the store for four pounds of compression or a blank verbal agreement form. I never ever fell for that sort of cock when I was a kid.'

He stopped, waiting for me to say something.

'Me either,' I said. 'In my case it was striped paint.'

322

'You see? Well this dog's the same. If you can convince him there's some sense in doing something, like if you do it yourself first—and it has to be done at a time when it's really necessary—he'll soon get the idea. He might even do it. But all the time he's telling you: I'm just as good as you are, mug. And if it sounds like an order, it's out. He won't have a bar of it.'

'I like the sound of this dog. Are they all like it?'

'That's why I'm trying. I'd be the first. Other blokes have had a go, but no dice. Make one mistake in handling 'em, and that's it: no second chance. It's as if they decide you're a nong and won't have any part of you. Boy, is this one loaded with personality? Independent! I don't think I'll ever tame him, but I'm having a go.'

He didn't succeed. Two weeks later the dog was gone. He'd made the mistake of confining it. Built a sort of cage. It ate through the steel pipe that formed the bottom rail of his neat cyclone wire prison.

'Steel!' I said. I believe most things, this was a bit much.

'Steel,' he said firmly. And we wondered about that for some time until he came out with something that threw me.

'You get around,' he said. 'You talk to a lot of people. I never did much in the mechanical line, apart from mucking about with cars.'

He leaned a bit closer and said, 'You know when you play a record on a record player?'

323

I knew what was coming. 'Yeah, I know.'

'Well, you wouldn't happen to know how the bloody thing knows what size the record is, would you?'

'Wouldn't have a clue.'

Why spoil it for him? He'd have a mystery now. There weren't many besides me that he'd care to ask. They'd rubbish him, roar it all over the pub.

Babies drinking their bathwater, we buried our mouths and noses in the froth of beer.

At a certain stage we hesitated, shaking our heads to disengage a thought. Perhaps the violence would be now, and we'd sailed too long and too far out on Beer River.

There's always that one fist you miss, one knee you don't see.

I should have used the phone. She'd always drop everything and come out and see me whatever time I rang or interrupted, but I just got in the car after work and dropped in on my darling.

There was a delay before she skipped out and cannoned into me. She didn't have her usual momentum—I wondered if she was losing weight or sickening for something—and didn't knock me over.

But the welcome was there. After the breathless kisses, she explained that she couldn't come and make love right away, she had this meeting in her office, very important for business.

I happened to look up—you can see her window from the street—and some of her business associates were there, looking down. She saw me looking, turned her little head and saw them, and said, 'Three friends of Roger's.' Roger was her brother.

'We're doing a promotion. Just getting our ideas together at the moment.'

'A sort of seminal session?' I said helpfully. I meant it as a joke.

She hesitated before replying.

'I suppose that would describe it.' She was looking at me differently. Estimating something. Her breath smelled of cigarettes.

'You smell of smokes,' I said stupidly. I didn't smoke.

'Oh, that. Yes, I've had one or two.' She seemed relieved to be talking of cigarettes and went on about it. I had to stop her.

'I didn't mean to criticise.'

'But you're right. I smoke too many. I'll try to cut down.'

'To one at a time,' I smiled, trying to get her good spirits back.

'Oh, I only ever smoke one at a time,' she responded gaily.

'Well, I'll be off,' I said. I felt a bit of a dill. After all, she was a businesswoman. It was pretty unreasonable of me to expect her every time I turned up.

The figures at the window of her office were still looking down. In shirtsleeves.

'Sorry, darling,' she said. I watched her walk back. The zipper at the back of her dress wasn't done up. She was a terror for little details like that. Ten to one the tiny thread-catch or hook and eye at the top was broken.

She stopped at the entrance of the building to turn and wave. She always waved me out of sight. Something I hadn't noticed before caught my eye. She usually wore a brassiere, her dresses were the sort that looked better that way, but from where I stood her breasts seemed lopsided. As if one of the cups had risen off that breast, or the other one had dropped.

By the time I was in the car and off down the street she was still waving. The men in shirts had vanished.

I was a bit sad, going away, but there was no reason.

That night, from my window I could see flashes, like someone lighting matches in the dark. And the wind blowing them derisively out.

Next day was Saturday. I woke feeling I'd like to iron myself out. I walked down hill to the Cross. Others came from all directions.

There, at ten, was the Red Bar ready for us to cross. Piles of shiny glasses waited on the nearer shore of this day's Styx. Sharon rose from a kneeling position, ready to help us aboard and ferry us over the river whose further bank we had glimpsed every time we got drunk, but never yet reached.

Alky Jack was nearer than the rest of us. He was already afloat.

I guess I was thinking of my darling while I was going along, or the light rain, or the water from the hoses Laurie had put out—mowing the fairways you have to go straight ahead, no curved tracks—trying to keep dry, but I rounded a green and nearly cut a schoolboy golfer's bag to pieces. He was about eleven.

My darling was thinking too. The day before, she told me she was going away to think. Combining the thinking with a business trip to last three weeks.

I wasn't too clear what she was going to think about, but I don't like to ask questions.

It was Christmas Eve and by tradition us workers on the course were allowed in to the clubhouse and given a special table to sit at, and all the dishes the rest had. I'd never seen such big plates full of such elaborate food.

The chef himself came out, wished us merry Christmas, and the nobs of the golf club sat with us.

After that dinner I felt about half as heavy again. I hoed into everything.

It was pretty empty having no darling to call up.

In the Great Lover's paper I saw a photo of one of the accidents that had taken place in the holiday period. The photo was of a couple of men and girls. Two of each. They'd been thrown out and the car caught fire and burnt to the chassis. One of the girls— the photographer sneaked a shot of them as they were being loaded into an ambulance—was pretty much like my darling. It couldn't be her, but the face reminded me of her. I guess I wanted to be reminded of her.

It was a blazing hot Christmas. In the suburbs, in thousands of stores Santa was saying Ho Ho.

And under his breath, 'This bloody suit itches.'

And, 'This year I'm Santa. Next year they'll have a robot.'

And little girls said delicately, 'Mum, he sweats.'

And Mum said, 'Not now, dear.'

'I smell him,' the children said. Millions of them.

'Hmm?' said mother.

'Like Mister Swartz next door Mum. When he does the garden. With no shirt on.'

'Yes, dear.' Mum was on automatic.

'Mum. Say, Swartz sweats six times quick.'

'Who's sick, dear?'

'Nothing, Mum.'

I helped this woman with her car which was stopped on the road, and drove it home for her. It was only a short way, but she was grateful, and I could see she wanted to reward me. I didn't mind a reward. My darling seemed a long way away.

'I live in with Mum,' she told me. 'We can't go inside.'

The only place was the laundry.

It was small as laundries go and no room for anything but to sit her on top of the washing machine.

That was all right. I kept thinking of my darling, though, which was unusual for me when I'd latched on to a bit of stray stuff, and I couldn't get the sight of my darling out of my head. It was as if she was standing in front of me, just like in the moment or two when she strips and stops a bit as if to say, Do you like what you see?

The result was I got out of control a bit. My darling really turns me on. I mean, just the sight of her. The thought of her. The thought of any bit of her. Fingers, elbows, anything.

I gave this woman heaps.

The upshot was I pushed and pulled—I had both hands round her, with the little fingers on the hips where

331

they begin to broaden out and both thumbs hooked in front of the sort of pelvic bones on either side of the navel—I pushed and pulled so hard and was just beginning to shoot the works when she overbalanced backwards into the washing machine. Doubled up like a jack-knife into the thing. It was a Malleys.

I couldn't follow her, I wasn't made to bend that way. He came out, firing all the way as she went down, and I was left gasping looking down at her.

I couldn't get her out. She'd gone in so hard and so far I simply couldn't get her out. I tried lifting. No good.

'Stay there,' I said.

'Don't leave me,' she whispered.

It was a waste of time her whispering. Mum heard the crash.

'Where are you Doreen? Are you all right?'

I turned the key in the lock quicksmart and put a towel over the laundry window. Then I pulled my pants up and got tidy.

'Help me,' she whispered.

'What's the matter Doreen?' came the voice of Mum.

'Mechanic,' I whispered to Doreen.

'The mechanic,' called Doreen to Mum.

As quick as I could I tipped the machine over on its side a bit and eased Doreen out. She put on her pants when she'd straightened up, then wiped down the wet on the front of her. I made noises with the washing machine.

'What mechanic?'

She opened the door to Mum and I busied myself down with the power point, stood up and said, 'She's OK now, Lady,' and barged out the door.

'What did you have the mechanic for?' said Mum.

'Free service,' I called back, then off down the road.

I didn't start laughing till I got the keys in the car.

Later I remembered the shot in the Great Lover's paper, and got lonely again. I never felt lonely for anyone before.

A storm blew up at eight. Wind got up on its hind legs and beat the walls and called in rain to batter the roof. Rain swept in under the doors, the floor for once was more awash than the red bar. Water even came in at the big crack in the end wall.

The day was all wrong.

They never did and never would make history: they endured it. Sheltered under the kind Cross of the South.

They were lords of the earth, and gods. But they did not know. They were gods and rulers of the world and the heritage of the ages was in their bones, but their shaving mirrors did not tell them.

They would age, and one day never come again. No one would remember their faces, or write their story.

The days passed as if they dragged a ball and chain. A new publican took over the Cross.

I got hold of Sharon in her lunch break and got her to knit me two little woollen things, just the size to go over the end joint of your little finger.

'What's it for, Meat?' she said.

I wouldn't tell her. She said OK just the same and next day brought them in. They were in red wool.

How could I tell anyone they were for my darling's two bent toes? I thought she might see the joke of having special pullovers for the two disadvantaged toes.

She'd accept them, anyway, whether she used them or not. She always seemed to brim over when you gave her something.

Alky Jack still hadn't died. You expect a man to die that's drinking himself to death.

I didn't want him to die. I didn't want any of them to die, but specially I didn't want Alky Jack to die in the same way I hated the thought that footballers of genius had to get old and retire from the game or that great men—men who did something no one else could do—had to die. I wished you could dig them all up again. All the old fighters too.

When I walked in, he looked round at me, lips wet, eyes strong and bright. But his hand shook, reaching for his glass. Before the words got going, his tongue writhed in his mouth like a gnarled root.

'It's the cost, mate. Think of the cost. Nothing's as important as the cost.' Continuing aloud what he'd been saying in his head.

'The cost can put shutters over men's eyes so they see nothing of what happens outside their doors. Why does the whole thing have to be built on the cost? Why does the whole thing have to totter along on cut-throat competition? Where's the place for generosity and sharing and honesty and laughing and enjoyment without harm? And love?'

I couldn't answer. He looked forward again, over the rim of his glass. I watched the leather of his face with the white stubble poking out. Somehow it seemed there was less stubble than last time I saw him, but that was impossible.

'Instead, they turn their backs on men and put their trust in machines. Before you know it, machines replace man's soul. Machines take away hope and meaning from men, take away the simple pleasure of making little things with their hands.

'You know what I think, Meat?'

And went on before I answered.

'I think they'll have to get to the place where they say the world owes everyone a living. Or wipe out most of the world.'

His hand waved about in the air. 'A man's got to do some little thing. There's got to be something for his hands to do and his brain to work on. Some little thing.'

He made as if to say more, but hesitated, his arm stretched to pull words out of the air. As if he heard the sound of wings beating in his mind.

I thought Alky Jack would have been content to lean there and drink all day every day, but maybe that came within having some little thing to do. That or his thinking.

He said nothing. I began to feel that the wavering, the hesitation, were Alky Jack's whole message for me.

Long after I'd been turfed out of the pub that night, his arm in my mind was still extended in that unfinished gesture. Perhaps he had reached the point where the alp in his brain was not the future but the past.

After all, what had he ever done but talk? He must have thought of what he might have done.

It was around eight and several of the boys had been pretending to fight up the other end of the bar. They'd been drinking too long past the time when they could think of anything more to say to each other, and when some clueless young kid new to the district said the wrong thing, one of them straightened him with an uppercut and three of them took him outside. Not out the back to belt shit out of him, but out the front. That was unusual.

Out they went, past the far glass door which had been broken three times in the past month and at that time was boarded up with a sheet of hardboard. I remember I was thinking at the time what would happen if the sun blew up. It lives by explosions; who says they can't get out of balance? It wouldn't be so tragic if we all went together.

Next thing I knew the new kid returned to the Cross.

He came in backwards through one side of the glass door near where we were talking. The door had been shut, he took out most of the glass. We looked him over.

Aside from alterations they made to his face, he had miraculously survived having his kidneys torn out or his neck severed on the thick jagged glass. All he had was a few dozen points of blood scattered over the back of him. Minor cuts. The three didn't come back in. I finished my schooner as if it tasted of blood.

I was at the Cross next afternoon when Bob arrived. He nearly bowled me over when he said he was following Shorty up Coffs Harbour way. Getting right away from the city.

'To a commune?' I said.

'Shit no. I'll get a job easy. One brother's up there already'—all his brothers were in the building game—'and he says there's a mile of work.'

I knew lots of guys down from the country to find work, but this was getting to be a habit, getting out of the city.

As I was thinking about it—he went over to drink with his father—two very old men tottered into the pub and waited for Sharon to serve them. Both had cold weather in their bones and eyes full of rain.

One was so old the other man had to order for him: he couldn't talk.

'Whisky and a brandy,' croaked the talker.

The non-talker shook his head, getting pale purple in the face. It was a while before the one beside him knew there was anything the matter. When he became aware of the head shaking, his own head turned unevenly on creaky vertebrae and he said, 'What?'

The man started nodding and shaking his head, his mouth moved jerkily, his hands waving about and shaking. Much more than Alky Jack's. Finally he got his fingers out in front of him and gestured a more or less fixed distance with his two forefingers.

The light dawned.

'Oh,' said the man giving the order. Sharon looked round.

'He wants a double.'

A double, and he couldn't even speak. I finished the rest of my schooner in one swallow. It tasted like a woman's mouth.

The next week was a repeat of the glass-breaking episode and the new publican decided to do something.

There had been talk for months that the old barn was coming down and a big new pub built on the spot, with proper parking for cars and carpet on the floor. All sorts of stories.

What he did was enforce the law. It was simple, yet no one thought to do it before.

When someone didn't leave promptly on closing time he told him to get out. Naturally the guy said up ya, he'd never had to do such a thing before. The police were called, the guy appeared in court, copped a forty dollar fine and was barred from the pub.

Plenty were barred before and always got back, but this was different. The publican was to report to the cops if he came near the place and it was for life.

No repentance, no getting back. The publican was really going to clean up the place. He even cleared out the kids with their air-rifles and BB guns.

Going out at night at ten I'd look up at the stars and see the Milky Way like lights on a distant shore across an unlit silent sea.

A week later, there were fourteen guys barred. Fined and barred for life. And the rumours about a new pub getting stronger. And the crack bigger, reaching up past the clock nearly to the roof.

Some of the guys got themselves barred just so they'd be in it; their mates had to drink elsewhere, they made sure *they* had to.

You see, it wasn't done to drink at another pub when you had a pub to call your own.

Being forced to drink at another pub was cruel. Like black men forced to leave their sacred places and water holes and become strangers in another tribe.

Fourteen.

On top of this, young Bobbie Gill, who played centre in the under eighteens, had his throat cut over the pool tables. There were only two local kids in the Cross at the time, early in the day, and the three strangers ran and were never seen again. He didn't exactly have his throat cut, they broke a glass and jabbed it at him and he had a cut throat. Eleven stitches. It wasn't even a fight. But there was no way for the Cross to hit back, they were gone.

They must have thought we were a weak old tribe.

On Saturdays the place was dead. There was no SP bookie, no fights, just people drinking to get drunk. Not even the friendly shouting and yelling. As for singing—if anyone sang, they called the police. And when they were drunk, what then? A bit of biff? Not on your life. Tamely home to bed.

The idea was sick, atmosphere sick: the pub was sick. The only people that thrived were butterflies.

What were they trying to push us to, with their comfort and nice behaviour? If everything was going to go on like this, all paved and carpeted and no biff, and no danger, and anyone—even idiots—walking free and safe all the time, then the sooner there was some sort of outlet the better.

There had to be *some* risk to living. If there wasn't, you'd have to create it.

Overhead, the sky looked silent and calm, but I knew it was full of earsplitting noise and unceasing explosions.

Wednesday when I went in off the course for lunch there was a telegram waiting.

'From Denmark,' Ray said. Ray's the boss.

'Back Thursday,' my darling wrote. 'Love.'

'Denmark?' he said.

'Just west of Albany.' How could it be *that* Denmark if it was spelled Denmark?

All afternoon my hands and feet felt light and airy and strong and able to do anything. Valuable, as if they were gold. I was conscious of how precious they were and how lucky I was that everything worked without me having to think about it.

Springy and marvellous, they felt; people in their own right. They ought to have separate names.

I breathed deep, looked at the sky. Day and night, night and day. Beautiful. The sun's hot, the moon's big and yellow or small and white. Beautiful. And the stars at night, what can you do with stars but shrug and shake your head and say nothing? And the sea—think of the sea. And her hand, resting on her belly with the fine white skin. Think of her hand. And her laugh, like little bells.

No one could ever want to die.

After work I lobbed at the Cross and began to drink like a fish. As I drank, the air outside got congested like an angry face. Thunders muttered in the distance, soreheads getting themselves worked up to put on a blue. I alone was calm and happy.

I awoke on a little island in a creek. I recognised it. Hunter's Creek, not far from the Cross, where that girl was found unconscious, ants eating her tongue. Where that kid from Merry Lands tried to hang himself over the edge of the steep part with a rope tied to the fence, but the fence broke and he landed up to his neck in the drink, unhung.

That was OK, I knew where I was, but I didn't feel like me. Who was I? I tried to see myself, but that was too hard. There was no information round me. My pockets. Not even a scrap of paper. Had I been parachuted into enemy territory? Was I on a picnic?

The creek murmured softly. I bent to listen to what it said, but it was in code, I could make nothing of it.

A bottle floated downstream. I captured, uncorked it. No message.

I began to fill it with water and empty the water on to dry land. This struck me as a useful thing to do. An hour and it was drudgery.

Then Fuse floated past, naked. Why was he dead? Should I try to fish him out? Too late, he had swept past towards the Parramatta, Port Jackson, perhaps the sea.

Then Danny. I should empty the creek. Yes. I worked like mad, the water tinkled on dry land like broken glass. The murmur of the creek became louder, angry voices detached themselves and broke off at the edges of its steady flow of sound.

Mick floated past, gloved fists spread wide. I was alarmed. Danger.

Flash and old Hugh floated by, face up. Mac and Aussie Bob. Why were they all leaving me? Behind me a shape grew out of the trees and advanced on me with a woman's panty hose taut between its hands. A strangler. I knew helplessness.

Sammy and Ernie went by towards the inexorable sea.

No matter how I turned and dodged, the strangler was behind me, but I never stopped baling for a moment. If I could empty the creek of water I could stop them all floating away. They might be dead but at least they wouldn't be leaving me.

Two young kids pool cues crossed, were followed by Red and the Darkfella, talking.

That wasn't right. I brought them back past me again, lips properly shut, tongues stilled.

The soft material was round my throat, a knot was tied.

A hill began to form above the creek. On top of the hill a figure sat at a table, bent over a typewriter. I waved, called out, then saw the man wasn't working at the machine, he had fallen asleep over it. Was he drunk?

I yelled, hoping the noise would wake him. No noise came.

The Great Lover and Tom passed quickly. The water was flowing faster.

The strangler tightened his hand in the stocking, but where I should have choked, it passed through my neck and fell to the ground.

Dog Man, Eh and Gibbo rushed past. Perhaps a weir further down would stop them and I could fish them out on dry land again.

The strangler dissolved into another shape. A thin man stood there, one arm steadying me, the other plunging a broad-bladed knife again and again into my chest. But where I should have crumpled, the knife passed through me without harm. No drop of blood stained my shirt.

347

The creek was choked with old publicans, bar managers, Sharon and young Sibley, the men that came round with supplies in baskets, Missus Mott and the old guys under the window, Serge and Ronny.

There was less water in the creek, my baling was reducing it, but there was little chance I could stop the flow.

The queer fella, the old man with the sack, Vivian, away they went faster and faster. Shorty and Blackie went so fast I couldn't properly see them, though Elizabeth Large was easy to make out.

The rest, from the new publican to Pat, his poem and the King, raced by. Only Alky Jack was missing. I pictured him; all the rostrums in his head deserted, mikes dead and audience gone.

I waited, baling furiously with the bottle. The creek was nearly empty when Alky Jack whizzed grandly past, nose in the air, mouth open, talking.

'We only came here on earth to say goodbye,' I heard him say.

I stopped. The creek ran suddenly dry as if someone pulled out the plug.

This young guy of my age appeared not far away. He was very big, it was easy to see every detail of his body, for he was not only big, but naked as the day he was born.

While I watched him, his body withered. Pieces of face slipped, chunks of flesh slid from his bones and rotted as they fell, crashing miniaturely to the creek bed and exploding in puffs of brown powder. Last of all, the bones cracked in sections and collapsed downwards in a heap of white dust.

Peculiarly, tufts of brown hair remained, undecayed, lying where they had fallen.

I knew.

It was *my* hair, *my* collapsing bones, exploding puffs of flesh; my body.

I had dreamed me.

THE DYING CROSS

I slept out in the grass at the back of the Cross till morning and woke, as usual, without a hangover. I washed my face at the tap behind the pub buildings, took a long drink to counter the dry mouth of drinking, got in the car and headed west by the median strip, made a U-turn and drove back past the pub on the way to the course.

Hunter's Creek wasn't dry, no dead bodies were floating away to sea, leaving me.

The Cross was as it had been for years: a mess. Today its flaws seemed more obvious, pushing out towards me, demanding to be seen. There were bits missing, side fences broken, gates bent, walls chipped and bricks gone from the carelessness of drivers; tiles had lifted and cracked across, the roof sagged as if very tired. I knew that inside were smells that strangers noticed and disliked but were so ingrained in the skin of the place they could never be got out.

As I passed I thought of the loss of the characters who made it a pub to be nervous in, to be excited in, to be expectant in, to be wary in, to be drunk in. Now they, its spirit, were gone.

The Cross lay sprawled on its uneven block of bare ground like a beached whale, a great wounded fish; old and damaged, spirit gone, parts of its body far on in decomposition, though not yet dead.

On my red tractor, cutting round the fourth green, the whole course lay below me. I stopped the motor and sat. The grass, as one brilliant green blade powered by energy of earth, sun, water, raced skyward to the white moon at voluptuous speed, my eyes following till the green of the blade was lost in blinding blue.

Looking into the sky I saw myself with an arm round my darling. I saw the sick and dying Cross of the South. I saw new bricks laid and rising and growing out of the old pub until a new shape sat there blinking and brand-new in the sunlight. I saw the uneven dirt of the yard paved and marked out for parking. I saw a host of young kids leaving off shooting butterflies and learning to drink well and play bad pool, and a younger host along Hunter's Creek shooting butterflies. I saw a new publican and a new staff, and carpet on the floor.

And one by one all the prodigal children of the Cross returning home where they belonged. I saw a surreptitious ring marked out at the far end of the carpark behind the new pumphouse near the creek, where fists could reign again. I saw the spirit of the old pub revive and get to its feet and shake its head and look round ready to challenge or be challenged and to put on the line the safety and comfort and wholeness of its bones and muscles and skin.

And on the bar, as at the edge of an ocean or the banks of a river, I saw endless rows of empty glasses being filled; those frail glasses men commit themselves to, some days floating calmly out onto broad reaches of water between sympathetic shores and willows and friends and waving picnickers on the bank, and other days whipping dangerously round a sudden bend toward nervous shallows and sharp aggressive rocks.

And now and then, as they drank deeply, they saw in the bottom of the glass, not the face of the man they knew, but the monster within that was waiting and all too willing to be released.

A ball plopped on the green, hit the pin and rolled away from the hole. I started the motor and went on cutting grass.

'Tonight's the night,' I said aloud. 'That's far enough into the future for you, boy.'

353

Friday, on the way to the course I had to stop at the lights outside the Vauxhall Inn. The car saw the pub and pulled over into the outside lane. It was ten past six in the morning.

'Silly old bugger,' I told the car. 'Won't be open till ten.'

I was a healthy animal, I lived a reflex life of hunger, thirst, desire, aggression, revenge; but mostly thirst, with hunger and desire a good second. I thought of my darling and how she'd been away a few weeks to think—I guess it was about us—and came back last night with her mind made up; how she had a laugh and a cry when I gave her the two red woollen pullovers for the bent toes; and how she ruthlessly drained everything out of me: life, affection, desire, the lot. Until I was fit for sleep and sleep only.

'Stay here,' she said. 'I'll wake you in time for work.' Then as she covered me she gave me a kiss, unlike any tempestuous or greedy kiss she ever hit me with before. It was so light.

So light.

I didn't say anything. But a moment later I shivered. I remembered the little house next door to Fortress Australia and the patient mother waiting for her children to come home from their foolish games. And her kissing them each lightly. After which they stopped their noise and laughter and playing and fighting.

And went quietly in her little house.

I don't remember getting to the course. I don't remember anything but sitting half asleep in the sun all day on a red tractor cutting grass.

It was the atmosphere. There were eight of them when I lobbed and one had a broad hat like you see at rodeos. By four o'clock a lot of the tribe were at the bar and pool tables, settling in for a good weekend, a wet weekend, sheltering from midsummer sun. In twos and threes another eight strangers came. Another ten. More broad hats.

They didn't bunch up together, stayed spread round the bar. Leaning not looking. Talking quietly.

Others began to feel the atmosphere. But there was no focus, nothing you could put the finger on.

I found Mick.

'Where's the King?' I asked.

'Doesn't knock off till five at the deathtel.' The King had a new joke, the funeral parlour was no longer a fun parlour, it was a motel for the dead; overnight stay, vehicular transport: deathtel.

'What do you think?' I said.

'Yes,' he agreed. 'Looks like it. Who are they?'

He didn't care. The calm mouth, contented eyes told the story. This was the beginning of a great weekend. And why not? He was made for combat. The monster peeped joyfully out of his eyes and got ready.

'The bar manager's at the races,' he said. 'Only the publican in the way.'

Then the clueless young kid walked in, the one that re-entered the pub weeks ago, backwards through the glass door. Round him were three guys that looked a lot like him, only much bigger. I watched. Groups of strangers glanced up briefly and did nothing. The young kid looked right round the pub carefully, not missing a face. He didn't seem to find what he was looking for.

'Who is it?' said Mick.

'A few weeks ago. They took him out the front then shot him back through the glass.'

'Who?'

'Barred now. Drink at the Bull.'

'There's a few of 'em,' he observed.

'More coming,' I added. Another car peeled off the conveyor belt and pulled in to the car park, red dust halfway up the sides. They were from one of the western tribes. The kid must have been visiting relatives for Christmas.

One came in with his arm in a sling. Keen.

Mick walked over to the three with the young kid and addressed himself to the one he chose as the most formidable. What Mick said seemed to please them. They almost nodded. Mick went up to the phone on the bottle counter, past which the accommodation part of the pub started. It was one of those red phones that have an extension to the occupier of the premises; it was just inside the publican's office.

He followed the flex back to the little white junction and eased out the male part to see if it was separate. It was. He turned and nodded. The men from the west caught the nod.

Mick came back. 'They agree.'

I wasn't the King. 'Agree what?'

'No weapons—knives and that. No glasses in the face. No outside help. No fighting out front where the public can see. And we isolate the place when it starts so no one can make phone calls. We'll lock the publican in his office.'

'What about the far door of his office?'

'I'll do that. Jam the bars into the sockets.'

'What's the signal?'

He looked at me, blank-faced.

'The first punch, Meat. What else?'

'But you'll be into it, Mick. You won't think of phones then.'

'You know how to isolate a phone?'

'I know.'

'You won't rip it out?'

'Cigarette paper.'

That satisfied him. He drifted away, having a word to the boys.

Only the rules were necessary, they had eyes. When they saw the tableau of young kid and three brothers and the pockets of strangers all round, they knew. Philosophers might dispute the nature of knowing till the earth falls into the sun, but the boys at the Cross knew what they knew and knew they were right. And they were.

Mick drifted further, doubling round towards the private entrance, to get that other door.

It was like a ritual. They waited until we were set and they had all the troops they were going to get. There were no neighbours either side of the pub after working hours, so as long as we kept it inside or out the back, we could go for our lives.

The politeness was intense.

When it felt like time, we got two guys to stay at both entrances to the car park to give the word to anyone that felt like leaving to keep his mouth shut. And to come in and yell if official interference lobbed. And one by one we folded back the rear glass doors.

Mick and Serge went to talk to the publican in his office. I pulled out the phone plug, wrapped a cigarette paper round each of the prongs, and pushed them back into their female part. I did it twice before I got a dead phone. Anyone could call from outside and get only the sound in their ears of the phone ringing, as if no one was in, but there would be no ring at our end.

After that, we stood around. Waiting for someone to do something. The time wasn't right. Mick and Serge stood talking with the publican, who had his feet on the desk.

We waited.

The pub roar was normal, but there was something about the way the door flew open. Everyone turned. The King stood in the front door, hands on hips, looking slowly round. A sort of relieved silence awaited his first words.

When they came, they were like a bellow. Like an affronted bull.

'What's all you fucken foreign cunts doin' here?'

Golden words. Every stranger and every Cross drinker swung at the nearest enemy. Several innocent travellers, just in for a drink, ran for their lives. The publican dived for the phone. Mick slammed the door behind him and Serge put three full barrels against it and wedged them with another barrel between the door and the bottle counter and followed Mick into battle.

GET UP. YOU'RE NOT HURT

I didn't have all that much time to lean on the bar and observe my fellow tribesmen, so I'd better tell you how things struck me.

The first thing was a fist that glanced off another shoulder and came to rest on the edge of my left cheekbone, its power gone; I got this glimpse of a big silver ring with a shiny black stone. Rings are abbreviated knuckledusters, the sooner that guy was down the better. I pushed past Eh and got stuck into him. I started quick and let go one of my favourites. It's a navel uppercut; hits the navel and travels up towards the arch of the ribs and in. Got him. He doubled forward. Another favourite: all knuckles together at the side of the head halfway between the eyebrow and the top of the ear.

The great thing about fist fighting is everyone keeps getting up. Gloves spread the impact and rattle the poor old brain like the milk in a coconut, but fists hit just one point. You bleed, but so what? If you didn't bleed you'd be dead. It's a way of keeping a check that its clotting properties are unimpaired. Cop that.

'Hey, Meat!' said Eh. 'He was mine, eh?'

The guy was down. Anything like knuckledusters you deserve to stay down.

'I don't need help, eh?'

'Sorry, Eh.'

Then he collected one and fell over and I was busy again. I bored in to another group but the guy that got Eh began hanging punches on me so I turned to pay attention.

He was taller and had a longer reach and drove me back to the one glass door that couldn't be folded back. I stumbled against the doorstop and this guy did the rest. Over I went, backwards, head through the glass. He went away. I shook my head, felt for blood and looked round. One leg rested on the welded barrel. Blood ran down my back.

Alky Jack was up the far end of the bar peacefully watching. The group of older drinkers that never mixed in fights were still sitting at their tables near the windows to the front of the pub. Sharon read the paper, the demand for beer had fallen off sharply. I got up after a bit, and troubled her for a seven. It was pleasant, watching.

Mick was busy and as he worked I saw how well he protected his hands, like a boxer should. When he worked on the head it was to the parts that gave or would turn with the punch. Sometimes he threw a deliberate glancing blow; I could feel the way he measured it, just to do damage and open the flesh—so his fingers and the bones of his hands would come up whole and ready for the next blow—yet not leave him off balance. Sort of cutting with blunt instruments.

I had a cut head and deeper cuts where I'd rested across the glass bits that stayed in the bottom rail of the broken door.

I got up amidst the surging battle and things weren't too steady. I put out a hand to steady myself on the Great Lover's back, but he was clobbered in that very instant and I ended up under him on my back again. Someone lurched above me, tried to recover balance and trod fair on my knackers.

'Taking it easy, Meat?' the Great Lover grinned, blood dribbling from his lip. He got up.

I got halfway up, to my knees.

'Saying a prayer, Meat?' Flash said, ducking a swing and poking up a right as if he pulled it out of his belt.

I rose to a standing position, legs bent, both hands on my only gift to the future. The pain rose on burning wires into my stomach.

While I was in this state, a guy that should have been busy with Danny spared time to uppercut me. Still holding them, I rolled over backwards like a hoop, came to rest at the barrel, which boomed when I hit it. It didn't do that guy much good, Danny got in several quick punches and flattened him. Danny's face was flushed, eyes bright, teeth flashing.

'Get up, Meat. You're not hurt.'

I'd said it enough on the field and sure enough it worked. The pain crippled me, but the magic words in that confident tone pulled me up like two strong hands under the armpits. Did I say confident? Any more confidence and it would have been contempt. Maybe that's what did it.

I got my hands away from there and let them swing. Felt like a beer barrel was tied to them. I put my hands up. The guy with his arm in a sling had the sling off and approached me valiantly. I didn't know what to do. He swung, not very hard, with his good hand. At the same time I threw a left. It wasn't very hard either. I wished he'd go away. Fighting with a cripple.

Next thing the cast hit me. It was one of those that enclose the forearm from the elbow down and end in a clenched hand, leaving the thumb and the last two finger joints nearly free. It felt like an iron bar. It was probably fibre-glass, much the same thing.

This guy must have flattened a lot of our tribe with his broken arm. I staggered back towards him, caught it again, this time on the shoulder. He was grinning.

'I'll give you laugh, you cunt,' I said uncharitably, and got in close, inside the range of the weapon.

I got his nose, with my fist turning over from the wrist, breaking it to one side. I didn't let him go and I didn't pull him down, I worked on that nose. I got it loose one side, then broke it back the other way. You use the lower knuckles: if you use the middle ones there's the risk that the lower ones will be cut to pieces on teeth. Remember they weren't knockdown punches, just jarring and cutting.

Flailing, his armour got me on the ears, the head, cut my lips against the teeth. I spun it out quite a while, propping him up.

In the end he was too groggy to stand—blinded with tears, swallowing his own blood, his nose swinging loose.

Covered in blood, he fell. Fibre-glass knuckles are unmerciful.

He was finished. Believe it. My hands were a mess.

A funny thing was happening up near the clock. They were fighting among the pool tables and manners were slipping. Pool cues whistled, teeth cracked, heads honked, skin split, blood squished. Serge caught two and snapped them, but this made two more weapons. Danny put money into a table and armed himself with coloured balls.

Flash ducked round, bent over safe from fists and whipped shoes off the feet of fallen strangers. He threw the shoes far out the back.

'The bastards'll cut their feet to pieces,' he rejoiced as I went past headed for the far wall. From the corner of my eye I thought I saw Ronny come in.

At the wall a mass of bodies struggled. Danny was clocking heads with fists half closed round pool balls. He met a cue swinger, the cue caught the knuckles of his left hand, one ball dropped and he got the guy on the side of the head. Alas, he copped the thick end of a cue over the eyes and retired, blinded, for a while.

Someone was down. Bodies leaned back and bobbed slightly. The kicking had started. I saw the King turn from an engagement in the corner, sensing the new situation. I saw the gleam of Mick's light hair. I into it.

The young clueless kid was in there and his brothers. I bored in and made a path and my rush carried their sort of standing scrum to the back wall. The wall shook, the clock clattered against it. My shoulders were in the ribs of two guys that I had my arms round, but they were two of the visiting brothers. The other one got me with the smooth end of a cue in the small of the back, as near as dammit to the kidney. I staggered, and their counter rush carried me back out of the fray to a sitting position against the bar. I came to rest in a pool of blood, sticky and warm on the palms of my hands, my head smacking the tiles.

When I looked up, the mass had closed again and Mick was still down. The King was ripping bodies away with both hands. Ronny and Serge, side by side, saw the kicking and left their work. They charged. But I had a better idea. I grabbed the twice-welded door-stop and raised it overhead and I charged too.

I met the first body—who was preparing a welcoming right for me from near the floor: I must have looked a lovely target—and let it go as hard and as high as I could. And dropped my hands like clubs on the head of the welcoming stranger.

The barrel took the four kickers round the head and shoulders and drove them back into the wall just as Serge and Ronny got there. Finding opposition gone, our two tried to stop, but stumbled and fell over Mick, who was crawling back out of it.

When the lot hit the wall, the crack shot right to the roof, opened up and half the wall fell out with a beautiful crash. The strangers fell with it.

The clock stayed up, swaying, half in the pub and half out in darkness with sky behind it. A roof beam with cross members, together with half the roof, fell on Serge and Ronny, pinning them. Ronny didn't move.

The King and I protected Mick, while Flash and others came jumping on the flattened wall to get stuck into Clueless and his family. Serge tried to lift the beam off himself, but without Ronny's help he was RS. The centre of the fight was still where we were, the chance to kick was such a strong temptation once manners had gone. I tried to get over to help, but I was occupied.

Next time I looked Ronny was stirring, and shortly after he and Serge pushed together and got free. They stood up, looked at each other, looked across at the King and down at Mick. The King came over and they lifted Mick behind the bar. He had trouble with his back and was a while getting to his feet. By that time we were a solid block, working together, mowing down everything. The three of them fanned out and I took care of the rear. We had a reason to be serious.

If they ran, they ran. We didn't follow them out to their cars. Our reverse wedge made a mess. Serge trod on an instep, you could hear the bones go. The King put his right hand into a face and the cheek went in and stayed in. Very depressed-looking, that guy; half his cheekbone in his mouth.

Ronny faced one of the brothers, who let him get too close. He grabbed, lifted, and threw him. The Great Lover, eyes peering through puffy slits, leaned with all his weight on one guy's arm that he'd pulled towards him across a small table, and was hammering the guy with the other hand. The one Ronny threw landed on this stranger, knocked him to the ground, but his arm stayed on the table up to the elbow. Which was broken backwards. The Great Lover peered round for the missing body, then let the arm flop off the table to be near the scream.

The invaders retreated a bit. They saw the empty barrels outside the cellar door. They came back bearing these gifts and tried to press them on us. They made no difference to Serge, Ronny or the King. No parts of their bodies were unpadded. Raised forearms warded off the high ones; they caught some and threw them back; others bounced off chests, hips.

One they threw landed on the clueless kid's hands. He had them spread out on the table in front of him and was gazing, dazed, straight ahead. His jaw hung down, one side more than the other. (It was split dead centre; when they opened his mouth there was a gap in the lower jaw where the two halves no longer joined. His bottom teeth looked funny in two sections and on two levels. They wired his jaw up in the hospital with metal screwed into the jawbone and coming out his cheeks.) The barrel landed on his hands and bounced off on its way. The hands stayed there, but broken, and if you had time to watch you'd have seen them swell as the blood came out of the broken blood vessels and the fluid came running to the damaged parts to help.

He copped it coming and going.

Things went on much the same for the best part of an hour. There'd be rests when a few got weary, and the rests got longer and more got weary. The really injured stayed out of it.

Mick was on his feet at the bar, drinking. His back hurt a lot and he walked very slowly. Ronny collected a barrel on the head and it ricked his neck; he was recovering at the bar. The King and Serge were still full of fight when the cockatoos raced in to say the police had come.

The few foreign tribesmen still on their feet sized up the situation right away and were drinking at the bar before the police looked in. Two officers on their usual patrol. I guess they couldn't understand why there were no drunks.

They asked the strangers where they were from and got civil answers. There was no disorderly conduct. They could see where it had been, but no one was going to tell tales to two men more foreign to our way of life than any other drinking tribesmen, no matter how far away they came from.

We got the publican out. We watched the decisions chasing each other over his face. But he made no accusations. Police go away, but the boys were from this tribe and would be here forever, and their kids after them. How would he bar the whole pub? He needed *some* of us there, to drink his beer.

Someone started the fight, someone we didn't know and now he'd gone. We were trying to stop it, of course we were. As for the wall, it was due to go any time.

'That crack was right up to the roof today,' the King reminded him. 'You saw it.'

Sure, he saw it. He nodded, anyway.

'The traffic. That did it,' Serge said helpfully.

'The vibrations,' I said, remembering the bone barrel. 'All that rain we had settled the foundations further down.'

'That's a point to remember,' said Mick intelligently, 'when you come to fill for the new foundations.'

'Yeah, when's the new building going up?' said Serge.

There was a sort of intermission while the publican thought. Now was his chance if he was going to put us in. But he *had* been locked away unsighted. He sighed. We'd say it was for his protection. He looked at us. We didn't go away. Finally he said, 'The plans are approved. The builder might be ready to start.'

'Might be here Monday if it's fine,' Mick said.

'Yeah,' said the publican a shade drily.

'We'll help you patch up over the weekend,' the King said.

'That's the shot,' said Mick. 'Stick around and guard the place. If that's all right.'

He looked at the officers, they looked at the publican. That was OK. He knew exactly how much they'd help. He'd have to call his manager in from his day off to guard the place at night and over Sunday.

'See if you can fix the far door, Mick,' the publican said. 'It seems to have the bolts twisted or jammed. I couldn't get out either door.'

Mick had the grace to look away as he went to fix it.

I spent a while bringing back the empty barrels and putting them in the right place. Walking wasn't pleasant, my balls were up like a football. Well, a cricket ball.

The wounded went to hospital, we drank with the strangers. They weren't bad guys. Came from a rather big country town, as country towns go.

What would I do with the doorstop? There was no future for doorstops in a brand-new pub. I didn't want it opened at the brewery, or thrown on a tip. I made a trip to the car while the cops were elsewhere.

The publican called his manager in from a party; they took turns to keep watch all night. We got bottles and cans, went to the Great Lover's place and drank till morning. The strangers told us stories of what it was like being a drinker out west. One was in the team that took the Amco Cup from the city teams. No one mentioned good manners or bad; it wasn't the time or the place.

They left round midday Saturday to pick up the wounded from hospital and called for a farewell drink on their way home and headed west around two. By then two jokers on ladders were knocking nails into fibro sheets and had the beam up where it belonged and the iron roof nailed down.

They found a broad-brimmed hat under the mess and nailed it up for a souvenir. Just under the clock.

The barrel bothered me.

The races were over. The Cross was full of stories and satisfaction, blackened eyes, cuts and bruises and limps. Like the aftermath of some gigantic game of football. Stories were being worked into legends.

Mick was limping, but he felt a bit better. He hadn't gone to the doctor yet and started the long business of X-rays and tests; later he had a big operation while the doctors tried to fix up the nerves that went down to his leg. There's a scar beside his spine now, a scar like a fishbone.

'The barrel, Mick.'

'Barrel?'

'The empties got thrown round. Mixed up.'

'Christ.'

'I've got it.'

'You?'

376

'Took it in case the cops kicked it.'

'Where is it?'

'My room.'

He thought.

'No one'll see it. Not ever. Could put a cushion on it, make a seat. Or use it for a swimming barrel for the kids up the Lake. To try and stand on while it's rolling. Unsinkable. Or could be a fixture up on the roof when they build a new pub. You could do the welding, a couple of chains either side, nice and shiny, see it for miles.'

I knew he'd want it where he could see it. If he did the welding it would never fall, and it would be awful hard to steal.

'The sign's a good idea. You keep it up your place till the time comes, OK?'

I saw him talking hard to Nick, the publican. Who looked dazed still. I guess he'd learned he wasn't the only one could bring about change.

SOME LITTLE MATTER TO
BE SETTLED

The man with the basket of food came round at six. He stopped at a group of the boys sitting in the sun at a table covered in slops and the water that dripped off the sides of glasses. On the table they carefully spread a road map. The water came up through the paper and formed lakes and inland seas in places that never even saw much rain. The boys didn't mind. They stocked up with garlic sausage and stuff and put it on the four corners of the map to hold it down at the edges. They began following roads with their fingers, calling out distances, remembering times they'd been at the different towns in the western part of the state.

I went over to look. Yes, they had the right town. Like all the other waterholes, it was marked in red.

As I walked past to the phone to ring my darling about our Sunday together—she wanted it to be special, she said—I heard them wondering what date the King and Serge and Mick would decide on. They were happy. It was like looking forward to a picnic.

There was a notice on the phone: Out of Order.

Out of order? I was just about to ask Nick if he'd reported it, when I remembered. I eased over to the little white junction, pulled it apart, ditched the insulating cigarette paper and put it together again. Dial tone. I put in money and called my darling.

Have you ever had someone climb all over you from the other end of a telephone line? I could feel her warm breath on my face.

When I got off the phone the King and Mick gave me a wave. Serge was there. I went over. Mick was holding his back.

'Are you in?' said the King.

'I'm in.'

'Thanks, Meat,' said Mick.

'How's the back?' I asked.

'Crook.'

'I don't like the slipper,' I said. It was the only word of comfort I could think of.

'How does Easter suit you?'

'Whatever suits the rest suits me.'

They nodded. Didn't speak for a while.

The King said, 'You're looking after the barrel?'

'That's right.'

They nodded again.

'A cute trick, that broken arm,' said Serge, grinning at me.

'Like an iron bar,' I said. No one said nose.

'Maybe we take some tricks with us,' he said.

We all thought.

'I don't know,' I said. 'Maybe.'

'What about that wall,' said the King innocently, not looking at Serge.

'What wall?' said Serge. Just then a BB tinkled on one of the glass doors. We all looked out the back, pleased. Even Mick.

'Butterflies are in season,' Serge said.

'And brick walls,' said the King. That was the nearest they got to laughing. I don't have any authority to keep up—I'm not a mountain peak—so I laughed out loud, thinking of the beautiful day it was going to be tomorrow. They watched me till I stopped.

Mick looked down at me and said, 'Now you know what a football feels like when it's kicked.' I looked down at the swelling. I had it held up with two pairs of briefs.

'How'd they miss the old feller?' said Mick.

'Easy. I strap him to the inside of my leg in three different places: one high, one halfway, and one just above the knee.'

'I thought you tied it round your waist like a belt,' Serge said.

'Not when there's glass on the floor.'

I went to the bar to get us a small fleet of glass canoes to take us where we wanted to go. I thought of the tribes across Australia, each with its waterhole, its patch of bar, its standing space, its beloved territory. It was a great life.

Down the back of the Cross kids were shooting butterflies.

Text Classics

For reading group notes visit textclassics.com.au